THE TENANTS OF THE HÔTEL BIRON

ESSENTIAL PROSE SERIES 92

THE TENANTS OF
THE HÔTEL BIRON

LAURA MARELLO

GUERNICA
TORONTO • BUFFALO • BERKELEY • LANCASTER (U.K.)
2012

Michael Mirolla, general editor • Chris Edwards, editor
• David Moratto, book designer

Guernica Editions Inc.
P.O. Box 117, Station P, Toronto (ON), Canada M5S 2S6
2250 Military Road, Tonawanda, N.Y. 14150-6000 U.S.A.

Distributors:
University of Toronto Press Distribution,
5201 Dufferin Street, Toronto (ON), Canada M3H 5T8
Gazelle Book Services, White Cross Mills, High Town, Lancaster LA1 4XS U.K.
Small Press Distribution, 1341 Seventh St., Berkeley, CA 94710-1409 U.S.A.

First edition.
Printed in Canada.

Legal Deposit—First Quarter
Library of Congress Catalog Card Number: 2011945663

Library and Archives Canada Cataloguing in Publication

Marello, Laura
The tenants of the Hotel Biron / Laura Marello.
(Prose series ; 92)
Issued also in electronic formats.
ISBN 978-1-55071-359-6

I. Title. II. Series: Prose series ; 92

PS3613.A7397T46 2012   813'.6   C2012-900002-7

Library and Archives Canada Cataloguing in Publication

Marello, Laura
The tenants of the Hotel Biron [electronic resource] / Laura Marello.
(Prose series ; 92)
Electronic monograph.
Issued also in print format.
ISBN 978-1-55071-360-2 (EPUB).--ISBN 978-1-55071-379-4 (PDF)

I. Title. II. Series: Prose series (Online) ; 92

PS3613.A7397T46 2012   813'.6   C2012-900003-5

Acknowledgements

This book was researched and written with the assistance of a National Endowment for the Arts Grant, a Wallace E. Stegner Fellowship from Stanford University and a University of California Regents Scholarship. Chapters from an early draft of *The Tenants of The Hôtel Biron* were published in *The Quarterly, Q22* 1992 (Gordon Lish/Vintage).

Special and heartfelt thanks go to Pavel Machotka, who introduced me to Rodin; and Frank X. Barron, who helped me to study Rodin and to travel and live in Paris. I must also thank my sisters Donna Graboff and Janis Barrow, my editor Chris Edwards, my publishers Michael Mirolla and Connie McParland, and poet Paul Nelson for his ongoing support and encouragement.

For Lillian Brigman Kane

Author's Note

At different times between 1908 and 1912, the rooms in the Hôtel Biron were rented to poets Rainer Maria Rilke and Jean Cocteau, sculptor Auguste Rodin, painter Henri Matisse and other artists. The Hôtel Biron is now the Rodin Museum (Musée Rodin) in Paris. The photographer Eduard Steichen worked with Alfred Stieglitz on his magazine *Camera Work*. This book begins with the facts stated above and departs from them into a world that is primarily fictional. Nothing in this book should be taken as actual historical fact without verification from accepted historical or art historical sources.

A collection of manuscripts by the tenants of
the Hôtel Biron, originally written for Alfred Stieglitz's
magazine *Camera Work*, collected by Eduard Steichen
from the tenants and their heirs in 1967, edited
and with an Introduction by Steichen.

The Manuscripts

Editor's Introduction

In 1907 I rented an upstairs room in the Hôtel Biron. I was twenty-eight. I had come to Paris at the turn of the century to live as an expat painter and to photograph Paris in the wake of Eugene Atget. On my way to Paris, I had met Stieglitz in New York and at his request designed the logo for his magazine *Camera Work*. This began our long and multifaceted collaboration. In 1904, just three years before, I had discovered the color processes that would later lead me to fashion photography for Condé Nast. So many things were beginning.

Picasso also came to the Hôtel Biron that year and brought Rousseau with him. Rousseau had lost his lodgings through a misunderstanding, so Picasso and Rousseau rented adjacent rooms at the Hôtel. Picasso retained his studio at the Bateau-Lavoir.

The Hôtel Biron was originally one of the most luxurious mansions in the Faubourg St-Germain. It was designed in the eighteenth century by Jacques-Ange Gabriel, the architect of the Petit Trianon and the palaces on the Place de la Concorde in Paris. For a time it served as the Couvent du Sacré Coeur — a convent and Catholic school for girls. After the nuns left, it was placed in the hands of M. Ménage, a liquidator of government property, who found the mansion in a state of disrepair. He left the mansion as it was, allowed the garden to grow wild, and rented the rooms to artists.

In 1907 Matisse's painting classes at the Convent des Oiseaux had become so popular he was obliged to rent a larger studio in the Chapel to accommodate his increasing number of students. In September of 1908, the German poet Rilke moved into the upstairs rooms in the southeast corner at the Hôtel Biron, previously occupied by his wife, the sculptor and former student of Rodin, Clara Westoff. In a letter to Rodin, Rilke urged him to move in and likened the rabbits scampering through the overgrown garden outside to a scene in a Chinese tapestry.

At that time Rodin was living at the Villa des Brillants with Rose, his long-time companion. Though he had many studios and residences in Paris, pied-à-terres and garçonnières, some known to friends and public, others secret, he was drawn to the huge estate at 77 rue de Varenne, in part because of Rilke's urgings, in part because of the wild gardens. Rodin said the place had a mischievous charm that intrigued him. He took over the ground floor rooms on the southwest side, using them as studio space and staying there for weeks at a time, until Rose sent their son to the place with threats.

Once Rodin had settled there, he installed his former mistress, Camille Claudel, a great sculptress in her own right and former student of Rodin who, since their stormy ten-year affair ended in 1891, had slowly begun to withdraw into her studio.

Also in 1908, the avant-garde writer Jean Cocteau, soon-to-be darling of the Ballets Russes, was wandering through the Faubourg St-Germain and stopped to take a look at the Hôtel Biron. The concierge showed him the former dance and music classrooms of the nuns, located in the sacristy of the Chapel and accessible only by passing through the Chapel's main area where Matisse held art classes. That afternoon Cocteau made an offer to the liquidator and kept the rooms until the artists were evicted after the war, at the end of 1918.

Erik Satie was the next to arrive. During his ten years of self-imposed exile in the suburbs, Satie had come to Paris only at night, carrying a hammer in his pocket. He earned his living by playing piano in the Auberge du Clou or Le Chat Noir. Fiercely independent, he reemerged in 1910. He settled happily with the other tenants at the Hôtel Biron.

The famous dancer of the Ballets Russes, Vaslav Nijinsky, was not long in seeking his lodgings at the Hôtel Biron. Soon after meeting Rodin in 1912, in the middle of his own *succès de scandale*, and against the wishes of the impresario and owner of the Ballets Russes Sergei Diaghilev, Nijinsky was invited to Rodin's apartments. A year later he moved upstairs.

The Hôtel Biron is a smaller house than you might imagine. It must not be more than a 3000 square-foot, rectangular, two-story building. We could all hear each other inside our own rooms, and see each other passing in the hallways. Only Matisse in the chapel and Cocteau in the sacristy had any privacy.

In addition to the Picasso-Satie-Cocteau collaborations for the Ballets Russes, and Picasso and Matisse sponsoring the Granados-Satie concert, there was another collaboration going on among the tenants of the Hôtel Biron. At the request of Alfred Stieglitz, photographer and publisher of the magazine *Camera Work*, I helped to arrange the shows of Matisse, Picasso and Rodin at Stieglitz's 291 Gallery. The exhibits horrified American audiences, a response not repeated until the 1913 Armory Show in Chicago.

Shortly afterward, also at Stieglitz's request, I solicited manuscripts from the tenants of the Hôtel Biron to be published in Stieglitz's great and important magazine. The cubist writer Gertrude Stein had already contributed portraits of Picasso and Matisse in the magazine, so there was a precedent for this kind of writing.

Unfortunately, these manuscripts were never published. Soon after Rodin's death in 1917, the French government locked the basement of the Hôtel Biron, where they had placed in storage all the letters, bills, papers, and documents relating to Rodin, together with many never-exhibited drawings and plaster casts. In 1918 the remaining tenants were evicted. In 1919 the Hôtel Biron became the French Republic's official Rodin Museum, and the basement archives were declared closed to scholars and art historians for fifty years, in accordance with French canonical law.

Early portions of the manuscripts I solicited for *Camera Work* were locked in that basement. Many times between 1918 and 1967 I appealed to the French Government to return these manuscripts to me, reminding them that they were my property, not Rodin's. I did not have any success. My anxiety grew. What would happen to the manuscripts? Would they fade out and become unreadable? Would rats eat through their pages?

In the meantime certain legends grew about the archive: one that Rodin's cache of erotic drawings was stored there, another (put forth by the Rodin biographer Gruhnfeld) that evidence of Claudel's sons by Rodin existed in Rodin's letters also boxed up somewhere in this basement.

In 1967 when the archives were finally opened to scholars, few people remembered that the Musée Rodin was once the Hôtel Biron, where Rodin occupied the downstairs rooms, and the upstairs was rented, flat-by-flat, by painters, poets, a photographer, a dancer and a composer.

While scholars huddled around Rodin's erotic drawings, mused over the remnants of uncast plasters, inspected his elaborate filing system of letters, bills and foundry receipts, I waited patiently while the director of the Rodin Museum brought me the initial manuscripts that I had commissioned from the tenants of the Hôtel Biron.

I finally had them in my possession, and with them, all my memories of those days at the Hôtel Biron with the difficult eccentrics who were now the canonized artists of their day came back to me. I knew it was my duty, my obligation, to share their ideas by publishing these works.

Care had not been taken with the manuscripts. The French officials moved the museum's belongings into the basement in great haste, in fear of sycophants who, after Rodin's death, came to claim valuable busts, small plasters and drawings as souvenirs. But the manuscripts were in my hands, and a cursory look through them convinced me they were salvageable.

I had urged the tenants to continue to work on new portions of the manuscripts, until 1967, when I could gain access to the Rodin archive and reunite the new portions with the old portions. Though *Camera Work* was no longer being published and my relationship with Stieglitz had cooled, I promised them I would publish their manuscripts as a book shortly after the original portions were freed from the Rodin archive. As each tenant grew old, I collected the manuscript from them either during their last illness, or if they died suddenly, from their heirs. Picasso was the only one of the tenants still alive in 1967 when the Rodin archive opened and was able to give me his manuscript as a vibrant man in his 80s with who knows how many more years to live. (I believe he may outlive me).

I can't describe to you my delight in uniting the original portions of the manuscripts with the later portions, and reading them in their entirety for the first time. Or, in some cases, opening up an entirely new manuscript. Each artist created a manuscript that is different from those of the others and peculiar to his or her artistic temperament. Picasso chronicles the artistic movements of the time; Satie celebrates life in Paris at the turn of the century; Rousseau describes Rodin's early years; Matisse creates brief biographies of each of the tenants; Claudel reveals the letters she wrote Rodin but never sent him, from the time she met him until her death; and Nijinsky creates his own spiritual exercises.

It was Satie's *Spiritual Exercises*, after St. Ignatius Loyola's famous work of the same name, that made me realize a few of the artists, having no professional writing experience, had fashioned their work and also titled it after a more famous work. Matisse's *Brief Lives* takes its title from John Aubrey's work of the same name. Picasso's *The Histories* takes its title from the 5th century B.C. work by the Greek historian Herodotus. After further research and reflection I realized Claudel's letters seem to owe something in content and style to *The Letters of a Portuguese Nun*, another found manuscript written in the seventeenth century by a nun to her lover, the Marquis de Chamilly, who promised to marry and subsequently abandoned her. Rilke was familiar with that work and had even translated it. He had showed it to Rodin; perhaps he also shared it with Claudel. Finally, I remembered that Satie did write a memoir called *Memoir d'un amnésique* — *The Memoirs of an Amnesiac*. His *Consolations* uses some of the ideas from his original work.

Originally I planned to publish these manuscripts as a series of discrete entities, collected in a book. But upon further reflection, I found that if I added my own journals written during my time living in the Hôtel Biron with the other tenants, and I also split up Camille Claudel's very large manuscript of letters to Rodin in the same way, the book, though still a series of individual manuscripts, reads much more cohesively.

I hope you will forgive the pedestrian quality of my journals compared with the quirky, eccentric, heart wrenching, and ethereal musings of the other tenants. But I hope it will ground you to what was happening in the house when the tenants were starting these manuscripts.

The publication of this book satisfies a fifty-nine-year obligation to the tenants of the Hôtel Biron to publish their manuscripts originally begun and commissioned for Alfred Stieglitz's magazine *Camera Work*. I hope you will enjoy reading them as much as I have enjoyed editing and publishing them. I hope they will provide a window into the art world in Paris at that time, and into our lives together at the Hôtel Biron.

—**Eduard Steichen**,
Topstone Road, West Redding, Connecticut,
November 30, 1967

THE MANUSCRIPTS

Camille Claudel's Letters Not Sent — Introduction by Eduard Steichen

▷

During World War II, I served in the Navy. I don't know how the letter found me, but at the start of the war I received a note in the post that said simply: *I am dying now. I love you. I will see you again.*

It was not signed and I had no idea who had sent it. It was 1943.

Two weeks later, I received a visit, also unannounced and unexpected, from Sandro and René Athanaise, Camille Claudel's twin sons. By then they had reached the middle of their lives. I had never seen photos of them, but I recognized them immediately, because they had Rodin's soft eyes under his stern brows, but Camille's beautiful nose and mouth. God had done very satisfactory work when he produced those twins.

They introduced themselves, and I asked them to sit down. Sandro seemed more at ease and he spoke for them. René was carrying a package under his arm.

Sandro told me that his mother had given him this box of letters to Rodin, that she had never sent him, and that she intended me to have them, to fulfill a promise she had made me. He said he knew no more. He and his twin brother exchanged glances then, and looked uneasy.

I explained she had offered the manuscript as her contribution to a book I was editing, with submissions from the artists who lived at the Hôtel Biron around the time that they were born.

They nodded. René shifted in his seat, and crossed and uncrossed his legs. Sandro put his hand on René's shoulder to still him. I was so glad they had each other. I envied them.

Sandro told me that he and his brother were uncomfortable having their mother's letters to Rodin published. He told me she had given them permission to read the letters, which they had done. Sandro said the letters made his mother sound like a bitter, angry woman, when in reality his mother had been loving, kind and patient, and cared about them more than anything in the world. He told me that she had borne her incarceration with grace and poise and an almost religious acceptance. He said she was a great artist and he didn't want anything she might have written to detract from that.

I told them that I didn't want to do anything that would upset them. I said they were free not to show me the letters and keep them for themselves — they had fulfilled their mother's obligation. I said they could also choose to take out any letters they felt were too personal or too disturbing.

Finally, I told them it would be twenty-five more years before the Rodin archive opened and the originals of some of the manuscripts were made available, so by that time their mother's name as an artist would probably be secure, and the letters would only enhance her reputation.

Sandro and René looked at each other; René nodded. Then Sandro handed me the box. *We have taken them out, Monsieur*, he said.

The two brothers stood up to go. They shook my hand. When they got to the door, they turned.

Did you know her? René asked. It was the first time he had spoken.

I nodded. *She was beautiful*, I said. *She was a great artist.*

Was she mad? René asked. *Or was it simply that my uncle Paul was embarrassed?*

No, she was never mad, I said. *She was quite sane. More sane than all the rest of us.*

René smiled and nodded. He put his hand on his brother's shoulder. *This is what I thought,* he said.

After they left I unwrapped the package and opened the box. It looked like the kind of box a store clerk would put a bathrobe in. All the letters were there, hand written, with drawings and sketches in the margins. Some had the tops or bottoms torn off them. In some places pages were missing. Yes, they had taken them out; just as Sandro said.

I realized the love note I had received in the mail was not for me, but for Rodin.

Letters Not Sent:
The Letters of Camille Claudel 1
(1881-1882)

1881

Monsieur Rodin,

I write to you now, when we have only just met, because in the moment of our acquaintance, I already envision a time when I will be apart from you and unable to tell you my thoughts.

But I would not write to you at all if I planned to give you these letters. In the first place, you would throw them away. (You see how after our first meeting I begin to know your wiles). In the second place, I do not reveal my thoughts to my brother or closest friends, let alone a complete stranger, who has assumed the responsibilities of my real teacher, Alfred Boucher, who voyages to Italy.

Perhaps one day, if you prove to be extremely kind to me, I will let you read these letters, but only in my presence, and only to prove to you that I was right. They will remain mine. They will be a testimony to what shall come. They will serve as a sort of prophecy.

I wish you hadn't left for London after we had just been introduced. I miss you. It seems all the more poignant now than if we were already friends. I am not a patient person.

Everyone discusses you here because of your piece *The Creation* in the Salon and your commission for the colossal doors for the Museum of Decorative Arts. I wish I had met you two years ago, before you had received the commission, and the emphatic reviews from critics at the Salon, before people had begun to notice you, so I could have seen what you were like when you were still unrecognized. But two years ago I was only fourteen, a girl from the provinces (I still have my accent, as you remarked), and even though I was studying with Monsieur Boucher, you would have thought me a child. I also wish we knew each other better because, for example, then you would post me letters filled with news of your adventures.

I wonder who tends your studio while you are away, and wish it were I. I am very organized.

October 1881

Monsieur Rodin,

I am relieved you have returned to Paris safely, and I might get to know you. I love listening to your stories of London, especially the ones about the museums and the Elgin Marbles, which you seem to admire so much. I am also happy that you have acquired a new student on the trip, the American Monsieur Natorp, who lives in London when he is not here studying with you. I know he will pay you well, as the English girls and I cannot. You need the money. Just because you have a new commission and the critics have stopped slandering you does not mean you can cover your expenses. I understand this.

I am also pleased that you have been asked to fashion more busts, and M. Legros will arrive in December to sit for one, because I know you need the money. But I must admit I envy the time you will spend away from the English girls and me.

I am not jealous of the time you spend at work on the colossal doors because I know you are creating art. If I ever fell in love with you I would have to watch you work, because I would love you as much for that as who you are when you're with me.

Since you will be visiting our studio to comment on our work, and we may even grow to be friends, perhaps I should tell you more about myself.

I have been sculpting since I was four. Do not ridicule me, sir. It's true. I have been carving marble since I was ten, and I engage one of our maids, Eugenie, to rough out the blocks for me.

I have studied with Alfred Boucher since I was thirteen. Under his tutelage I have completed busts of Bismarck and Napoleon, completed a figure that M. Boucher named *David and Goliath*, and many groups of figures, some drawn from ideas in the poems of Ossian, much the way you have chosen Dante's *Inferno* as the inspiration for your colossal doors.

When I decided I must follow my profession as a sculptor to Paris, my mother, sister and brother felt obliged to accompany me. I am afraid my family does not like me very much, because they feel they are forced to make compromises for my art. I was willing to venture out alone, but my mother forbade it. Here in Paris (and already in Soissons), they feel crowded because my work occupies so much space. My younger brother complains I tyrannize his boyhood. I think he envies me. They all condemn art. My mother and sister feel adamantly that the artist's profession is amoral, and fear for my chastity. My brother believes the artist's life is too messy — what with the clumps of clay, chunks of plaster and wax, the stone chips collecting in layers of dust everywhere. He also objects to the messiness of the works of art being produced in our time. He says they are gross and ugly, products of vice and sloth.

They oppose my calling so strongly you must wonder why they followed me to Paris. They should have been happy to see me take my "mess" away to the city. I believe they came for three reasons. First, in the provinces they grew accustomed to their martyrdom for the sake of Art, and now are reluctant to abandon it. Second, they sense, in spite of themselves, a meaning in my pursuit of art, and they would feel empty without it. Finally, I believe my sister and mother are sincere in their concern for my reputation, and hope to save my chastity by accompanying me.

You wonder how I can proceed in the face of so much opposition. But I suppose you know that for me, like you, art is not a choice, it is a calling. I never doubted what I would do in life; I never considered any other occupation. I have always felt that I was born to sculpt, that my whole being was styled to this enterprise. At sixteen I have acquired the manual skills I need.

I don't know if I could prevail if my entire family were against me. But my father has always loved me, and understood my destiny. He has not made life difficult for me. He holds the rest of the family at bay.

You will think me domineering because of the way I've organized my group of English sculptresses, chosen our studio and models, invented their poses, divided up the chores and arranged for the collection of rent. I have no family money for my training here in Paris, so I must devise a situation in which I can pay my own way. The English girls are not in their own country, they are timid about taking the initiative and making decisions. Like you, I might be shy or indifferent when it comes to social life or family life, but for anything that has to do with art, I have plenty of initiative and I am not afraid to order people about.

1881

Monsieur Rodin,

You ask me if it bothers me that sometimes you conduct yourself like my younger brother. Of course not. It is only natural, since you had an older sister you loved so much, and I have a younger brother I love very much. It's true that I am only sixteen, and you are forty, and the separation in our ages might make this liaison seem absurd to others, but who cares about the others? What do they know about us?

I was very moved that you confided in me the secret of your sister. I understand why you have been unable to love a woman so completely again. But you seek my approval in this, and even though I respect and admire you, and am touched by your confession, I cannot consent. I don't believe a person should promise another not to love. However grievous the sin, that is too much to exact for penance. If you are still so desolated by the loss that you cannot love, I can sympathize deeply sir, and offer you all the comfort and tenderness I have to give. But if you choose not to love, I cannot approve. You kill yourself by half measures, and you impede the true expression of your art if you refuse to let yourself feel deeply. I believe that emphatically.

But I do not think you pathetic when you entreat me in your childlike way, like a younger brother. I receive it as a token of friendship and I cherish it, much the way I cherish you.

You mustn't mistake my pride for heartlessness. I have cultivated it as a way to succeed in the face of my family's opposition. I am capable of love. I am not brittle. Surely you must see that.

I am thrilled that you showed me your initial drawings after Dante. To have passed a whole year at nothing but that! I did not count on you being so singular in purpose. What a black, evil world to have inhabited so long. You frighten me now—to think that Dante's *Inferno* could conjure up such stories in your mind's eye!

You had reason not to utilize these sketches for the door, and instead to model from real figures to see what it might become. But certainly the year was not lost, because you would not have been able to imbue these new figures with the sense of torment, of anguish, of despair and especially of longing, if you had not spent that year in hell yourself.

It is ridiculous to say that I inspire the longing and desire in the new figures for your colossal door. You barely know me—longing is for someone lost who cannot be recaptured, not for what might be.

I liked our walk to the Church of Madeleine yesterday afternoon. Perhaps I just like to walk with you. I miss my walks with my brother, which we undertook when we lived in the country. I would like to walk with you in the countryside, but even our trip a few blocks to the Church of Madeleine was an adventure for me. With you everything is an adventure because I see everything with new eyes, as if the world I have been living in for so long has been transformed all at once, and has become more intimate.

You have reason to glean from the Church of Madeleine that your colossal doors would be improved by abandoning the separate panels, employing figures on the doors that are almost whole, and by adding some freestanding figures. I think you discovered this beforehand, and the Madeleine just confirmed what you already knew. Of course you must demand more money and the Ministry must approve. It is all very tiresome. I myself don't understand how you can bear to execute commissions and at the same time create art. But you do, and in this case you need the extra funds.

1882

Monsieur Rodin,

Let us correct one thing right now, sir, if you are to be my new teacher. The remark your colleague Monsieur Dubois made about my work owing something to yours is not only false, it is erroneous. I assure you that, when he made the remark to me, I had never even heard of you. He did it to compliment you, because he feels sorry for you, and rightly so, on account of the false accusations of *surmoulage* made against you.

And yes, perhaps he saw slight similarities in our work—we do have things in common, you and I, make no mistake. But I have found my secrets in the Florentines; I am not ashamed of it. You have found yours in Michelangelo. That is the fundamental difference between us and always will be. So do not flatter yourself by believing Monsieur Dubois when he thought I had already studied with you. He simply phrased his remark in that way to impress upon my real teacher Alfred Boucher, who was also present, that he might put me safely into your hands while he was voyaging in Italy.

Do not misunderstand me. This is not to say that I don't respect your work, or I don't have anything to learn from you. I do. Only a student lacking in confidence would be afraid to admit that. You have great talent and mastery, and even genius, and I, your very first student, will learn many things from you, I'm sure. But my work does not resemble yours and never will. I will be your student, but do not try to make me your disciple. Do not try to cast a shadow over my art in order to diminish its importance. History has proven that one great artist can study with another. You had no teacher because you did not have the confidence to be able to learn from one and hold to your own truth. I do. But if you insist that your students live in history under your shadow, I will leave you.

Do not try it. I know you have these ideas because you are jealous, because my work was exhibited and reviewed in the newspapers by the time I was fifteen, and you are only now getting exhibited and reviewed at the age of forty. My brother is also jealous; already at his young age I see him conspiring to be a greater writer than I am a sculptress. He does not seem to understand that brother and sister can be great. But I will not let him subjugate me and I will not let you.

No, of course I don't think it's wrong of you to seek out an audience with Hugo, and to obtain permission to do his bust. Of course it would be an honor and it would be great art. I complain of the busts because I feel that you want too much to be a part of Parisian society and you are willing to sacrifice your art to it.

And no, I do not think you were wrong in inviting the journalist Bazire to your studio, even if it was a way to obtain an introduction to Hugo. I do think it was unkind to call Bazire's festival in Hugo's honor a rehearsal for his funeral, even though you may be right in saying so.

Pursue what you will within the realm of art. You don't need my approval in all things; though I'm flattered you seek it. After all, we barely know each other.

1882

Rodin,

I am afraid I am falling in love with you. What makes me more afraid is that you might be falling in love with me. I like and dislike these ideas for several reasons.

I have never been in love before. Not truly, like this. It strikes me as the culmination of something I have been striving for in my art. I am not sure yet what that means, but that is the way it feels. Everything is so heightened. Everything matters. When you brush against me, or I feel your breath against my neck it gives me the strangest sensation, as if my whole body were filling up and every muscle had contracted.

It makes my senses more acute, makes me notice things I wouldn't otherwise. I watch you move, blink, watch your eyes, watch your expression change.

Even at a distance it gives me pleasure. I am thrilled to watch your work develop. Your ideas grow more sophisticated, you change and adapt them, you use what you know, and you bring such intensity to it. I am learning in a different way now. Even art has been brought to a sweeter level. I am so young, I am afraid I do not explain these things with enough precision.

I worry about this love because of the promise you made to your sister. Will you be able to love completely? It seems only natural that we, two great artists who are about to become recognized, should work together and fall in love. But I am afraid you are not willing.

And I worry because I see very clearly that you are trying to make me jealous with the attentions you pay my companion, and your student Jessie Lipscomb. But it is you who are deceived. The English are rarely swayed by false flattery. She realizes it is me you are falling in love with. She first brought it up to me. I did not even have to call it to her attention.

So Jessie will not fall into your plan. You will not be able to use her complicity to make me jealous. She will remain loyal to me.

You will have to admit sooner or later that you are falling in love with me, so you might as well do it now. Your tricks will not work anyway. And, if you must be told, Monsieur (since you do not seem to be catching on), even though I am proud, and confident and a great artist, and see through your ploys to win me by trying to hurt me, this does not mean I am incapable of love. On the contrary, I can love you because I am confident, because I am proud, because I see through your ploys, and because I am a great artist. If I were not, I would be in great danger, since you, like my brother, try to hurt me. So you need not try to play with me because you fear I will not love you. That is nonsense. But if you fear an equal both in love and art, if you fear the truth, then I cannot help you with that, can I?

The Notebooks of Eduard Steichen #1
(1906-1908)

FEBRUARY 1906

I don't plan to stay in Paris forever, but I'm glad I've come back for a second visit. As much as I enjoyed my success doing portrait photography in New York I confess it frightened me. I felt as if my work were stagnating. I do believe it is possible to use photography for both art and practical matters like portraits, but I also believe that I need to continue to move forward. I wasn't doing that anymore, so I came back here to Paris, where six years ago, at the age of twenty-one, I discovered so much about art. I hope I can do that again, and this visit to Paris can be a rejuvenation of my spirit that will sustain me when I return to New York.

MARCH 1906

I went to visit the great master Rodin, who was so kind to me six years ago when I first visited him at Meudon. I told him about Stieglitz's new 291 Gallery in New York, and how we would like him to be the first to exhibit there. He was flattered and told me I could send whatever I chose. I explained to him that the gallery was small and I would need to send drawings and watercolors.

January 1907

Since I had told Rodin that the first exhibit at the 291 would be his work, I was horrified to learn that Stieglitz has opened the gallery with a show of Pamela Coleman's watercolors. I am extremely disappointed, but also worried that Rodin might take offense. He has broken with several friends lately as the result of misunderstandings such as this one.

June 1907

I borrowed a Goerz-Anschütz Klapp camera from a friend yesterday, thinking that I would take up documentary reportage, and headed off to the horse races at Long-champs, filled with purpose. I was surprised to find, how-ever, that the people who go to the horse races here are not so much interested in the races as they are in showing off the latest fashions, in seeing each other and being seen. I took some good pictures, but I had to revise my intentions a great deal before doing so.

A company called Lumière has introduced something they've named autochrome plates that produce color photographs. The results are amazing and the process is relatively simple. Stieglitz was here briefly on his way to the Alps, and I had the chance to show him some of the experiments I had made with the new process. He was astounded and took some plates with him.

August 1907

I have been to London where I photographed George Bernard Shaw. He is a delightful man, so puckish and whimsical. I used some of the color plates because I hoped they might complement his complexion (red-blond hair and beard). Stieglitz likes the results so much he wants to publish them in *Camera Work*.

DECEMBER 1907

I have taken a room in a big house called the Hôtel Biron. It is a seventeenth-century mansion, originally built for a Duke, that had for some time been a convent, but which has recently been given over to the French state. While the government decides what to do with it they are renting the rooms out very cheaply to artists. Henri Matisse holds painting classes in a building near the chapel and also has a room downstairs in the main house, where he works and sometimes stays. A young Spanish painter named Picasso also has a room here though his main studio, the Bateau-Lavoir, is located in Montmartre. A sculptress named Clara Westoff was living here in an upstairs room facing the garden, but she has returned to Germany, and her husband, the poet Rainer Maria Rilke, is staying in her studio. Rilke used to be Rodin's amanuensis, and has written two monographs on the master. Picasso has recently convinced the primitive painter Henri Rousseau to live here. Picasso found one of Rousseau's portraits in a junk shop and greatly admires the older man, who seems very lively and good-natured.

1908

Rousseau is sulking over Apollinaire's review of his work at the Salon des Indépendants. Rousseau says Apollinaire recognizes and praises every other artist of genius except him. He says the review is condescending and incorrect. He insists he must not lose his ingenuousness as Apollinaire warns he must, that no artist knows exactly where he is going or what he wants so there is no point in singling Rousseau out on that score, and that he does have pride but also modesty.

FEBRUARY 1908

I had been unsuccessful in trying to persuade Matisse to agree to exhibit at the 291 so I enlisted Sara Stein to encourage him. As the result of her coaxing Matisse has agreed to exhibit. I've been having a similar problem convincing Picasso, so Gertrude Stein has agreed to speak to him in my behalf.

MARCH 1908

Matisse will be exhibiting at the 291 this month. It will be his second show outside of France—the first one was in London in January. He is very pleased about it now that he has agreed to do it. He came up to my room tonight to ask me details about the gallery and how I thought the Americans would react to his work.

Matisse introduced Picasso to a Russian art dealer named Shchukin, who has purchased several of Picasso's paintings. Shchukin says he will stop by every few months, and Matisse claims he is a man of his word. Shchukin said Matisse and Picasso are the best painters of their generation.

Jean Cocteau, the young poet who is determined to distinguish himself at all costs, has just rented the sacristy and decorated it with goatskins. If any visitor to his new bachelor apartment looks askance at them, he will snatch one up, inhale its scent, and with great theatrical fervor exclaim that he adores the smell of furs.

Cocteau says the Hôtel Biron reminds him of the Hôtel Pimodan on the Île St. Louis, where Baudelaire used to live. I think he aspires to become one of the Decadents. In order to achieve this aim he invites Catulle Mendes over to recite poetry and Reynaldo Hahn to sing Venetian ballads. He believes that in this manner he pays homage to the Baudelairian reception.

Cocteau, in his impatience to be famous and loved by great men, insists he wants to meet Rilke but is afraid of coming inside the main house. Rilke, for his part, wanders around the house in a trance and doesn't speak to anyone. He is working on a prose piece entitled *The Notebooks of Malte Laurids Brigge*. Sometimes he refers to it as a novel, sometimes as memoirs. I believe if Cocteau tried to introduce himself, Rilke would dismiss him as impertinent. This sounds unfair, since Rilke himself has sought out great men in Tolstoy and Rodin, and should understand the impulse. But he wouldn't reject Cocteau out of insensitivity. He would reject him because he is working. He works in long sprints, without resting, for weeks or months at a time, and when he does it is as if he's caught up in a whirlwind. Nothing can touch him.

1908

Rousseau says there are ghosts in the house. At night I can hear him chasing them and swatting at them with magazines and paint rags. He says that when he worked for the Municipal Toll Service he used to shoot at them. When I asked him why he doesn't just leave the ghosts alone and let them live in the house with us, he said it is because they ridicule him with foul smells and keep him awake at night.

I suppose I shouldn't be surprised that so many women come to visit Rousseau. He is good looking and I imagine his ingenuousness is charming. He loves these women while they visit, and asks each one to marry him, but they refuse. When they leave he goes right back to his painting, as if nothing has happened. I think the difference between Rousseau and Rodin is that Rousseau does not use women for inspiration, he doesn't seek them out, he doesn't mind when they refuse him marriage, and he doesn't seem to miss them when they're gone. Unlike Rodin, he doesn't mix with high society. As a result, Rousseau seems to suffer much less over women, even though he is just as popular.

Picasso is working less at night now so that he can receive visitors. The poet Max Jacob and critic Apollinaire come by most often. No one disturbs him in the morning except those innocents who don't know he sleeps late.

I was invited into Picasso's rooms yesterday while some other people were also visiting and noticed his Sherlock Holmes and Buffalo Bill novels. When he caught me looking at them, he explained that he likes adventure stories.

1908

Rousseau has started to throw his own art parties. He holds them on Saturday nights. He sends out formal invitations that list what events will take place at the party, like a theatre program. He dresses up in a dark high-buttoned suit with a rosette in his buttonhole and wears a large beret over his white hair. He relies on a cane, except when he plays the fiddle for his guests. He arranges chairs all facing front to a makeshift stage, greets his guests at the door and seats them in the order of their arrival. First his students play their instruments or recite poetry, and then the guests are allowed to perform.

These parties are becoming fashionable. Apollinaire and Delaunay often come, Picasso and Braque like to come, Max Jacob often comes. I think these painters are really in awe of how much fun the old man can have and still paint such amazing pictures.

1908

I am not sure what to think of this banquet Picasso gave in Rousseau's honor. I know Picasso truly respects Rousseau and his paintings, but so many of Picasso's friends have ridiculed Rousseau and played tricks on him, taking advantage of his childlikeness, that I'm suspicious of them.

But Rousseau did have a good time. I think he knows when people are making fun of him, and it's possible that Picasso's sentiments dominated the party despite what some of the guests felt. Picasso put Rousseau in a special raised seat at the head of the table, hung Chinese lanterns around his studio (he held the party at the Bateau-Lavoir in Montmartre) and decorated the Rousseau portrait he'd recently bought with streamers.

Marie Laurencin got drunk for a change. Apollinaire brought Rousseau, who brought his violin. The guests, primarily Spaniards and poets, sang Rousseau songs and recited toasts in his honor. Laurencin and Apollinaire got in a fight and Gertrude Stein had to settle it. Afterward Apollinaire sulked in the corner and pretended to write letters. Then Cremintz and Salmon ate soap so they'd foam at the mouth and faked an attack of delirium tremens to scare Miss Stein, but she only thought they were brawling. Rousseau pretended hot wax was not dripping on his bald spot from the Chinese lantern above his seat, and Miss Stein took him home when he started dozing.

1908

Stieglitz wrote me that, to follow up on his Rodin, Picasso and Matisse exhibits, and because of the interest in Stein's articles on Picasso and Matisse in *Camera Work*, he would like to publish an issue of *Camera Work* that would consist of articles written exclusively by the artists who live at the Hôtel Biron. I guess my letters to him about life in the house have made its inhabitants sound intriguing. In contrast to his Stein article on Matisse and Picasso, Stieglitz wants to try something different, almost oppositional: he wants to exclude articles by writers, in order to let the other artists speak for themselves, so I asked everyone except Cocteau and Rilke. Picasso says he wants to write about what's happening on the Paris art scene. Matisse isn't sure what to do. He thinks he might like to write brief biographies of the artists here at the Hôtel Biron. Rousseau says he plans to write about Rodin's life. Rilke doesn't mind being excluded, but he said he might write some poems about the garden at the Hôtel Biron. Cocteau is hurt and says he is planning to write a play in which the tenants of the Hôtel Biron talk to each other. He says it will be so incredible Stieglitz will feel obliged to include it. I think for my article I might edit these notebooks and submit them.

Rodin's Apprenticeship:
A Fictional Account by
The Douanier Henri Rousseau

(1850-1862)

That is what they are interested in this century, the Primitive Man. I am a Primitive Man, or so they say, but Rodin is a Primitive Man and I should be the one to tell his story. Even now, I see him getting old and see him getting famous, and we are both about to die, and still he falls for the ladies' charms and doesn't see that they are taking away his busts and drawings after their appointments with him. He was a ferocious appetite in his day, and so they say he took advantage, but really he knows only his work and the love of women, and needs someone to protect him. He is prey to them.

So I will tell you the story, and the parts I don't really know I will make up, but in a way that, although I don't know exactly, like his childhood, I will make you know him better than if you had the facts, the way I make you know better the man in a portrait by Henri Rousseau, though he doesn't look the same, because they say his face is flattened, and his nose is out of whack, and I'm a Primitive. And then, I will hide the parts that I make up inside the parts that are true, and so, you won't know which is which. Pretty soon, you will grow tired of guessing, and then you will forget that I lied to you at all, and then you will become so intrigued in my story that you won't care, and I will have my way with you.

1850

Rodin's family didn't think much of him, except his Aunt Thérèse and older sister Maria. Maria was older by two years, bright and cheerful, and devoted to her little brother, so much that she would convince their father to let him study art at the Petite École. But before Auguste went to the Petite École, his father sent him to his Uncle Hippolyte's boarding school in Beauvais.

Rodin's father, Jean Baptiste, moved to Paris during the Industrialization, and settled in the workers' quarter of Saint Médard, an ancient quarter of narrow streets once inhabited by artisans. Jean Baptiste wanted for his son what every man wants—a job that is stable, where he could have some dignity. But Auguste couldn't read. He wasn't good with figures. Instead of studying, Auguste lay out the magazine pages the grocer used to wrap their bread, and copied the pictures on them.

When Maria noticed, she started saving the sheets for him. She would quibble with the grocer until he gave her the sheets with the most pictures. She made sure they didn't get dirty or torn, and that her mother didn't throw them in the fire before dinner. When Maria unwrapped the bread at night, she laid the pages down flat, and smoothed the creases out with the palms of her hands.

Such love. It infuriated her father. "He should study his books at night," Jean Baptiste would say when he saw her smoothing down the pages. "He should learn to read."

"But he draws so well, Papa," Maria would say. Then she would look to her mother for help, but Madame Rodin kept her eyes on the soup.

Madame Rodin was a pious woman, a mystic and a stoic. She knew what Jean Baptiste wanted for Auguste but the boy was stubborn. He refused to pursue anything unless he was inclined to it. "When he wants to read, he will learn," Madame Rodin would say. But her husband had no foresight and was disbelieving. Finally one night he said: "He would learn to read at his Uncle Hippolyte's boarding school in Beauvais."

"Would you listen to Aunt Thérèse?" Maria asked her father. Thérèse was Madame Rodin's sister and had three sons of her own who were training to be artisans.

"Three years at Beauvais and he will learn to read," Jean Baptiste said. He had made up his mind.

"What will become of him?" Maria said.

"The soup," Madame Rodin said, and while they filled the bowls she tried to imagine how she would tell the boy that he would be going away.

⌐

On the day Jean Baptiste decided to send him away, Auguste had been studying Ovid at the École des Chrétiennes. Daedalus was homesick, but Minos held him on Crete by the force of the water on all sides. Only the sky was open. Icarus watched his father lay out the feathers and work the wax between his fingers.

Auguste tied up his schoolbooks with a rope, swung the satchel over his shoulder and fled the classroom. The Saint Médard quarter of Paris was a shabby rundown workers' quarter, a confusion of dance halls and cathedrals, high narrow apartment buildings pitched against low squat ones, neighbors squinting up and down the narrow shafts.

Auguste wandered through the rue Mouffetard marketplace toward home, ducking under the wooden tables of the fruit-sellers, jumping crates of wine, piles of linen and sackcloth. Behind the window of the creamery a woman sliced through the leafy crust of a monk's cheese, the gray ash of leaves wafting down to the cutting board — Icarus, his singed wings.

As it was getting dark, Auguste passed the dance hall and stopped at the bookseller's shop on the corner. He set his satchel down and stood on top of it. He was a quiet boy with carrot-colored hair and grey-blue eyes, the color of a gas flame where it burns from the wick. He examined the little square panes of the bookseller's shop window, running his finger along the leaded seams connecting the panes, and watched the rust colored light inside flicker against the glass. Why did the single light make an illumination in every pane? Why were all the reflections identical, all moving together the way the light moved? Auguste fogged up the window and watched the light absorb the uneven surfaces his breath had made on the pane. He could feel the answers there, on the other side of the glass, just out of reach.

The bookseller came outside and took off his spectacles.

"What is it?" he said.

Auguste climbed down off his satchel. "Old newspapers, sir?" He looked at his shoes.

"For reading?" the bookseller asked, taking in the boy's small stature, his rough hands and worn jacket.

"For copying the pictures, sir."

"For copying the pictures! Better to line your jacket with." The bookseller turned to go inside. "No old papers for copying the pictures." He pushed the door handle down; Auguste grabbed his satchel. "What did you study today?" the bookseller asked when he saw it.

"Icarus and Daedalus."

"Ah." He motioned the boy inside.

The shop was too warm. Auguste followed the bookseller through the narrow aisles, where stacks of books rose above his head and shelves reached to the ceiling. He trailed his finger along the bindings — Minos, a path through the Labyrinth. When they had reached the back of the shop and were so completely surrounded with books and papers that Auguste could not make out a wall, a window or a door, the bookseller brought out a painting in oil and set it on top of a book stack for the boy's inspection.

Auguste's eyes went first to the center of the painting where he saw the water splashing, the idle leg in the air. He cocked his head, imagining Icarus upside down underneath the water. Next Auguste saw the cliff in the foreground, where the ploughman stood on the ledge, looking down. Then he saw the cliffs on the far side of the water, and finally, off to one side, the sun.

"Who did it?" he said.

"A boy at the Petite École. It's a Breughel, copied in the Louvre."

They stood there for a moment, not saying anything, looking at each other, neither one knowing what the other wanted. "You live close?" the bookseller asked, and led Auguste back through the narrow aisles to the door.

Auguste mumbled thank you, gave a little hunched over, stumbling bow, and in doing so got a better grip on his book satchel. He hesitated at the doorway, thinking the bookseller might give him the papers now. He expected the bookseller to say something cryptic or sage. But the bookseller only looked past him into the air, drew in the side of his cheek and began to chew on it.

Auguste scrambled down the Mouffetard, passing the rue d'Arbalète. In the fifth floor apartment of the corner building, his mother stood over a pot of boiling soup. He looked up at the window, felt the tang of hot cabbage against his throat, then continued down the street and ducked into the Église Saint Médard. Inside, he lit a candle and fixed it in a holder next to the others. His mother, father and sister lit candles for the dead, but he did not know the dead, so he just lit them. Auguste held his hand up at different angles to block the light, sending gargantuan shadows up the church walls, way up, into the arches, where only the light and shadow, where only the birds could go. He recited from his schoolbook: *And they named the sea after him, and Minerva turned his soul into a bird who stays close to the ground, who is fearful of all high places.*

In the steamy kitchen Maria brought the full bowls of soup to the table. She wanted to tell Aunt Thérèse that Papa was sending Auguste to Beauvais. Thérèse might be able to talk him out of it.

After dinner, while the others busied themselves with their reading or mending in the main room, Auguste sat hunched over the table, his head bowed close to the paper, squinting. He clutched the pencil in his hand, and conjured up the dizzy tilt of Icarus' leg above the water, the splashing and the wings. He tried to make the cliffs rise up behind the water, but he could not make them recede. The cliffs in the foreground were stacked below the water instead of in front. Auguste stubbornly drew and redrew the leg at different angles, changed the shape of the cliffs. He drew the splash again and again, changing it slightly each time, and then he did the same with the floating wings, until he could no longer remember what he had seen in the bookshop. He drew the ploughman off to one side, looking down, and then built the cliffs up underneath him. When he was satisfied he put the sketches aside and began a new series.

Maria stood behind her brother and watched. His concentration was fierce. With a steady plodding hand he drew sweeping vertical lines that started at a distance from each other at the bottom of the page, and converged in a point at the top. Maria recognized the shape as arches, built very high, and seen from the inside, the inside of a church.

Then his hand burst into quick motions, like reflexes. It was as if he'd reached out by his sudden motions and captured the figures he saw in his head. The shapes were curious and striking; they resembled tiny leaves or feathers, all of them similar shapes but drawn at different angles and volumes. When Maria saw them, she wanted to cry out—they looked like tiny birds falling down along the sides of the arches.

Then, very slowly, and with great care, as if he were handling something precarious and fragile, Auguste drew the outline of a boy. He was upside down, falling through the air past the birds. Maria recognized one of his legs; it was the leg kicking out of the water in the drawings Auguste had just set aside.

In the morning Maria ran off to Aunt Thérèse to tell her the news. When Auguste got up, he found his mother in the kitchen, cutting a sheet of flattened dough into shapes and dropping them in a pot of boiling fat to fry them.

Auguste watched the cakes twist and bloat in the fat. "Mamma," he said, "Can I shape some *men* to fry?" She still hadn't told him that he would be going to his uncle's boarding school. He looked up at her and, when she didn't say no, he took the flattened dough in his hands, and fashioned it into two thick men, one slightly larger than the other, their heads cocked, their arms and legs akimbo. They took up all the dough that was left. Madame Rodin shook her head. *All the dough.* She carefully dropped the two dough men into the hot liquid.

Mother and son watched the dough men stretch and pop in the fat, throwing their legs and arms against the sides of the pot. When they were brown, Madame Rodin laid them out on some paper to dry. She shook her head again, *dough men*, wiped her hands in her apron.

That was when Auguste began to laugh. He had frightened himself by what he could make, the men burning, Icarus and Daedalus. Some longing had been released in him, seeing the men move like that, from one peculiar shape to another.

Maria came into the apartment breathless from running. Auguste and her mother stood in the kitchen, clinging to each other. On the counter beside them were the two boys Auguste had drawn in his sketches the night before, falling down from the cathedral arches. They were fried up as cakes, arms and legs thrashing, all browned and hot from the cooking.

Maria inspected the fried boys. They looked grotesque, trapped in that moment right before death. "What on earth are we going to do with these?" she said.

Mother and son looked at her. She was so offended and earnest. They turned to each other with a glint of conspiracy between them, and Madame Rodin began to laugh. Auguste laughed too, until Maria thought they were lunatics.

"What are we going to do with them?" Auguste stood up and shook himself in an effort to regain his composure. "We're going to eat them!" he told Maria, pulled off the head of the larger one, Daedalus, and popped it whole into his mouth.

1854-57

Auguste spent three years at his Uncle Hippolyte's boarding school in Beauvais. He moped in the corner of the schoolyard, intractable and sullen, and drew everything he saw going on around him. His reading and numbers didn't improve much. He didn't learn Latin. His spelling was odd, sometimes outrageous. When Auguste came back to Paris in 1857, Jean Baptiste could see his son would never learn the skills to manage a clerk's job like his own. Jean Baptiste's three nephews were still studying drawing with an aim to becoming artisans. So Maria, with the help of Aunt Thérèse, convinced her father to let Auguste study drawing at the Petite École.

In the early mornings the old painter Lauset taught Auguste to work in oils. From 8 a.m. till noon he went to the Petite École, where he studied drawing with Lecoq de Boisbaudran. He spent his afternoons copying the sculptures and drawings in the Louvre. In the evenings he took a life drawing class at the Gobelins factory, and at night he drew at home from memory, the way Lecoq had instructed him to do.

Lecoq didn't let them draw the whole figure at once. He started them on the eyes or nose, then the whole head, feet and hands, an arm, a torso, before he let them try figures. Little by little he took the figure away, and the boys found their own means to fix the image in their minds. He made them draw the lines in the air, and then with their eyes shut, and then on the paper without looking.

Sometimes Lecoq held his life drawing classes outside in the garden. Out in the yard the models stretched and played, while the boys sat on the grass or wandered among them sketching, or waving their pencils in the air, to give practice to their memories.

When the boys had mastered the outline, Lecoq made them start all over again from the inside and draw from the bone. They made a skeleton, then added on the muscles and tendons, until they'd produced scores of little flayed men and women who gestured and stooped, bent their arms and legs and pointed, but had no skin.

Lecoq drove his students out of the studio. He told them to take their sketchbooks into the streets, bathhouses and markets, and draw what they saw there. He complained when they knew nothing about history or literature. He said they should read. And it was Lecoq de Boisbaudran who noticed Auguste was myopic.

The boy had been wandering around the École, opening doors and searching the rooms, when he walked into a modeling session where the second-year boys were working with clay. Auguste took a small lump of the moist clay and made a tiny foot. He smoothed out the angle of the arch with his index finger, pinched the toes into place, rounded over the curves of the anklebones and stroked in the sides along the tendon. Then he took a position right next to the plaster model and made a tiny replica of its arm, copying exactly the way it bent at the elbow. He shaped a leg and twisted it into different positions. Then he tried a miniature head, cocking it at angles on the neck. When he finally tried a figure, it was so small it fit in his hand. He was delighted to work with clay -- he could hold it, and when he was through he could touch the surface of what he made. He could take it apart and put it back together a different way. Nothing was written.

Auguste was holding a tiny figure right up to his face, pressing his thumbs into the clay to arch the back, pinching the legs into shape, when Lecoq came into the room. The teacher put his hand on Auguste's grey linen jacket and drew him back from the plaster model so the other students could see it. Then he took the boy by the wrist and pushed his hands away from his face.

"There," he said, "you see the figure better now, no?" Lecoq retrieved the little clay feet, legs and heads that Auguste had left on the floor near the plaster model. When Lecoq came back to him, Auguste had the clay up against his face again. He held it so close it looked like he might devour it

"Can't you see?" Lecoq asked.

Auguste crossed the Pont des Arts eating a chunk of bread with a slab of chocolate hidden inside — a trick of his mother. He walked quickly, eating through the bread until he came upon the chocolate, then he slowed down. By the time he reached the quai du Louvre, he had finished it all.

Auguste learned a great deal in his mornings at the Petite École, but it was his afternoons alone at the Louvre that he loved best. Upstairs were paintings of all sorts, 16th, 17th, 18th century, the Italians and French, Rembrandts, and Titians in full colors. But that boy, he was wise. Already he knew what he was about. Auguste went downstairs to the basement. Down there were the big rooms, and in them the art came from ancient lands, where the sun was hot, the ground was dry, the sky so blue it was crippling, and there was water, everywhere: islands and deserts, and the sea.

In one room the sphinxes crouched on their stone slabs, the Egyptian cats sent long shadows across the floor, and great Pharaohs stood upright in their coffins. In another room Auguste saw the silver-winged ibex standing on a satyr's head, the winged lion with ram horns in glazed bricks along the wall. Then he took notice of all the winged creatures: griffins and bulls, scorpion men, demons with lion heads, and the Six-Winged Genius. So many animals with men's heads, he saw, and beasts with their own heads who acted like men: a lion playing the lyre, a bear and gazelle bringing vessels, a fox and donkey dancing on their hind legs.

In a third room Auguste found the black shaft of an obelisk, the amber statuettes of kings, the granite head of Hammurabi. Stone lions bared their teeth, guarding the entrances to temples and tombs. From a raised pedestal the demon Pazuzu snarled and stretched a claw.

For the École Auguste sketched the classics and the Renaissance. He copied Borghese's aggressive *Gladiator*, Puget's anguished *Milo of Crotona*, Pilon's solemn *Entombment*. But for himself he went to the lower rooms, where the sculptures were so old they had no guile. These sculptures frightened the boy; they enchanted him, and filled him with longing.

Sure, in the end he would tell them he had been too poor to buy colors, but I say he makes a loveable sad story out of his childhood. He was too poor, but he is too physical a man for colors to hold him. He would have gone down there, no matter. When he got old, he wanted to keep the pleasure to himself, that special magic of the ancients. He's bought quite a lot of those sculptures now that he's rich—the headless torsos, the gods' heads with their faces cracked off, the black cats in onyx. He keeps them upstairs above the sacristy. I can see him there when there's a moon. He walks among them, crumbling the dust of the broken edges in his fingers, smoothing his hands along their stone rumps, and quick, squeezing their tails in his fingers. But even there, in the dark, in the middle of the night, they won't yield up their secrets to him, like his women will. So he crosses the garden and goes back to bed, a cranky insomniac like myself, back to the certain nightmare that he's spent his whole life toiling, toiling in vain, after some charismatic whimsy, some hidden twist of bemusement the ancients had as natural as they walked. They were incapable of guile, I tell you. No pose, no fake attitude, and so all the terror and strangeness, all the swoon and wit sweeps through their work like a glare, like that crippling blue of the sky.

The young Auguste, he sat entranced in those cold rooms; he ran his fingers over the terracotta and gypsum; he examined the fish eating each other around the vases; he stroked the head of the tiny limestone monster. Who were they to make these things so ingenuous, so moving? Who were they to know so well how the world felt, to avoid everything false? Who were they, so candid, to lay everything bare—just like that, without mask or exaggeration, without refinement? And the young Auguste was so astounded by it that he never told anyone, anyone at all.

1857

By the time Auguste was seventeen, his cousin Henri had become a typographer, Emile a draughtsman and his namesake cousin Auguste an engraver. Jean Baptiste believed his son too was grown up now, and would apprentice himself to an artisan of this type. He was sorry that his daughter Maria was the one to do so well in school, have so many brains, when all she would do was marry and raise children. But it was alright. Auguste had trained for a dependable job and was ready to apprentice himself.

This was when Auguste announced, at a family picnic no less, without warning and without consulting anyone that he intended to become a sculptor. Not a craftsman, but an artist. He wanted to apply to the Grande École des Beaux-Arts.

"The hubris!" his father shouted. He knew where that led: a life of dissipation, women lounging everywhere with their clothes off, rich women fully clothed, patronizing him, total financial instability, unheated rooms. In short, complete madness.

"But you're not making any sense, Papa," Maria said. "You haven't yet mentioned two things that go together. How could naked women be lounging around if there were no heat? How could he be penniless if the rich matrons were beating down his door!"

Auguste didn't even know what women were about. Not yet. He wasn't the old goat they lampoon in the newspapers now. Women were mysterious creatures to him.

All along he pretended he was training to be a stonemason or an engraver like his cousins, Jean Baptiste thought.

"Look how hard he's worked, Papa. Look how good he is. Have you seen the clay figures he has locked up in Mama's kitchen cupboard?"

The three cousins nodded their heads vigorously over the young Auguste. There was something eerie about his diligence that awed them and made them afraid.

"How good is he?" Jean Baptiste said. They were all talking furiously now as if Auguste weren't sitting there on the grass at the picnic with them. "Just how good is he, after all?"

"Why not let Maindron decide," Madame Rodin said. A canny woman — she acted like she didn't take sides, but then, when the moment arrived, she did what was necessary.

"Hippolyte Maindron?"

She nodded. He was the one who had sculpted *La Velleda* on display in the Jardin du Luxembourg, and two groups on the Pantheon. Why not let him decide if Auguste's work was good enough for the École des Beaux-Arts?

It took several weeks of letters, arrangements, whisperings at the table after dinner, before the interview was arranged. Auguste took the time to sort through his sketchbook and clay figures, and pick out the ones he would show the Master.

He took a week to choose. In the evenings after dinner he ransacked the kitchen cupboard, spreading the clay *maquettes* on the table. Jean Baptiste stayed in his chair reading; if Maindron thought Auguste was good enough for the École des Beaux-Arts, Jean Baptiste would let him apply.

It was all the same to Maria, one clay figure revealed his talent as well as another. Her loyalty did not discriminate. But Auguste — dogged in front of the clay feet and knees, tiny figures he had carried home from the Petite École in the pockets of his jacket — he could see the difference. The figures he made the first year were confident, but there was something naïve in them that embarrassed

Auguste—who thought he had come so far. The figures from the second year were more deft and richer in surface, but by then he had received more instruction than he could absorb: the advice and warnings had made the work self-conscious. At the beginning of the third year he made the instruction his own, lost the deliberateness, reclaimed his instincts. Those figures were the most successful, but they'd lost the quirky charm of the earlier ones, which were out of whack. He saw the stages all crowded together on the table.

"It's all the same," Maria said. She thought he had looked at the work the way he imagined Maindron would, and despaired. But no. He looked at his own awkwardness; he saw the things he'd been too ignorant to grasp missing from his work, skewing it. He took each figure in his hand and held it at different angles, ran his fingers along the surfaces, as if he could decide by touch, like the blind.

At night, when the others had gone to bed, he pored over his sketchbooks. When he looked at each drawing, he remembered the day he had made it, the incidents that occurred, the ways he had troubled over the work. The whole surround of the moment came back to him. He looked at the figures from the bathhouse, and saw the skinny boy again, shivering in his towel, the men jostling each other on the tiles. He hadn't thought of them since that day, yet when he saw the sketch, he remembered the day exactly. When he came to his sketches of the carriage plunging down the street, he heard the loud clatter of the wheels against the stone; he felt the panicky forward rush.

He came across the Greek figures he'd copied at the Louvre. The guard eyed him again, suspicious. Auguste shivered in the chilled stone rooms. The three years came back to him, the early mornings, concentration, long walks across town, condensed into his notebook.

Once he'd been through those three years all over, he made his decisions easily. He chose several clay *maquettes* executed from the model at the École, two sketches of Antiques at the Louvre, some clay feet and an elbow. And with a reckless superstition, he included his favorite sketch of Icarus.

On the day of the interview Auguste hired one of the hand carts found on any corner, and arranged his clay *maquettes* and sketches carefully inside. He made the boy pushing the cart follow behind him, and they went down the Mouffetard like that. Auguste shot stern looks over his shoulder, and pretended the boy wielding the cart was his assistant. Auguste would have a real assistant soon, a faithful worker in his companion Rose. She would keep his clay figures wet with rags, and pose for him in the unheated studio, carrying on his business in Paris when he was away in Belgium, having casts and pedestals made. But in the meantime the boy pushing and dragging the cart had to do.

The baker came out of his shop to watch them, and likewise the bookseller, the woman who ran the creamery, the produce vendor. They knew Auguste's father worked for the Préfecture de Police, that Madame was pious, that the daughter Maria sold religious trinkets to help the family income. They watched in awe, in secret horror, some with hidden triumph as that boy of their neighborhood went trooping along in broad daylight with a servant at his back and a cart full of naked figures — horror that he would do such a thing, the crime of hubris, secret triumph that it was one of their own, off to ask a famous sculptor the Big Question.

So Auguste made his way out of his own neighborhood, and when the shopkeepers no longer came to stand in the doorways, his confidence began to waver. The boy dragging the cart caught up with him and began to yell at Auguste for walking so fast, making the cart so heavy and taking him so far out of his way. Auguste didn't know Hippolyte Maindron was a darling of the Salons, at the height of his career. All he knew was that the man had his sculptures on the Pantheon, and he was the only man alive famous enough to make his father consent.

When they had walked so far the boy dragging the cart threatened not to go a step further, Auguste found the door and knocked. A servant who seemed to be expecting them led Auguste and the boy with the cart into a vast studio, bigger than anything Auguste had ever envisioned, until he saw Hippolyte Maindron, who was also big. He fit the room.

Rodin would never be very tall, but he would fill out later. His square head, great beard and myopic eyes would give him power, and this power would make him seem larger. But now he was a frail boy, and his future was resting on the decision of this very large man who filled this very large room, and for a moment Auguste thought about what this might mean as he gazed absently into the cart.

Hippolyte Maindron was at the height of his career, at ease with himself. He could afford to be generous. He was conservative, as much as he tried to avoid the technique admired under Louis-Philippe and Napoleon III. He had a streak of the romantic in him. He thought he could recognize talent, could see the spark even in the most plodding copies done under the pressure of the École. He prided himself on being able to recognize early genius, the passion lurking in the mundane exercise.

He approached Auguste, who was still looking glumly into the cart. "I see you brought your assistant," Maindron said. Auguste nodded gravely. He had just looked over his meager production there in the cart, and all of a sudden it seemed to be not nearly good enough—just the way a boy feels when a man is about to judge him.

"Let's have a look," Maindron said, and they brought the clay figures and sketches out, and laid them on the Master's worktable. Putting his hands on the objects, Auguste began to feel himself again. He saw the surfaces; he remembered the moments, the discoveries, and the pieces began to interest him again. He watched the Master's face. In it he saw that he was a very young boy who knew next to nothing, but that this could be fixed. Then he watched Maindron discover the shiver of the boy in the bath, his hair showering droplets in all directions, the stupefying charm in the plaster elbow, the ingenious curve of a back. Maindron began to nod.

So it was true after all, Auguste thought. That little thrill when the men were wrestling on the tiles—he had communicated it through the shivering boy. That particular suspense in the back, Maindron could see it. Auguste was not imagining. It was there. Someone else saw it. This big man was nodding his head, reluctantly, with the great weight of a young boy's future on him, who has much hope. And then he asked Auguste, picking his words very carefully, and a grave voice to match that extra seriousness young boys have, as if they were all on the verge of suicide, he asked Auguste if he was prepared to work very hard. Auguste said, Yes, yes, he was.

Maindron began to put the plasters away. He said: "Because you will have to work very hard. And you will have to be patient and things will never come quickly or easily."

Auguste understood that the man had given his consent, and so his father would, and he clutched at the great man's coat sleeve, just for a moment. Maindron was putting the sketch of Icarus back into the cart, and he stopped to look at it again, cocking his head to one side. Auguste gave a weak smile, and released him.

On the way back home he was running so fast the boy with the cart could barely follow. On the Mouffetard the vendors and sellers nodded their secret triumph, their secret pleasure, snuffing out the candles they had lit superstitiously and let burn all afternoon, candles that should have been lit for the dead.

1857-1862

Auguste applied to the Grande École des Beaux-Arts three times and was refused. Oh, he was accepted in drawing, of course, but he had no use for studying drawing; he wanted to become a sculptor.

No one understood why he was turned down. Jean Baptiste thought he had been right all along: his boy was suffering from the sin of hubris. He would become an artisan like his cousins, and rightfully so. Then someone decided the Grand École rejected the loose surface modeling Auguste had learned at the Petite École; they wanted a stiffer, cleaner style.

Who knows what Auguste thought. He just went on with his plans to become a sculptor. Later he would take each rejection and make it into the biggest public insult he could, capitalize on the scandal that followed. But he wasn't canny enough yet, in no position to make a *succès de scandale*, so he just went on. To help support the family, Auguste took a job working for an ornamental mason. He made friends with the son of Bayre, the great animal sculptor, and took the Master's anatomy course at the Museum of Natural History. But the women made him uncomfortable, so he moved down into the basement and worked alone there in the early morning before his job, and in the evening, when Bayre's son would join him. They spent hours copying the animal specimens they found there, or ones they borrowed from the lecture rooms. Sometimes Bayre himself would come down and watch them work.

Other evenings he spent reading the books the bookseller had been so generous to loan him: Hugo, Michelet, Lamartine. Auguste was obliged always to return each book. At these visits the bookseller would cause him to talk a little about the books. The bookseller, who fashioned himself Auguste's tutor, went about it slyly so it would seem like friendship and not A Charity of Pity. He knew the boy had been rejected from the Grand École but was going about his studies anyway, as if the Grand École didn't matter and he would become a great sculptor nevertheless. The bookseller thought this showed fine pluck and mettle, and a boy like that, approved by Maindron himself, would go far. He should have some reading, and someone to help him along with it.

The family moved to an old house in the rue des Fosses Saint Jacques, just off the Place de L'Estrapade. They took the third floor; from the windows they could see the walls and garden of a convent of penitents. One day Rodin came home from his job working for the decorative sculptor Constant Simon, and found Maria sitting at the window, looking down from their rooms at the gardens behind them. She sat there for hours, her eyes fixed on top of the wall. She caught the light refracting off the winged bonnets that seemed to float by.

But this time Auguste found her and shook her shoulders. She tried to explain to him the awe of the place, its hushed static, its condensed suffering. At night she snuck to the window, believing she could hear their sobbing. She could feel some otherworldly presence descend from the sky, like her brother's drawings of the feathers falling.

"It's only the leaves scratching against each other," Rodin scolded her, and he pointed to the trees and bushes brushing up against the convent walls. He paid particular attention to leaves, since he had to make some in his decorative work for Constant Simon. Simon had showed him how to turn up the edges, give them movement. So he saw the movement his sculpture should have in the wooshing sound, and he shook his sister Maria.

But Maria was all moony those days anyway, the good girl who sold religious trinkets and was going to teach school. Most of her time at the window, she spent mooning over Barnouvin, a friend of Rodin—Barnouvin who had been coming to the house three or four times a week to paint her portrait.

"Is your friend coming this evening?" Maria asked her brother.

"Which friend?" he said. It didn't occur to him how often his friend Barnouvin had dropped by. It didn't occur to him that Maria would be flattered he'd painted her portrait. He had painted Rodin's portrait too. To Rodin, this Barnouvin was just using them as models.

"Barnouvin," Maria said. She pronounced his name carefully, staring off into the garden. Maria was a good girl, devout, with wild blue-grey eyes that had a feverish sparkle in them those weeks. She was not inclined to folly, but this handsome boy Barnouvin had come to the house like this, paying her attention and charming her. Maria sat at the window when he wasn't there, and everything began to intertwine: images of the garden behind the house with its floating bonnets, images of the boy Barnouvin laughing behind the canvas. By then she had fallen in love with him. In her mind she mixed the boy with the garden the way people nowadays mix the erotic with the spiritual, the way later Rodin would mix Dante's *Inferno* and Baudelaire's *Flowers of Evil* in his drawings, the way he would mix a woman's longing with Christ on the cross, the way some men confuse the love of women with the love of God, because the combination of awe and catastrophe feels the same in each.

They would get married — that's what she thought. The boy Barnouvin would ask her. Now Maria wasn't rash. But too many images had become tangled up in her mind, and she had given herself over to longing the way people put faith in God. Rodin learned the lesson through her, and afterward he would never lose himself again except to his work in the studio. But you can understand how she did, when you see her so religious, and the boy so charming, and him at the house four days a week, laughing. Women lose themselves all the time, especially to God.

"Barnouvin's not coming to the house tonight Maria, or at least he didn't say he was. Why would you think that?"

"He was painting my portrait."

"But he's been finished with that for days," Rodin said. "So why would he come?" And Rodin was right: Barnouvin had stopped coming to the house. Pretty soon he was engaged to someone else. The following week, Rodin came home from his job one day and found his mother and father staring out the window. Maria was gone.

"Where is she?" he asked, startled. They pointed over the wall, at the floating bonnets. "At the convent," he said.

They shook their heads. "Not that one."

"Which one?" he asked, as if he were the only one hurt.

"The Sister of the Doctrine," they said.

At the end of her two-year Novitiate, Maria came home again. But it was not because she had given up the church. She was sick with peritonitis. *"Mal au coeur,"* her mother said—heartsickness, a disease too apt to be caused by the cold, or an open window, or a predisposing weakness. It had to be her lovesickness, her broken heart, Barnouvin, God. The young Rodin blamed himself.

Rodin sat by her bed. When she opened her eyes, he took her hand. When she groaned, he fluffed the pillow up. When she shifted in the bed, he arranged the covers. Rodin had spent the two years of her Novitiate asking himself why he hadn't known she was falling in love with his friend Barnouvin, why he hadn't seen it coming. He should have known, intervened, secured his friend for Maria or kept him away from the house before his sister was lost. Everyone else took it for granted a courtship was in progress; Maria was so restrained she would never dare to say anything. The family believed in curses and omens as much as God.

When Madame Rodin came in with Maria's food and medicine, Rodin insisted that he feed it to her himself.

"You should go to bed now," Madame Rodin said. "You have to get up early for work in the morning."

"I have to stay with her," Rodin said. The voice inside his head kept saying, *You could have prevented this. The hushed whispers, the floating bonnets, you thought it was a religious fervor. You thought your sister was there only to take care of you, to model for you; you never imagined she had a desire of her own, a weakness, an unhappiness.*

Madame Rodin waited while the boy fed Maria and gave her medicine. Then she led him out into the hallway toward his bed. But he had to stop at the window. The garden of the convent of penitents was still out there, to remind him of his shortsightedness, as if to say that world of home and women had trapped him.

—

The priest of Saint Jacques was knocking at the door. Auguste had been in his room for the two weeks since Maria had died. He wouldn't come out. He hadn't gone to work. He had stopped modeling clay. Madame Rodin could barely convince him to take the food she left. She thought he might go crazy, so she summoned her priest-friend.

The sound of the priest's knocking was different than his mother's. His mother's said: *We know how you grieve. Come out. We'll console you.* The priest's said: *It is hubris to claim responsibility for what God has done. It is hubris to covet what God has taken.*

Or so Auguste thought. On the second day, when the priest came back, the knocking sound said: *You're to blame. Confess. Repent.* Really what the priest was saying through the crack in the door was: *Be brave, put your faith in God.* But Auguste did not hear these voices.

Auguste sat very still. He had to if Maria was to come. And she did come. In the early morning she brought the bread wrapped in the magazine pages with the pictures to copy. One afternoon she yelled at Papa for planning to send the boy to their Uncle's boarding school in Beauvais,

and threatened to talk to Aunt Thérèse. On another afternoon they were picnicking; she took his head in her hands
and defended him. He should go to the Grand École. Art
was not a life of dissipation, reckless poverty, rich women,
favors. She enlisted their cousins' support. She made them
nod their heads while she stood by. In the evenings they
went over his sketchbooks together, and this time he let
her pick out her favorites, as he hadn't done before his
visit to Maindron. To her the best was Icarus, falling from
the cathedral arches, the startled feathers wafting around.
Finally one night she stood at the foot of the bed. She
wanted to take him with her. He shivered and pulled the
covers up around his shoulders.

In the morning from the other side of the door, the
priest knocked and knocked. "I want you to meet someone," the priest was saying.

Rodin opened it. "I'll come with you," he said.

Madame Rodin stood behind, and made as if to argue
the point, but her priest-friend gave her *The Look* and she
shifted her eyes. They were not lost, her children, they
were with God. But she had thought they were stronger.
Life is so sudden. They went to the Pères du Très-Saint-
Sacrement, where her son met Father Eymard. Two weeks
later he joined the order, and took the name Brother
Augustin.

⌒

Father Eymard thought he could save the world — or at
least save the urchins, the Arabs, the street gangs of the
Butte-aux-Cailles and Fosse-aux-Lions. Other priests
brought the lost souls to him

Father Eymard made his establishment at the Faubourg
Saint Jacques and the boulevard Arago. He possessed a

run-down house, a chapel, and a shed stood at the end of the garden.

At first Rodin was only allowed to pray. But Father Eymard was a crafty one, he was sly for all his holiness, like Rodin would become later. Whenever Rodin was in the garden, Father Eymard went down to the shed and occupied himself near it, opening and closing the door, walking in and out, leaving the door wide open.

Soon enough, Rodin came down to the shed when Father Eymard was not around, and he put his head in. There was plenty of floor space, long wide workbenches against the walls, a wooden table, a few rickety chairs. Rodin stepped inside. He ran his hand over the workbench, and leaned against it, checking it for height. He grabbed the chair back and rattled it, then sat down. He sat there for a while, just looking around. The shed looked even bigger from the inside, a useless place ready for Rodin to fill up with clay and purpose.

Father Eymard had seen him go into the shed. He had a way of turning people's minds to his own desires, the way Rodin would learn to do. Lucky for Rodin that the Father Eymard was practical and proud, and did not want to keep a new priest who had come, not to choose God, but to escape the world. Can you imagine Rodin shut up in a monastery his whole life, with no women to make love to, no *Gates of Hell*, no erotic watercolors? It would have been a crime against Art.

Rodin kept returning to the shed. One day he swept up a little, another he stared out the window. Some days he just sat in a chair, looking around. He was planning all the sculptures he would do, and how he would fit them in the shed. He imagined some busts in progress on the workbenches, full figures on the floor where the roof was highest, and fragments of and torsos on the back workbench. Once he brought his sketchbook in and drew, letting the full sheets fall around his chair.

One day while Rodin was drawing and letting the sketches fall, it occurred to him that this could be his first studio. Then he remembered his vows. But he reasoned with himself, as Rodin always would to get his own way. Didn't religion, didn't God, require artistic endeavors to celebrate them? What about the cathedrals?

⌒

When Madame Rodin heard the knock on the door and the voice announce it was from the Pères du Très-Saint-Sacrement, she thought they had brought her son home; so she was puzzled when they asked her to collect some paper, pencils, chalk, his clay and sculpting tools. What kind of strange waffling was a priest-artist, like a drunken man staggering from one side of the road to the other?

Rodin spent every hour between his rounds of prayer in that shed. He had no models to wander around the studio the way he would in several years. But Rodin worked, no matter. He rolled the clay into little balls, and pacing around the shed he worked quickly, nervously, making little *maquettes* of feet, heads, elbows, torsos, the way they had done at the Petite École. He drew what he could see from the shed: the garden, kneeling priests, rabbits. When he had had enough, he drew from memory, as Lecoq had taught him. He shut his eyes, fixed the shape of the lines in the air, then transferred them to the page. When he couldn't remember any more, he made things up. He made fantastic drawings of skeletons and flayed men. He drew the scenes from the tomes the bookseller had given him.

Work has its own healing power. When my children and my wives died, how disconsolate I was. Nothing helped me, no bottle among friends, not even the flute between my lips. But those tiny canvases I was working on, cluttered in the small room, crammed into the hours before and after my clerk's job at The Municipal Toll Service, the little worlds of canvas I could enter in despite the fact that the figures didn't want me there, and I could walk around on the clipped lawn or the shoulder of the man in the portrait, took me away from my own sadness better than anything for the time I had the brush in my hand. So it must have been with Rodin. No loss is ever as great as the first one.

One day when Rodin was working in the shed, Father Eymard stopped in to see what the young sculptor had done. Eymard walked very carefully through the shed, bending over and twisting his head so he could see the different sides of the clay sculptures. He used his hands to hold his cassock down in front when he leaned over, so it wouldn't brush against any of the figures. Then Father Eymard looked up to find Rodin was leaning against the workbench, his hands idle, watching. "Please, please, go back to work," Father Eymard said.

Having a man in the shed like that, especially Eymard, with his fine chiseled face, and his tough swagger, and his wild hair that reminded Rodin of a goat's horns, made Rodin want to make a bust of him.

Rodin took a roll of clay in his hand, and appeared to be fiddling with it, when really he was fashioning a tiny *maquette* in the shape of the priest's head. When he was finished he tried another, and then another, little lightning sketches, trying to capture the volumes and contours of the priest's face. When he couldn't see enough to make any more progress, leaning there at the workbench, he followed the Father around the shed, fiddling with the clay, capturing angles of Eymard's head.

"I shouldn't say anything," Father Eymard said, "because I don't know about sculpture, but this work looks very serious to me."

"If you like the work so much Father," Rodin said, "I would be very grateful to make a bust in your likeness, and have a bronze cast for you, Father, at the cost of materials." He continued to finger the clay, looking up at the Father now and then when he dared. He was working on the angle of the jaw as it went up toward the ears.

When Father Eymard came to sit for him in the shed-studio, the Father sat very still while Rodin measured with the calipers the width of his skull, the space between his eyes, the distance between his nose and mouth, across his jaw. But the Father was unnerved when all of a sudden Rodin began to dart around him, making frantic sketches of him with wild movements, as if there were some insane precision to be found in the speed he used, as if through speed he could bypass self consciousness, and all the other Impediments To Art. Sometimes Rodin worked so fast he didn't even bother to look down at the page, and he kept filling the pages and ripping them off one by one, letting them fall to the floor.

Father Eymard put up with all this, even though he was beginning to worry that maybe some demon had been released in the young man. Rodin began to peer down his neck and at the back and top of his head. No, no, that was just too much, looking down at a priest, and from behind. So he twisted and fidgeted to avoid it.

"You must be still Father," Rodin said, as reverently as he could.

But didn't the boy know what the problem was? "Come around here, come around where I can see you," Father Eymard said.

Rodin obeyed. Father Eymard pointed to the block of clay on its pedestal. "Why don't you start working on that now," he asked "and stop worrying so much about the back of my head, and all these preliminary drawings?"

Rodin should have known right then that it would always be this way: important men were vain and could not bear to sit still, that they would object to the time it took, complain about his way of working, fidget under his scrutiny, and refuse to cooperate after a few sittings. When they saw the bust, it wouldn't look the way they had hoped.

Father Eymard always left the sitting a little early, and came back for the next sitting a little bit later than the hour they had agreed upon. At the fifth sitting, Father Eymard asked Rodin if he could see the bust.

"Oh no, Father, it's not finished yet," Rodin said.

But the Father would have none of it. He looked at the bust and was horrified. The man in clay looked so bony and severe to him. The bust had a vanity that didn't suit a priest; and what was all that hair sticking up and out in such a fashion that he looked like Satan? The cheekbones were so sharp, the temples and the hinge of the jaw so prominent. It hurt to look at that face; it seemed starved, ravaged, bold—not dignified and holy. Of course, to the street boys, the Father looked just like this.

"But what's this?" Father Eymard asked, pointing at the bust.

Rodin lowered his head. "Your likeness, Father," he said.

"And do I have horns for hair?"

"No, Father," Rodin said quietly.

Eymard ran his hands along the workbench to prepare himself to lie and said: "Your work is startling, like the work of great artists before."

"Thank you, Father," Rodin said. He covered up the clay bust with wet cloths. Father Eymard walked to the door of the shed. The air was too thin and there wasn't enough light. "But you don't have models here," Eymard said. "Maybe this is what God meant for you to do." He bristled at the idea of his satyr-like bust and whispered, "Others are here, to pray."

Father Eymard cast a meaningful glance into the studio, and then made a theatrical sweeping gesture with his hand, as if to take it all in, and maybe even bless it. Then, Father Eymard looked out into the garden, up at the sun, and left the shed at a brisk walk, crossing the garden to the chapel. As he went across the garden, the Father decided to store his bronze bust in the basement, and vowed never to pay for it.

On his way up the rue Saint Jacques toward his parents' house, with a small sack of tools in his hands, Rodin made preparations in his mind for how he would come in a few days with a hand cart to take the bust and the other clay *maquettes* home. But it was hard to think about it now, because the sounds and smells in the street distracted him, and the things close enough that he could see. Eventually he stopped thinking and walked down the street as if he were in a dream. He even thought he could feel a girl's fingers press in on the bones of his shoulder, he felt the presence of her at his back, and heard a young voice call his name. Finally he stopped and turned around.

No one was behind him. But he had stopped in front of the Église Saint Médard. He wanted to go in, light a candle, as he had on his way home from school as a boy.

The candles were in the back by the door. He drew up very close to them, and watched the lit flames flicker in the draft. After a while he felt hot and dizzy and he leaned against the cool stone pillar behind him. He put his satchel down. The times he had lit candles before, he hadn't known the dead, so he just lit them. But this time the candle could be for his sister Maria.

He asked her if she could forgive him for not realizing she was in love with Barnouvin. He vowed he would work hard all his life, and become a great sculptor. He told her he would never make anyone a promise again, since he failed with hers, and obviously didn't know how to keep them. And he told her he would never love anyone or lose himself so completely again, because it just did them harm.

A bird flew in through the open door of the church, and up into the arches above his head. Rodin could hear the echo of its wings flapping. He took this as a sign that his offer had been accepted, set the candle into its holder, and thanked his sweet sister Maria for a kindness and generosity he himself did not own.

The Notebooks of Eduard Steichen #2
(1908-1909)

JUNE 1908

Picasso has left to spend the remainder of the summer in La Rue des Bois, a rural area north of Paris. People in the house say he's very despondent over his friend Weigel's suicide. Apparently this is the second close friend of Picasso's to kill himself.

AUGUST 1908

Rodin asked me to photograph his *Balzac* by moonlight at Meudon. I spent an entire night at it, experimenting with different exposures. Some of the negatives look interesting, but I plan to wait and show Rodin prints. The morning after the all-night photography session I found two thousand francs under my breakfast plate. That's about four hundred dollars. I protested that this was too much for a night's work, but Rodin waved me off as impertinent.

LATE AUGUST 1908

Rodin loves the prints of his *Balzac* that I showed him. He says people might eventually understand the sculpture through my photographs. I was very flattered.

September 1908

Stieglitz bought a set of *Balzac* prints. He says it's the best thing I've done.

September 3, 1908

Rodin had lunch today with Rilke in Rilke's wife's upstairs rooms. Rilke quoted Beethoven, gave Rodin a wooden Saint Christopher, and argued with him about the role of women. Then they reconciled. They had quarreled several months ago when Rilke was working as Rodin's amanuensis and wrote letters in his own behalf to Rodin's colleagues, which angered Rodin.

The end result of all this is that Rodin has rented the lower rooms on the right back corner of the Hôtel Biron and Rilke is taking over his wife's rooms since she will not be returning.

But Rilke did not succeed in convincing Rodin of the ability of Woman to transcend desire. Rilke even dragged out his translation of *The Letters of A Portuguese Nun* as proof, but to no avail. Rodin is convinced that women are an obstruction and a trap, but at the same time necessary as an elixir. He refuses to be convinced they can be equals, artists, transcendent, though he claims he would like to believe it. Rilke was very discouraged by Rodin's attitude and blames it on his race!

September 1908

Rodin has a cold. Instead of working he reads Plato, writes his thoughts down on scraps of paper, and sends them sailing across the room in all directions the way he does his quick drawings from the model.

LATE FALL 1908

Picasso has returned from La Rue-Des-Bois and has been spending a lot of time with his friend Braque. A few weeks ago he decided Braque should get married and arranged to introduce him to the daughter of the owner of Le Néant, a cabaret near his Bateau-Lavoir studio in Montmartre.

They brought Max Jacob and some other poets dressed up in top hats, cloaks and canes, and arrived at the cabaret. The owner and his daughter were impressed until Picasso and his group drank too much and started clowning around in their usual way. The owner asked them to leave and they took the wrong top hats and capes on their way out. Now they're afraid to return them.

OCTOBER 1908

Stieglitz is very excited about the Matisse, Picasso and Rodin exhibits at the 291.

NOVEMBER 1908

Rodin has offered Camille Claudel the use of one of his rooms here at the house. Since they have not really been friends now for ten years, I doubted she would use it at all, but she does occasionally come and sit in it, and stare out the window overlooking the garden. More often though she stands outside the house and looks in the windows. When she does come in the house, some of the artists here try to engage her in conversation, especially Rilke, who seems very sympathetic toward her and asks her about her work. I asked her if she would like to contribute something for the tenants of the Hôtel Biron issue of *Camera Work* and explained to her what it was.

She said she had been writing some letters to Rodin that she planned never to give him, and she thought these might be appropriate for the magazine!!!

1908

Cocteau went to a party at the Baron de Pierreborg's with his companion Maurice Rostand (son of the famous Edmond, of course — who else?). Maurice and Cocteau were admiring the Decadents, as is their wont, in particular Aubrey Beardsley, when Paul Claudel overheard. Paul is Camille's younger brother. The tenants of the Hôtel Biron have nicknamed him "The Catholic Puritan of Letters." He happens to be in Paris between diplomatic appointments. Anyway, Mr. Claudel couldn't let this admiration pass without condemning it, so he whispered in a loud voice, so Maurice and Cocteau could hear (apparently so everyone could hear), that men of their ilk should be ostracized. Maurice shot back: But who would come to the Salons?

Cocteau told us the story in the presence of Camille and she laughed louder than the rest, the kind of forced laughter that makes people uncomfortable. I think it reassures her that people realize what a prig her brother is, and how insensitive to art. But I believe she loves him, and it hurts her that he disapproves of her profession. I also think she must resent the fact that her brother does so well both at literature and in the foreign service with such little effort, while she works so hard and is still only recognized in the most esoteric art circles. I hear she blames it on Rodin, but I believe she'd be more correct if she blamed her heartache on Rodin and the limited success of her career on her sex. There are such good women artists, and yet so few get any recognition (except perhaps the dancers and actresses), and when they do they're looked upon as freaks of nature, women who have somehow defied or transcended their sex.

DECEMBER 1908

Our dear Mr. Rousseau is planning one of his famous parties for Max Weber, the young painter who has befriended him. Mr. Rousseau assures me that he is inviting a lot of Americans to the party, but Rousseau refers to anyone who is not French as an American, so there is really no telling what range of foreigners will be represented.

JANUARY 1909

Rousseau is on trial for forgery and embezzlement. One of his students put him up to it. The defense lawyer is trying to prove his innocence by showing he is too naive to have suspected his student of any wrongdoing. To do this the lawyer is reading excerpts from Rousseau's scrapbook of press clippings and showing his jungle paintings to the jury. This creates a carnival atmosphere in the courtroom and the newspapers are capitalizing on the festivities, but the jury seems sympathetic.

Since Rousseau made no financial profit from the embezzlement (the student kept all the money), that fact seems the most compelling way to prove his innocence, but the lawyer seems to be reaching for more theatrical effects. I wish there were some way to protect Rousseau from ridicule, but he doesn't seem to mind it. He treats it as superfluous, the way a wise man disregards gossip.

END OF JANUARY 1909

Rousseau was given a suspended sentence. He's very pleased and offered to paint a portrait of the judge's wife. Rousseau has also invited his defense lawyer to his Saturday parties.

1909

The Friends of the Louvre Society gave a tour of the Hôtel Biron today. It regularly gives tours of historic buildings and, since the state is considering restoring it, we were on the society's list. We were notified in advance of the tour, so we were all able to be on our best behavior (e.g. Cocteau wasn't in the midst of throwing a wild party; Rodin refrained from drawing women in erotic poses; Rilke kept his windows shut and did not recite yesterday's work to the garden at the top of his voice; Matisse managed to keep his pupils from imitating his style when copying the plaster model; and Miss Claudel was nowhere to be found). I was quite proud of us and everything was going along smoothly until the tour headed into the sacristy and discovered Cocteau living there.

In addition to the sacrilege involved, Mrs. Cocteau, Jean's mother, is a member of the society and was one of the ladies conducting the tour. Evidently she had no idea Cocteau had rented a "bachelor's" apartment here. Of course she was horrified by all the bohemian implications, but she managed to squelch her horror for the duration of the visit, and was very diplomatic while everyone sat in the rattan chairs and sofa in Jean's room, ate cakes and drank orangeade off his packing crates, and admired the lilies and doves Matisse recently painted on the walls in preparation for Jean's next party.

But a few hours after the tour was over Mrs. Cocteau returned to tell her son what she thought of the scandal. She's threatening to cut off his allowance if he doesn't give up the rooms.

1909

I was wandering around downstairs this morning and found Rodin's new secretary, Maurice Baud, going through the pockets of all the trousers and jackets Rodin has worn in the last few days. The master changes clothes at least three times a day, so this is a gargantuan task. Mr. Baud must have thought me suspicious because he was very eager to explain to me that Rodin leaves all his receipts, invoices and checks in his pockets, in armchairs, on modeling stands, etc., and many have been lost. At present he was searching for a check for fifty thousand francs that had arrived yesterday from America. Rodin could remember the check but not where he put it.

Cocteau is circulating through the main house, trying to solicit poems and drawings for his new magazine *Scheherazade*, but no one wants to contribute. Cocteau claims it is the first deluxe magazine for poets but everyone here is skeptical. Rodin has seen the first issue and does not like the Art Nouveau style of the magazine, which he calls the "internationalist" style. He also dislikes the fact that the magazine says it is published here at the Hôtel Biron. When he confronted Cocteau with this tidbit, Cocteau said: *But I am the publisher!* Rodin shrugged in the French way and went back to his erotic sketches. Cocteau left with a wave of his hand, saying Bonnard's drawings would appear in the next issue and Rodin would be envious.

MARCH 1909

Rousseau is trying to get everyone in the house to write letters to his new girlfriend Léonie, attesting to his stature as a painter and to his good character. Apparently Léonie won't marry him, and he is not about to forget about her the way he has about the other ladies who visit him. Léonie is a clerk in the Bon Marché and apparently doesn't know what to think of Rousseau. Rousseau wanders around the house pouting and playing his violin. He's still painting, but I am afraid it will all end badly.

MAY 18, 1909

The preview (dress rehearsal) for the opening of the Russian Imperial Ballet at the Théâtre du Châtelet was held today. Diaghilev completely renovated the theatre for the occasion. The high society of the Paris art world was invited, as were journalists. Cocteau is sulking because he wasn't invited. He claims Diaghilev feels threatened that Cocteau might steal Nijinsky away from him. Cocteau insists Mr. D. would not be jealous if Cocteau were not so irresistible. At present Cocteau is plotting ways to be introduced into the ballet company's inner circle. I'm sure he will succeed.

1909

Rodin has taken his student Malvina Hoffman to the Louvre this evening for what he calls "The Candle Test."

He performs this ritual for one of his students at least twice a month. Miss Hoffman says he takes her at closing time, and holds the lighted candle up to one of the Egyptian sculptures so she can see the shadows reflected by the contours. While he moves the light along the sculpture, he discourses on the beauty of the ancients.

Apollinaire challenged Max Daireaux to a duel because he was insulted by Daireaux's review of his poems. Then he asked Picasso to help him out of the mess. On the day of the duel Picasso hid Apollinaire in his Bateau-Lavoir studio while Max Jacob, dressed in a top hat, tails and monocle, acted as a go-between among the seconds, who were installed in two nearby cafés. Max Jacob managed to get both sides drunk on aperitifs and then drew up a document that both groups signed.

Cocteau and Picasso were in Rodin's rooms admiring his Greek and Egyptian artifacts. They were trying to discern which ones were real, which fakes, and which contraband, but neither knows enough about it to judge. Picasso says the Greek drinking cup was made in the 19th century and the Tanagra figures are fakes, but he concedes the charm of the copies and understands why Rodin would want to collect them even though he can't verify their authenticity. Rodin himself conceded that the Hermes statuette is a fake and can be bought for a few francs in a plaster cast dealer's shop in Montparnasse. Then he looked dismayed and victimized for a moment. When he does catch the swindlers, he buys the pieces anyway, but so much cheaper.

Picasso is a collector of African sculpture and jewelry. He wants Fernande to wear the jewelry, but it makes her self-conscious. Picasso asked Rodin many questions about how he approaches dealers and how he determines whether a particular piece is real or fake, so he could apply these lessons to his own collecting. But since Rodin doesn't worry too much about authenticity, and buys what he likes for the sheer pleasure of it, he couldn't help Picasso very much. Picasso has gone back to Spain for the summer. People in the house say he's homesick.

Picasso's The Histories —
Introduction by Eduard Steichen

In the spring of 1954 I went to Picasso's ceramics studio in Vallauris, in the south of France, to collect his manuscript. When I asked him to send it to me, I thought I was doing him a favor, saving him the time of a visit, but he insisted I collect it in person.

By that time, you could not say no to Picasso, nor would I have been inclined to do so. I thought of him then as the most famous person in the world. Perhaps he was. He had conquered the art world. He had won his rivalry with Matisse. I might have been the only one who thought that Picasso had earned Matisse's respect as a result of that contest.

Picasso's son Paulo let me into the studio. By then he was a young man in his late twenties, shiftless, with a propensity to drink and a lack of ambition. He was serving as Picasso's driver.

I sat with Picasso at a long wooden table, while he painted the plates and bowls that his assistants spun out on their ceramic wheels. He was immersed in his neo classical period then, and liked to paint women with elongated faces, their arms stretched out, or doves and leaves, some stolen from Matisse's cut outs.

At first he told me there was no manuscript beyond what would be locked in the basement of the Hôtel Biron until 1967. *You've done nothing else on it?* I asked. I was not surprised. He always worked quickly, and let his work stand on its own without revision. Why should his writing be any different?

He smiled and nodded. He told me he had done enough and I should be satisfied, that in fact I would be satisfied, when I saw it. I nodded and fell silent. But Picasso liked to toy with people, and my acquiescence didn't please him. He coughed. He pushed away the plate that he had been painting. An assistant took it to a wooden shelf to dry. The studio was monochromatic — wooden floors, tables, chairs, shelves, a wood-burning stove a slightly darker shade than the wood, nothing more.

Picasso got up, and went to a locked cupboard at the far side of the studio. He was wearing one of his French striped sailor shirts he was later photographed in, and a pair of slate gray cotton pants that matched the palette of the room. From the locked cupboard Picasso brought out a large handmade book, loosely covered in leather. He brought it to the table and pushed it toward me. He watched me. I opened the book. The paper was hand made. There were drawings everywhere — of paintings on walls, people chasing each other, the usual things. But there was also a text, in his own hand, entitled, *The Histories*.

That is what you came for, he told me. He watched my face. His focus was something I have never seen before or since in anyone. I told him that this manuscript with its drawings was too precious to be part of a larger book, it should be published on its own, perhaps by an art dealer or gallery in connection with *Les Éditions de Minuit* or *Les Éditions Gallimard*. He had done other collaborations like this with the Greek poet and publisher Stratis Tériade, for example.

Picasso scoffed at this. He said he didn't want it published as a stand-alone book in the traditional French
literary style. He wanted it included in mine. I told him
I didn't know if I could include the illustrations. *You can't,*
he said. *I don't give you permission. You can use the text only.*

And this marvelous book? I asked, lifting it up and feeling
its weight.

That is for you, he said. *A gift.*

I was stunned. I asked him why.

Because you are American, he said. Then he laughed at
the incredulity he saw in my face. *I joke with you,* he added.
It is not because you are American.

I wondered if he was making reference to the fact that
after World War II the center of the art world had shifted
from Paris to New York. I wondered if he felt somehow
superseded, but the thought was too laughable, so I dismissed it.

That was the end of the interview. Picasso's son Paulo
showed me to the door, and to my car.

He is very fond of that book, Paulo said, pointing to it.

I will treat it with the utmost respect, I said.

Paulo nodded.

He loves you, you know, Paulo said. He almost sounded
wistful.

I told him I didn't understand. Paulo shrugged. He
watched me drive away, before turning and going back
into the studio.

The Histories by Pablo Picasso

BOOK ONE: TRIBES AND TRIBESMEN

THE ANCIENT POST IMPRESSIONISTS OF PARIS

The Post-Impressionists were a nomadic tribe of painters who only lived in direct sunlight. Like their grandfathers before them — the Impressionists, they insisted on scientific accuracy. They allowed no spontaneity, inspiration or temperament in their work. They wanted to paint what they saw. A tribe member named Degas saw women bathing in tubs in small rooms. He painted them without spontaneity. A tribesman named Monet saw a cathedral and painted it at different times during the day when the light looked different. Clemenceau, a leader of all the Paris tribes, showed him a lily pond, and on his command Monet painted that to be shown in a room called the Orangerie. They didn't paint the way the woman in the tub looked to them, or the way the cathedral or the lily pond made them feel, they painted the way the light looked on these objects. I say objects because that's all they were to these Post-Impressionist tribesmen. Without spontaneity, inspiration or temperament, the woman or lily pond is just an object that attracts light.

The Post-Impressionist tribesmen didn't realize the apocalyptic character of their painting. So when people complained that the women in Degas paintings weren't women they were just objects, Degas didn't say: *Yes, that's my point exactly.* He said these women were honest simple folk concerned with their own physical condition. And when the Americans and English said they are not nude they're naked the French didn't know what to say because they don't make the distinction. They have one word for both conditions.

But the Post-Impressionist tribesmen did not agree about everything. They agreed that they should paint the way the light looked on objects; they agreed that women were objects and they agreed that there should be no spontaneity, temperament or inspiration in their canvases. But they did not agree on where to put their canvases in a particular room. When two of the elder tribesmen, Rodin and Monet, tried to put their work together in the room called the Galerie Georges Petit, Rodin insisted on keeping all the best locations in the room for himself, and his tribesman Monet got very angry. Rodin blamed the argument on Monet and the two tribesmen did not speak to each other for a long time, despite their interest in medieval architecture.

THE ORIGIN OF CÉZANNE'S POWER

Cézanne did not depend so much on the light; he liked to paint things over and over again the way Monet painted the cathedral.

Cézanne lived in the foothills near the Mediterranean, far away from Paris. He preferred to paint Mont Sainte Victoire over and over again. Nobody knew why. The

Symbolist and Nabi tribes liked his paintings, but they didn't understand them. Cézanne didn't try to explain. What he did say didn't make much sense.

Cézanne didn't paint the way the light hit the objects. He painted the forms he saw in the objects. He didn't do anything but work. He couldn't use models because he was embarrassed to hire them. As a result his nudes are oddly shaped.

Eventually, when they put all his paintings in a room in Paris called the Galerie Ambroise Vollard, painters from the other tribes thought they understood what he was doing. They didn't. At least they recognized the importance of his work.

I appreciated Cézanne's paintings, and created my own tribe called Cubists. The Fauve tribe also credits Cézanne for their innovations.

THE SYMBOLISTS' REVOLT

Some members of the Post-Impressionist tribe decided that there should be inspiration, spontaneity and temperament in art after all. They decided to break from the Post-Impressionist tribe and start a new one called the Symbolists. They believed that painting should be a synthesis of feeling and form. The Post-Impressionists said the Romantics had already done that but the Symbolists thought painting should express this idea, not explain it, as the Romantic tribe of their great-great grandfathers had done. Only two of the tribesmen actually showed these ideas in their paintings. These tribesmen were called Gauguin and Redon.

Henri Bergson, a tribesman from an international tribe called Philosophers, said that intuition was the only path to knowledge and art the only way to depict that path. Charcot and Freud, who belonged to an international tribe called Psychologists, argued the importance of dreams and psychic life. The Symbolist tribesmen repeated these word paintings to prove they were right. Gustave Kahn, of the international tribe called Critics, said introspection knows no limits. Mallarmé, a tribesman who made word paintings called Poetry said art should reveal the mysterious meanings and aspects of existence.

THE ORACLE'S ANSWER

That tribe called Critics, who made word paintings about the tribes and tribesmen who made art, claimed four painters as the true grandfathers of the Symbolist tribe: Gustave Moreau, Puvis de Chavannes, Odilon Redon and Eugène Carrière. Gustave Moreau lived on the slopes of Montmartre, never came down, and never put his paintings together in a room where people could see them. Puvis de Chavannes painted murals that were too large to be put in a room. Redon was well known and well loved by the Symbolist tribesmen. He put his paintings in a room with them called the Durand-Ruel.

PAUL GAUGUIN DEFINES HAPPINESS

Gauguin was still a member of the Post-Impressionist tribe when he left for Panama and Martinique. When he returned, he was a Symbolist. He had found pure color and expressive power. A trip to a hot country can change a painter this way. In a big room in Paris called the Exposition of 1889, he saw prehistoric art from Central and

South America. These are hot countries. No one in Paris had seen this art in a room before. Gauguin liked it very much. He said he had savage blood. His family had settled in the hot country of Peru and he had grown up in Lima. He wanted to paint with power from the hot countries. People said painters with that power belonged to an international tribe called Primitives.

Gauguin painted experiences that could not be explained by the senses. When he came back from the hot countries, Gauguin could not stay in Paris. He went to other wild places, some hot but wet like Polynesia, some cold and wet like Brittany, some temperate like Arles, but all wild and emotional. Gauguin craved wildness and emotions. Of the emotions, Gauguin liked unsatisfied desire the best. He liked to depict the fox because it was the Indian symbol for perversity.

After six years in the Symbolist tribe, Gauguin had spent all his money painting. At the Exposition of 1889 he put all his work in a room called the Café des Arts with other paintings by Symbolist tribesmen. Gauguin didn't make any money. He moved to Tahiti where he painted both satisfied and unsatisfied desire. He had an auction and sold a painting to Degas. Aurier wrote a word painting about the auction and published it in a newspaper called the *Mercure de France*. Now people knew who Gauguin was. People liked Gauguin's Tahitian paintings better than his French paintings, the same way they preferred Rousseau's jungle paintings to his French paintings, even though they're the same paintings. They want to see the exotic, but they want it painted in Paris.

No one liked Gauguin's Tahitian paintings when they were first put in a room together in Paris in 1893. He hadn't painted these pictures in Paris. He didn't live in

Paris, and he used new colors. Strindberg, who belonged to the tribe of Playwrights, called him an inferior to Puvis de Chavannes. Gauguin said that Chavannes explained his idea but didn't paint it. To Gauguin each color had its own scent. Each scent had its corresponding color. Color vibrated the way musical notes do.

In 1903 Gauguin died in the Marquesas Islands. In 1906 his work was put together in a room in Paris called the Salon d'Automne. The new Fauve tribe saw it and especially liked it. The new Expressionist tribe in Germany also liked Gauguin. Mirbeau says his work reveals the irony of sorrow that is the threshold of mystery.

The Story of van Gogh

Van Gogh's paintings were so expressive that a new tribe formed and called themselves the Expressionists. Van Gogh wanted to paint what he felt. He was unteachable and self-taught. His family came from international tribes of Pastors and Art Dealers. Before he joined the Symbolist tribe, van Gogh tried to work for the Art Dealers called Goupil & Co. He failed. He tried to work as a missionary with Belgian miners. He failed again. When he painted, he thought he was failing too, but he kept painting. He didn't stop. He couldn't believe anything other people told him, so he had to discover everything for himself. He moved to Paris to live with his brother Theo who belonged to the Art Dealer tribe. He began to find his own colors, his own paintings. He began to express himself the way he wanted. He saw Impressionist and Divisionist Paintings and Japanese prints and took what he needed from these. He met Gauguin. He painted flat areas of unbroken pure color.

Van Gogh was cranky and fought with everyone in Paris. In 1888 he moved to Arles, a hilly place away from Paris and closer to Aix and the Mediterranean. He was alone. He drank a lot, worked a lot. It was calm. At first he made his best paintings.

GAUGUIN AND VAN GOGH COME INTO CONFLICT

Gauguin arrived in Arles in December. Van Gogh quarreled with him about aesthetics and values. Van Gogh attacked Gauguin then cut his own ear. Van Gogh had frightened himself. He admitted himself to an asylum. He did not feel better. He shot himself.

In 1901 they put all van Gogh's paintings in a room in Paris called the Galerie Bernheim-Jeune. This is why the Fauves started their tribe. They put his paintings in rooms in Amsterdam in 1905, Cologne in 1912 and in Berlin in 1914. This is why the Expressionists started their tribes.

THE CONQUEST OF THE NABIS

After Gauguin left for Tahiti, Bernard and Denis started their own tribe called the Nabis. They admired Gauguin's work and its sources in medieval sculpture, Japanese prints and primitive art. Many painters from other tribes lacked respect for the Nabis. They said they were only a French version of the decorative Art Nouveau tribe, and simply a path from Symbolism to Expressionism. The path from Symbolism to Expressionism is not simple.

Bernard was the first to arrange van Gogh's paintings in a room. It was called the Galerie Le Barc de Boutteville. He did this only four months after van Gogh died. The

Nabis put their paintings together in a room called the Café Volponi in 1889.

Every year during the 1890s, the Nabis put their paintings together in the room called the Galerie Le Barc de Boutteville. Until someone put Cézanne's paintings together in a room in Paris in the 1890s and the Fauve tribe put theirs together in the room called the Autumn Salon in 1905, the Nabis' work was the most original and alarming anyone had seen in Paris.

Paris Dismisses Bonnard and Vuillard

Some people say Vuillard and Bonnard belonged to the Nabi tribe. They didn't. Not every painter belonged to a tribe. Vuillard and Bonnard's work looked like the paintings of the Symbolist tribesmen, the Nabis and even the Fauves. They painted secrets in the form of small corners of rooms or parks with a person or two together inside. But regardless of the objects they chose, they painted the secret mystery of those objects.

The Bones of Toulouse Lautrec

Toulouse-Lautrec would have been a sportsman but he broke his legs and they never grew up like he did. He grew up a dwarf and frequented Montmartre dance halls. He drew, painted and studied them. When you looked at his paintings, you felt at least eight different unpleasant conflicting sensations. Toulouse-Lautrec did not allow censure or caricature in his work. He captured the disillusionment and excitement of the cabaret.

Toulouse-Lautrec used an aspect of Japanese prints in his paintings that no one else had used. The Impressionist tribesmen had used their manner. Degas and Monet had used their space. Gauguin and van Gogh used their colors and patterns. Toulouse-Lautrec used their way of conveying movement within flat linear patterns. He made posters into works of art.

Painters respected Toulouse-Lautrec when he was alive. He showed his paintings, posters and lithographs for ten years in a room called the Indépendants. He died in 1901. He was thirty-seven.

Toulouse-Lautrec painted with oil on cardboard. He didn't steam his pencils into syrup the way Degas did.

MAILLOL REDUCED TO SUBJECTION

Maillol came to Paris from a fishing village called Banyuls-sur-Mer near the Spanish border. Vuillard convinced Vollard to cast Maillol's wood and terracotta statuettes in bronze and put them together in a room in Paris in 1902. Gauguin and Rodin admired them. They put them together in Paris in the 1905 Salon d'Automne. Gide said Maillol's sculpture *Mediterranean* was beautiful because it signified nothing.

SIEGE OF THE FAUVES

Of the several Expressionist Tribes, the Fauves are one. Fauve means Wild Beast. When Vauxcelles said "Wild Beasts," he meant the colors not the painters.

Matisse, Derain and Vlaminck were Fauves. In 1905 they showed their paintings together in Paris at the Salon d'Automne. Matisse was thirty-six.

The Fauves tried to make their colors bolder, surfaces flatter, brushwork more chaotic and feelings more expressive than any Symbolists or Nabis had. They admired Cézanne, van Gogh and Gauguin, and wanted to continue their discoveries. They introduced deliberate color disharmonies, refused to draw contours, insisted on the integrity of feeling, depended on intuition and instinct. They admired Mohammedan and African Art, and how these reflected cultures outside Europe. No one else admired cultures outside Europe. They were shocked when they saw these cultures admired in Fauve paintings. Élie Faure said: *Look at these paintings anyway.*

THE RADICAL DEVOTION OF MATISSE

Matisse said his feelings and his way of expressing them were inextricable. Matisse left the Fauve tribe to paint other pictures. He found a balance between what he felt and how he painted. He made colors move, condensed meaning, followed the desire of the line.

THE REBELLION OF KANDINSKY

Kandinsky was a Russian painter who lived in Munich. In 1910 he asked me, Braque and some Fauves to put our paintings together in a room with his in Munich. It was the biggest collection of work from the new international tribes that anyone had amassed. In 1912 he published *Concerning The Spiritual in Art*. It explains why paintings do not need to represent objects. Kandinsky was upset after Rutherford bombarded the atom and discovered substances don't really exist. It was important to Kandinsky to show emotions and spiritual essences in his paintings.

In 1912 Kandinsky showed paintings by himself, Klee and Marc all over Europe. These paintings did not represent objects. He called this his Blue Rider Exhibit. Kandinsky published *The Blue Rider Almanac*. In one he reprinted Rousseau paintings.

In 1913 Kandinsky showed *Improvisation No. 30* in London. Roger Fry called it pure visual music and said it expressed emotion without representing anything.

THE CULT OF ROUSSEAU

Rousseau wanted to paint poorly but couldn't. He painted well in spite of himself. People call this Primitivism.

Kandinsky says Rousseau's reality is greater than ours. Rousseau showed in the Salon des Indépendants from 1886 to 1910.

Rousseau dislocated each piece of an object from its adjacent pieces, and showed them side-by-side. He was the first painter to do this. I was the second. He made the objects that were important to him bigger than the objects that weren't. Pierre Loti's forehead was very important. So was his hand. His cigarette was not. Neither was his cat. Rousseau's objects lock together in a geometric design that the viewer cannot detach.

Rousseau admired Japanese prints. Rain slashes diagonally across his first jungle painting. Rousseau conveys his feelings in his paintings. Rousseau felt whimsy and magic.

CUBISM DEFENDS ITSELF

Form creates space. I started the Cubist tribe. In 1907 Braque saw my painting *Les Demoiselles d'Avignon*. In 1908 we showed at the Salon d'Automne. Apollinaire said our work was composed of tiny cubes. Then he said Matisse had said it. Later, Gleizes and Metzinger said that form is inseparable from the space it creates. We admired Cézanne. In 1910 and 1911 Braque and I painted the same pictures. We painted the forms as we thought them not as we saw them. We didn't use colors. Braque put sand, sawdust and metal filings into his paint. Then the paint had form. I made a collage and pasted a piece of oilcloth to my canvas.

In March 1911, Gleizes, Metzinger and some other Cubist tribesmen showed in Room No. 41 of the Salon des Indépendants., Gleizes and Metzinger published *On Cubism*. In October 1912 a group from the Cubist tribe showed at the Galerie de la Boétie. They called it the Salon de la Section d'Or. Some of the older Cubists wouldn't let Marcel Duchamp exhibit his *Nude Descending a Staircase*. Apollinaire in 1913 wrote *Aesthetic Meditations on the Cubist Painters*. The War started. I left the Cubist tribe.

The Flight of Marcel Duchamp

In 1902, Marcel Duchamp joined the Impressionist tribe, in 1907 the Fauve, in 1910 the Cubist. In 1912 when the Cubist tribe refused to let him show *Nude Descending the Staircase* with their paintings, he took it home in a taxi and quit the tribe.

In July 1912 Duchamp painted *The King and Queen Surrounded by Swift Nudes*. In 1913 he started making sculpture from kitchen stools and bicycle wheels. In 1915 he called these ready-mades. He began work on a large glass painting called *The Bride Stripped Bare by Her Bachelors Even*. He is developing a new physics, mathematics and a fourth dimension for the painting. He says that the act of love is an ideal fourth dimensional situation. In 1913 he made the painting *Coffee Grinder*, which is a study for his *Bride*. He is using glass because he used a glass palette when he painted on canvas and wants to protect the paint from oxidization. He used paraffin to outline the shapes on the glass. He etched them in fluoridic acid. He glued lead wires with varnish and sealed them with foil. He's made two preliminary studies this way. One is called *Glider*. The other is called *Cemetery of Uniforms and Liveries*. Duchamp created his own system of measurements through accidents called "oscillating density," "uncontrollable weight" and "emancipated metal."

Duchamp keeps all his notes for the painting in a green cardboard box. He has a large schematic drawing on the wall of his studio where he works out his ideas. Duchamp has a weak heart and couldn't fight in the War. In 1915 he moved to New York. Everyone there already knew him because in 1913 they had put his *Nude Descending a Staircase* in the Armory Show. Everyone was outraged. They didn't think a nude should descend a staircase. Most people think nudes should stand still. They should lounge, or bathe, or reflect. But, above all, they should not descend a staircase.

Marcel Duchamp is the most innovative painter of our time. He will become esteemed. This may take fifty years or more.

De Chirico and the Dolphin

De Chirico was in Paris from 1911 to 1915. He started a tribe with Carra called the Metaphysical School. He painted canvases of people dreaming in deserted squares, read Nietzsche and wrote against Impressionism. De Chirico was Italian, grew up in Greece and lived in Munich. He read Nietzsche and believed his statement that underneath the reality in which we live another altogether different reality lies concealed. De Chirico said his art consists of two lonelinesses: the plastic loneliness and the metaphysical loneliness.

BOOK TWO: CUSTOMS OF THE PARIS TRIBES

SACRIFICIAL BULLS

Stein bought most of her paintings from Vollard, on the Boulevard Lafitte. Vollard did not show the pictures he had for sale. He turned them against the wall and piled them in stacks. Stein would come in and ask to see a Cézanne landscape. Vollard would go upstairs and return with a Cézanne nude. Stein would ask again to see a Cézanne landscape. Vollard would go upstairs and come down with a Cézanne still life. They went on like this until Vollard made Stein laugh. Then she would buy two pictures. If Stein got impatient, she would go to Fouquet's, eat honey cakes and nut candies, and come back. If she were really unhappy, she would go to Fouquet's, buy a bowl of strawberry jam, and not come back.

THE COST OF ENTERTAINING

When Gertrude Stein had lunch at the Matisses', they ate Jugged Hare in the Manner of Perpignan, and a Madeira wine called Roncio. Matisse brought Derain to one of these lunches. He and Gertrude Stein did not like each other. When Matisse had dinner at Gertrude Stein's, Helene the cook would fry the eggs instead of making an omelet.

Arabian Spices

Mallarmé had people over on Tuesday nights, beginning in 1884. The Goncourts started having people over the next year. Gauguin had his soirées on Saturday nights in the 1890s, when he was back from Tahiti. Degas, Strindberg and Mallarmé came. Rousseau came uninvited. He lived down the block. He played his violin. He offered to help Degas to get exhibited. Gertrude Stein had her gatherings on Saturday nights. Germans, Hungarians, Americans and Spaniards came. People danced and looked at the canvases. Once I got in a fight with Fernande about the difference between painters and Apaches. Rousseau was afraid to knock at the door. A Scandinavian came and would stand in the courtyard.

Tactics

At the Salons des Refusés in 1863, Manet showed his *Le Déjeuner sur l'herbe*. Napoleon III didn't like it. Neither did his wife. At the Salon des Champs-Élysées in 1885, Rousseau showed *An Italian Dance* and *Thunder*. Spectators slashed them with knives. Afterward, the paintings were taken out of the show and exhibited with the Refusés.

The exhibition of the Société des Artistes Indépendants in 1886 was their second show. Seurat showed *Summer Sunday at Grande Jatte* and Rousseau *Night of the Carnival*, and *Thunder* again. Seurat was accused of imitating Chavannes.

At the Salon d'Automne of 1905, Cézanne, Derain, Braque, Roualt, Vlaminck, Friesz, Vuillard and Dufy all showed. Rousseau showed *Hungry Lion*. Matisse showed *Woman with the Hat*. Vauxcelles named the Fauves. Maillol showed *Mediterranean*. People laughed at Matisse's *Woman in a Hat* and tried to scratch it. Gertrude Stein bought it. Matisse went the first day and heard what people said about his *Woman in a Hat*. Afterwards, he sent his wife instead.

At the Salon de la Nationale in 1912, José Maria Sert exhibited a large dining room ceiling. At the Futurist exhibit in 1913, Boccioni showed a construction containing human hair, glass eyes, and fragments of a staircase.

MUMMIES

The Sun Went Down Over the Adriatic: This canvas was painted entirely by movements of Lolo the donkey's tail. It was exhibited at the Salon des Indépendants.

THE FESTIVAL OF THE PHOENIX

Rite of Spring, May 29, 1913, at the Theatre des Champs-Élysées: The Theatre des Champs-Élysées had just opened. Denis and Vuillard had painted it. The theatre was full. The audience wore pearls, aigrettes, ostrich plumes, tail-coats, and tulle. According to Cocteau there was snobbism, counter-snobbism, and super-snobbism. The audience shouted, whistled, booed and hooted so loud the dancers couldn't hear the music. Countesses thought they were being made fun of.

Parade, May 18, 1917, Paris: The curtain goes up to the Prelude of the Red Curtain, composed by Satie and dedicated to me. Then the First Manager tries to get everyone's attention by dancing a repetitive dance to repetitive music. Then the Chinese Prestidigitator comes in. He bows, eats fire and has an egg that vanishes and reappears. Then a mime comes in. He brings the American Manager with him. He is wearing a skyscraper costume on his back. He stamps around the stage. The Little American Girl comes on stage and dances the Steamship Rag. She pretends to catch a train, drive a car, swim, act in a movie, and botch a holdup. The third manager comes in on a horse. He introduces the two Acrobats. They tumble while a waltz with xylophone plays.

THE ORACLE SPEAKS

Gertrude Stein said that Cubism was Spanish. She said only the Americans and the Spanish understood Abstraction, the Americans through disembodiment and the Spanish through ritual. Rousseau said the couch was not in the jungle, that the jungle was in Jadwiga's dream. He said he kept his naïveté because M. Gerome told him to keep it. He said we were masters, I in the Egyptian style and he in the modern. Matisse said you have to seek the desire of the line. Max Jacob said that personality is a persistent error. Degas said Gustave Moreau wanted us to believe that the Gods wore watch chains. Vlaminck said he loved van Gogh better than his own father. Apollinaire called Redon's work mystical blobs. Robert Mortier, a distinguished billiard theorist, said that no man is a prophet in his own country.

Letters Not Sent:
The Letters of Camille Claudel 2
(1882-1886)

1882

Rodin,

No, I am not sorry we made love. If I were going to be sorry I would not have done it.

You needn't fear for my chastity. No artist has a chaste heart, that is what my family fears. I am a passionate person like you, a tender person, like you. And like you, I have never felt quite this way before.

I understand how unhappy you must feel, but please do not despair. You should not be surprised that the master of literature, Victor Hugo, is really a cranky, tyrannical old man who refuses to pose for you, and is suspicious because some third-rate sculptor modeled an inferior bust of him ten years ago.

At least he has consented to let you roam the house and be near to him. Certainly, with your great ambition and fierce will you can find a way to approach near enough to him, and at all the necessary angles. Perhaps you will need to sketch him now, even though this goes against your new sensibilities.

Please do not give up, my little wise man. You will prevail.

JANUARY **1883**

Rodin,

I do not enjoy the time you are away from me and at the great Monsieur Hugo's, but I admire how you persist. And no I don't think you wrong in enlisting the help of Hugo's maid or Hugo's mistress, or his daughter, or whoever else is necessary to gain you access to the great man. For art must be completed at all costs.

It is truly cunning the way you manage to have your place at the dinner table changed to suit whatever angle you need to gaze upon the great writer that day, and the way you can draw so skillfully on those tiny cigarette papers without Hugo noticing. I'm surprised you have not lost even more weight than you have; I cannot imagine you getting a chance to eat anything at these bizarre sittings. I cannot imagine anyone, not even the Pope, being so difficult sir, so I truly sympathize when you complain about how hard it is, and I don't think you're becoming as cranky as he is.

And even though I cannot be with you, I am touched by the way you bring all the small incidents at his house back into the studio to tell me, in little asides while you work, as if you must relive the events to better shape the bust. But I am glad it is to me you recount the story, and not some other student or model or artisan. I want to believe that you love me.

1883

Rodin,

You need not look at my move from my studio on the rue Notre Dame des Champs to yours on the rue de l'Université as your triumph over me. It is not. It is only natural that now that I am working with you I should want to work close to you. Anyway, it is not as if I am living with you. I live with my family. And do not fool. yourself: I do not belong to you. If I belong to anyone, it is myself (and even that is in doubt, since above all I belong to my art) and perhaps a little bit, I belong to my father. Unlike you and my brother, my father is kind to me. He understands that I am seriously devoted to art, and he helps me as much as he can. I wish I loved only people like my father, but I have not met any other people like him.

I devote myself to art, not to you. I moved to your studio for my own reasons. I did not like feeling torn between the two places. I am not like you who cannot make a commitment to one studio or one place of residence, or one woman, or to his art. You have many studios, and it is not because your work is so voluminous. You have many places of residence, and it is not because you need a change of air and scenery. You have more than one woman, and it is not because one woman cannot fill your needs; you are at work on more than one sculpture at a time, and it is not because you have a vast creativity. This multiplicity (do not confuse it with abundance) persists in all facets of your life and art, because you are unable to commit. You are frantic, running from house to house, woman to woman, studio to studio, sculpture to sculpture. You are running away from yourself, from your feelings, from your art. What would happen if you stopped to look at it, to feel it, to concentrate? You might break your whole world apart, and find something inside. What? That is the secret you hide from yourself.

I must admit, I enjoy making the hands and feet for your sculpture. It is a job for me, just the way you, in your earlier years (and sometimes still now), worked for Carrier-Belleuse and the others making vases and cornices and decorative cupids. It's an honest job, to support my art.

If I make the hands and feet in your style, it is not because I can only copy your style, but because it is my job and because I am a skilled craftsman who understands your work well, perhaps better than you would like me to.

So why do I like the hands and feet? I like them because they are small. My work is not like yours. While you create these colossal white doors, and populate them with masses of figures, I do the opposite. In private, on my own time, I create tiny figures that I can lay in the palm of my hand. You do not appreciate them, because you are too busy running away to understand what is precious. But these figures are the key to my art and some day you will understand their secret genius. If you ever do understand, you will be filled with grief, because you will be forced to admit that I became a great artist in my own right.

But the shaping of the hands and feet are good practice for me in developing my true art, the art of the miniature if you will (which has not been tried in modern sculpture).

But in addition to practice, it is a joy to work with the hands and feet, because of their special character. They are so expressive, as if the joy or grief or love of an entire human body could be expressed simply in the gesture of the hand or the curl of the toes.

You should not worry so much that I am quiet and absorbed when I work in your studio, and I don't socialize with the others. I don't act this way because I am uncomfortable or because I feel you are a taskmaster who insists we work unceasingly. I am simply absorbed in my work. By nature I am a very restless, passionate person, and as a result I find it hard to find peace. One of the reasons I love my profession so much is that when I concentrate on my art, I lose myself in it, and this dissipates my restlessness and gives me the peace I need.

Furthermore, it is silly to be worried about me working for you. I do not mind it. There is no shame in it. Even now you do an occasional vase for Sevres. You worry too much about how I feel, and you misinterpret my pride. It will make your dyspepsia and insomnia worse. I am flattered that you would confide these troubles to me, but I don't want to be the cause of them.

I would never really tell you this because it might make you vain, but there is another reason I don't mind working for you. You will become the greatest sculptor of your time. Already the critics are beginning to sense it, as you set about to create your colossal doors. I am not threatened by genius; on the contrary, I thrive on it. It will make me a better artist. I will use you in this way. I hope you will not mind it.

1883

Rodin,

I am not surprised to learn that all these years Hugo has been betraying his mistress with his maid; great men seize all the advantages, and most of them are at the expense of women.

I do believe we should be free to love, men and women alike. Every young artist in Paris this decade believes it. But there is enough suffering in the world, why choose to inflict more? Why not be content to love one person, and in doing so, spare the feelings of others? I understand how I could love more than one man. But if I insisted upon exercising that right, wouldn't I be causing all three of us torment? That is the part I could not do. For certainly I could love another man but I could not torment us all by being another man's lover.

I do not like the way you examine my face when you give me this kind of news. It makes me think you are trying to look into the future. Perhaps you already have, at Monsieur Hugo's.

No, I do not mind posing for you. I think it helps me as an artist, and that perhaps you have lost something as an artist by never having had the occasion to pose yourself. When I pose I can see the artistic process from the other side; instead of looking at the object, I become the object. It is almost like two sides of the same experience, loving and being loved for example. Perhaps I will ask you to pose for a bust, so you too can have the experience. An artist who does not pose is like a composer who never listens to music and does not know how to play an instrument.

Also, I do not mind posing for you because I am not like the other models. You love me; you do not love them. I am an artist; they are not. And I especially do not mind, because of the way you look at me so intensely, as if you crave the beauty of the female form more than any other man in the world. You hide this feeling under a mask of lechery because that is acceptable, but I know the true nature of your feeling.

Then, what is even more delightful is the way you look at me so closely, as if you understood what it is to be a woman, as if you've imagined it so thoroughly, you crossed that line that God has made between us, and become a woman yourself. That is why you like to make figures of two women at love with each other. They are not really two women at all, but rather you — so deeply ensconced in womanliness that for a moment you have become a woman yourself, making love to another woman. This to you would be the ultimate union, the ultimate merging, and to others of course it is the ultimate heresy, more unthinkable than Leda and the Swan.

I love the way you draw so close to me, and without touching me examine my skin, your hands and lips remaining just a hair's length away from my body, so that the air between your hands and my skin becomes like a blanket covering me, warming me with the strangest sensation, until suddenly it sinks into my skin.

This is so delicious, almost better than making love. It is like the moment right before satisfaction when you feel yourself filling up inside and you believe you are about to attain everything you have always wanted.

I wonder if other men could make a woman feel this way. I wonder if losing yourself and becoming a woman is as exciting for you as it is for the woman you're gazing at. I wonder if you even realize what you are doing. Perhaps you do, since you try to hide it in the manliness of your long beard and thick frame. The other models, whom you don't love, do not understand what you're about — which is why they're afraid of it and believe you when you pretend it is only lechery.

But I don't understand how you can make love to your models when you don't love them. Yes, of course I could understand how you would have wanted to before when you were dissatisfied at home. But now that you love me it seems superfluous. I can't imagine it could be interesting to make love to someone you don't love when you can make love to someone you love like you love me. I will not ask you about it; we would only argue. You would say that men are not like women, that men make love to attain a variety of different pleasures and therefore can make love to a variety of different women. Or you would say that you were more in love with Woman in general than in any one, and to deny yourself Woman in deference to the one you love, would be denying yourself life itself.

I doubt you would deny you love me. I hope we are beyond that charade. But I doubt you would admit that you are trying to subjugate me by not acknowledging my rights as your beloved. If you did not sleep with the models, you would be granting me this equality. That is why you continue to sleep with them. That is why you continue to deny me my rightful place by your side and instead grant it to someone who is not even part of your artistic life.

Does your wife, Rose Beuret (whom you subjugate by not making your legal wife, and by not allowing her to participate in your artistic life) know that you will never love anyone the way you love me? If she did, perhaps she would not want to stay with you.

You say you need your wife to take care of you, but that is not true. The cook prepares your meals, the housekeeper cleans and sews and mends, the apprentices keep your *maquettes* damp and your plasters safe. You need her because you need someone who is beneath you to submit to your selfish, cruel treatment.

But then you complain that she harangues you and torments you because you will not give her her way. Then you conclude that all women are shrews because men will not give them their way. Did it ever occur to you that you have made her a shrew? Yes you, through your unjust treatment. If you cannot treat a woman as an equal and share your life with her, then you should not live with her and subject her to such torment.

You claim she clings to you and will not leave. Maybe so, but she was young and beautiful once; she could have met a kind man who would marry her. But you occupied her, you had her model for you, keep your clay *maquettes* damp, take care of your affairs when you were away. And then you did not give her what was her right.

Perhaps that is why you will not leave her. She will put up with your abuse and you can complain that she has clung to you.

I do not envy her, but I do wish I had met you when she did, twenty years ago, when you were young and frail, embarrassed and shy. Perhaps it would be different between us. Perhaps you would have been able to give me the kindness and equality I require. But I wonder why I believe this, since you did not give it to Rose.

And then you complain that I don't give you my heart. Look at all you have from me; don't you see it? Look at the figures you've made for the colossal white doors — don't you see the love of women, the bliss and torment? I do. And so many brilliant, usable figures at once, when before it took you months to create one — and so many figures with my body, with my face. People will say I have benefited by our acquaintance, but it is you, sir, who reaps.

November 1883

Rodin,

You should not have had such little confidence in Monsieur Ballu. You see how he is catching on and beginning to appreciate your colossal doors. You, who often tell me patience is a form of action, are too impatient — with the ministry, with the public, with the critics, with other artists. Now that everyone is beginning to notice you, you should forget all your bitterness about the past. Saying you will forget it because you love me is pure silliness. You finally have the recognition and approval you are seeking, not just for the doors, but for all your work, even that of the past.

I am touched by the way you have begun to consult me in all that you do. I know that you are a great artist with ideas of your own, but it pleases me that in addition to loving me, you also value me as an artist and now you feel hesitant to act without knowing what I think. It is as if we are growing up together, you and I, through our love for each other and our art. I know you don't notice these things. I suppose you cannot admit them. But Jessie notices, and even your friend Monsieur Morhardt has spoken to me about it.

1884

Rodin,

Of course I am pleased you have been chosen for the Calais monument. And since you asked, of course I don't think it's wrong that you want to portray more than one Burgher. Even if it wasn't what the committee had in mind, and it will cost more, you must do what your heart tells you to do. They have chosen your genius, not your artisanship to sculpt the monument. In doing so they choose to submit to your will in its conception and design.

Furthermore I think it is very diligent the way you do reading on your subjects' history and visit the local countryside. You make every effort to immerse yourself in your subject. Many sculptors would not take such pains, or would not be willing to lose themselves in another time or place or personage the way you are willing.

I am happy you are so satisfied with the first *maquette*. I have never seen you content with a sketch the way you are this one. I know you will make many studies and sketches before you are through, and the work will go through many transformations, but I wonder if the process has become easier for you as a result of working so prodigiously on your colossal doors. You seem to have acquired élan, an ease of execution you didn't have before, as if something inside your mind that was troubling you has been set free.

You are not wrong to ask certain friends who are close to the committee to speak to its members on behalf of your ideas. You must bring whatever pressure you can and use whatever connections you have to do what is right.

Thank you for confessing to me how much you love me, and what exactly I mean to you. To tell me you have not felt this happy since Maria was alive, to tell me it's the happiness of always being understood, of always having your expectations exceeded. I'm overwhelmed.

Now I am ashamed of all the times I've complained about your treatment of me. But you must understand I could not have imagined you felt this way. Yet I feel the same way, as if being with you was my destiny shaking my hand. But I am afraid now that you've been so candid and tender, I will want you to always be so, and it appears you cannot. Perhaps now that I know how you feel in your heart, I will not mind the things I minded before.

JULY 1884

Rodin,

I miss you and wish I could have traveled to Calais with you. At least I would be able to comfort you in the face of so much harsh criticism. Judging by your letter it appears they don't understand at all what you are trying to do. To say the Burghers' dejected poses offended them! To say they are insufficiently elegant and are an offense to their religion! How do they expect a group of men to feel who are going off to be unjustly executed? I suppose they want from you what they are used to seeing from academy sculptors: a false nobility that masks the true wretchedness of the moment. Well don't give it to them. The time is over when sculptors give their figures' poses and expressions a syrupy coating like brandied cherries. I should not be surprised they do not understand this yet. Perhaps they would rather be reminded of the Burghers' nobility than the true horror of their predicament in this moment, but that is no excuse.

I know it is no consolation to you when I say you have worked hard on this *maquette* and you have done the right thing. Don't let them sway you.

1885

Rodin,

I am so pleased with my two figures being shown in the Salon, I did not even mind when I read the catalog and found that I am listed as your student. I suppose I am and should not care as long as I am not thought of that way much longer.

It never ceases to astound me how different figures look at an exhibition than they did in one's studio. At an exhibition you cannot help imagining you are all sorts of other people, and look at the figure through their eyes. How odd it looks! How enigmatic! What mystery! And why that pose? Why this expression? As you know it is quite another matter altogether in the studio. I wonder where art would lead if the concerns of the critic and the public were identical to our concerns in the studio. Would that harmony allow us to explore new ideas in art un-impeded, or would that lack of tension make art deterior-ate? It will never happen so I imagine there is no use pondering the question.

So what do you think of these two figures now that they are exhibited? I do not know which is worse, not knowing what's wrong with a figure the first place, realizing what's wrong but not knowing how to fix it, or realizing what is wrong too late, when you no longer have the heart to fix it. I suppose you postpone indefinitely all these states of despair by never considering any of your work finished.

April **1886**

Rodin,

I wish I had been present at Edmond de Goncourt's visit to your studio. One hears so much of him; I would especially like to know if he is as people say — perspica-cious but petty. There is no doubt he is a very powerful man, but so are you; I would have liked to see how he sized you up, how he reacted to your figures.

I suppose now you will be invited to his Grenier meet-ings, and of course you will go. No amount of invitations from influential people is enough to satisfy your need for respect. Instead you should accept his solicitation of your dry points as a sign of respect. After all, he is a serious collector.

You mustn't worry too much about money for the Calais monument. You have enough to worry about already of things that are within your control. It is no reflection on you if the city has financial problems. The monument will be cast and erected in good time. Try to be patient.

1886

Rodin,

This might truly be your moment of triumph. Last year Dalou told the ministry that your colossal doors might be the most original work of the century and now Mirbeau has written in *La France* that it is the most important.

I know you understand the power of the press, since it was you who taught me. And coming from a poet you admire. I am sure you feel as glorious as I do now about your colossal doors, as satisfied.

I do not understand why you refuse to have your colossal doors cast in bronze. Of course you could work on it a little longer, make changes and improvements, but to what purpose? You could even go on working on the doors for your entire lifetime if you chose, and never let it out of your studio until you are quite dead.

I believe that is what you plan to do, but not for the purpose of making improvements. You do it out of meanness that is really selfishness. It is your persistence at work, carried to obsession. You want to keep everything that is dear to you, every lover, every woman you've possessed, every figure. You do not want to let anything go. That is a loss for you, not a triumph. It's a tiny death of a part of you, and you fear that too many of these tiny deaths might eventually whittle you down to nothing.

You are being coy when you say that the colossal doors remind you of me and, if you are going to lose me, you do not wish to give up the doors as well, which are your memory of me. First of all, you would not "lose" the doors by having them cast. Second, if you really wanted to keep me, you would be willing to give up these models you sleep with.

Furthermore, I do not like the idea that other artists are beginning to pay you visits because they have heard of your reputation as an eroticist as a result of your figures for the colossal doors. I like to think of you as a sensualist, a man who loves the idea of Woman, and perhaps one woman, and indulges his senses and feelings to the fullest in these realms. But an eroticist is a collector of women, and I would not like to think of myself as part of a collection.

The Notebooks of Eduard Steichen #3
(1909-1910)

NOVEMBER 1909

I spent part of the summer at Voulangis, where the painter John Marin came to visit me. I convinced him to try my color box, and sent the results to the 291 for his most recent show. Now the critics say Matisse influenced him, when it was really my color box!

The American Duchesse bought Rodin a phonograph that she winds up for him, and some recordings of Gregorian chants, that Rilke claims that until now only the Pope possessed. Rodin didn't know what to make of the music until Rilke said it was beautiful. Rilke says the purpose of the Duchesse is to bring Rodin back down from the heights of his art. Miss Camille Claudel agrees with Rilke with an almost malicious glee. Rilke has mixed feelings about it — he believes it is both necessary and unfortunate.

FALL 1909

Picasso exhibited the new paintings he did in Spain this summer. The show was held at the Vollard Gallery and was a great success. He sold so many paintings he moved out of the Bateau-Lavoir (though he will retain it to work, and will keep his room here at the Hôtel Biron), and into a studio and apartment in Montparnasse. The new place is so big and luxurious compared to the Bateau-Lavoir that Fernande says she feels anxious and uncomfortable there. They even have a maid in uniform to serve meals, and have begun to hold their own Sunday afternoon receptions instead of relying on the hospitality of the Steins.

A controversy is waging in the Hôtel Biron over whether or not Picasso should be allowed to bring his pets over from his Bateau-Lavoir and Montparnasse studios. He has cats, dogs, a tortoise and a monkey. The Duchesse detests the tortoise and monkey but everyone else wishes *she* would leave. Rodin is trying to be diplomatic and please everyone.

Picasso congratulated Matisse on the new Apollinaire article which just appeared about him, but Matisse shrugged it off, saying that he was embarrassed by the article because it made him sound like a snob.

1909

When Rodin met Lou Andreas-Salomé and her friend Ellen Key today, he pressed Ellen Key's hand and said with great exuberance: "I know very well Madame, that you were Nietzsche's mistress!" Everyone was embarrassed except Rodin, who seemed quite pleased with the meeting. I do not know if afterward anyone told Rodin that it was Salomé, not Key, who had been Nietzsche's friend, but I am certain someone had explained this to him beforehand.

1910

Cocteau is installing an exotic bathroom in the sacristy so that he may stage a series of Roman parties.

Matisse came up to my room this evening and asked me to come down and look at something in his studio — he wouldn't tell me what. He seemed very agitated. When we got down to his studio, he stood me in front of *The Dance*, a painting of five vermillion figures dancing in a circle on an emerald lawn against a cobalt background. The figures in the painting seemed to be actually moving.

I explained the Purkinje effect to Matisse, in which warm and cool colors change their values at twilight. I did not feel this was really an adequate response to the genius of his color selection, which in my mind was what had transformed his painting. I was about to add this but he put his hand on my arm to stop me. He didn't want to know any more. Later I realized why. Though the effect of light on colors might seem a dry, inadequate and overly scientific explanation to me, it was perfect for Matisse. After all, the Impressionists had insisted that light was what mattered. Matisse had gone off in his own direction, yet here was a photographer telling him his use of color was intuitively correct. It had engaged the light to create vibrancy and movement.

For once I had said the right thing. For once the scientific answer was also the aesthetic answer. We were both so pleased that Matisse gave me his painting called *Landscape at Collioure* and I accepted it. He also let me roam around his studio and look at his new work before returning to my room.

What he's doing really is amazing. He uses pure color, the brightest ones he can find, and chooses the most astonishing ones. Then he applies them to figure or landscape, not according to nature, but according to some more appropriate inner plan or scheme that is more suited to the painting. So for example, a bather might be a rose madder, or cerulean blue, the ocean might be ochre. Once the viewer accepts the fact that these colors are not laid out according to nature, but according to the forms and groupings in the painting, the rightness and expressive power of that color is overwhelming. No one else is doing such compelling work; no one understands better the relationship between color, form and content.

Letters Not Sent:
The Letters of Camille Claudel 3
(1886-1891)

1886

Monsieur Rodin,

You needn't try to turn the head of my friend Jessie Lipscomb to get what you want from me. I will not write you any additional letters; we will not return to Paris any sooner and Jessie will not extend to you any invitation to visit us in England. So your letters to Jessie are quite useless and do not make me in the least bit jealous.

Furthermore, we do not think the reviews of your work in the newspapers you send to us are the least bit ridiculous. What we do think is silly is the way you pretend you do not love me, pretend you are not preoccupied with me, pretend you are humble and meek and frank instead of stubborn and intractable and vain. In short, we find all these ruses laughable, sir, not your art.

If you could grant me a little respect by admitting a little more, or, if you cannot do that, at least refrain from these naked ploys, perhaps we would want to return early from England.

And what's more, you shouldn't write me such pathetic letters. I know they're not sincere and you are just trying to win me back—but on your own terms. What if I have come to England with Jessie to get away from you? I don't deny it. I wish I could stay angry with you long enough to be rid of you.

When I first met you, I told myself that if you fell in love with me you would put things right between us, and so I needn't worry. When finally you did love me, and you still did not want to live with me or marry me, I thought you needed more time, perhaps to realize how much you loved me, or how different this love was from the way you felt before. I thought maybe you needed to trust me more, to know that even though I am young and Independent and have my art, I would be loyal to you and never leave you.

So I gave you more time, and now I see that not only do you not plan to live with me, or marry me, or leave Rose (who would be happier without you), now that you have become famous you are deceiving me with models and students and even visitors.

I finally see that it is not so much that you want me, or you want Rose, or you want any particular relationship or woman. You simply want to have your own way at all costs, and so whatever anyone else wants, you oppose.

That is why I have come away to England with my friend and fellow artist Jessie Lipscomb, and none of your simpering, whining letters about how sad you are without me can disguise this fact of your nature. If you don't wish to change it, please do not keep sending these entreaties to Jessie and myself. You ask me to accept you on your own terms, but your terms are completely unreasonable. I will not do it.

JULY 1886

Rodin,

I really wish you hadn't come here to the Lipscomb's to visit us. Wotton House was a peaceful, comforting place until you arrived. Your travel to London on business was a ruse, I certainly saw through it. It is underhanded to obtain an invitation from Jessie's parents, by pretending to be gracious and posing as our teacher after all these years.

Your presence irks me a bit, because it reminds me of how much I love you. But none of your wiles, attentions, flatteries, or promises to obtain commissions for me will change my mind about things. You must understand that what I want (a life and a home with you) you are too stubborn to give me. So you must leave me alone now. I won't yield to your tricks and entreaties.

1887

Rodin,

No, I am not mad at you. I try to be angry with you, as you would see if you could read these letters, but it does not last long enough.

I understand why Jessie Lipscomb and Mlle Fawcett can no longer share a studio with me. They still want you to instruct them, and since I do not want to see you anymore, you would be unable to visit them in the studio. I can certainly understand how awkward it would be for all of us, and I certainly don't want to be reminded of you (you know how they talk about you) when I am trying so earnestly to forget you.

But I am sorry to lose my friends Jessie Lipscomb and Mlle Fawcett from the studio. It's not just the expense. It will be so dreary without them. You must know (or perhaps you do not) how much I yearn for a group of artists, especially women artists, to work together and bolster each other in the face of the public's indifference, and male artists' sense of competition.

I suppose I will have more room, and therefore I can make a big mess as you do in your studio. Perhaps this will make me feel more important. Perhaps I will be able to work longer hours or concentrate more, without the distraction of the other sculptresses, their projects, their needs, their banter. It may be quite pleasant after all.

So don't think I'm angry at you. I don't really want that, even though sometimes, when I am very hurt, I act as if I do. They say you ask after me constantly and relay your invitations for me to come and work with them on Saturdays in your studio. I am reassured to know you have not forgotten me altogether but please don't ask. It is so painful to try to forget about you. If you are sweet and kind to me, and ask me to forgive you, and invite me to work with you (which you know I love), I'm afraid I will abandon all this unhappiness just to be with you again, and you know that would only make us both miserable after a time, when you begin to deceive me again with other women.

I am not accusing you; I am just trying to explain to you why you please should not send me any invitations or messages through my friend Jessie Lipscomb.

1887

Rodin,

I think you are spreading yourself too thin. I know you need to meet expenses, and so you feel obliged to take on more students from London, especially the poet's son Browning. I know you feel you need to accept commissions for busts of prominent people, since they have begun to approach you, and even to decorate vases, beds and sideboards as you have been doing recently.

But is it necessary to socialize with every poet, critic and dignitary who invites you to their weekly breakfasts, their Tuesday afternoon Salons, their Saturday dinners? I thought you were a loner, like I am, and did not feel comfortable socializing with these people. I am not saying you're incapable; I'm sure you could attend them as I could, act charming and make witty conversation. Even your timidity is winning. But shouldn't you devote this time to your art? Isn't enough time wasted in decorating furniture and fashioning busts for these people?

I'm afraid I do not understand this desire of yours to mix with society. I know you say you must, that you will not remain in the minds of the critics and ministers without socializing, and without their approval you will not win future commissions that will bring you notice. Perhaps I am jealous, perhaps I want to be more important to you than these parties and dinners, but I also believe the way to create great art is to spend time working at it, not socializing to secure your position. You say I am idealistic in believing this — perhaps you're right, perhaps I am young, provincial and naive. But beyond jealousy and naiveté something is truly wrong with this undertaking.

It is true that my brother has taken up with Mallarmé and his gang. He admires Mallarmé the way he did Rimbaud. Mallarmé, in his turn, admires my brother Paul, and will make him an equal. That is how it is among men. Paul will follow, certainly, he is only twenty, but when he does achieve stature it will be at the same height Mallarmé reached before him. Mallarmé will not relegate him forever to student status.

It makes me wish there were great bands of women artists, sculptresses, who steadily pulled each other up into fame. But there is no such group. You and my brother Paul, and all the others like you — won't allow it. Fame is allowable for each other, yes, as a form of protection—but not for us. You tell me to beware my bitterness, that it will ruin my art, but isn't it you who has made me bitter by keeping me always your student in the eyes of the world? And what of Paul, whose fame is now secured at the age of twenty simply because the older poet has taken him in? But you would not do the same for me. You did something that had the appearance of being the same, but it is really designed to ruin me. And then you reproach me for being bitter.

1887

Rodin,

I followed you to the model market this morning. I told myself I did not know why I wanted to follow you; I was not willing to admit the reason.

I wanted to see for myself how you looked at them, how you chose them. I knew if I did not feel jealous—watching you there at the Place Pigalle; I needn't be jealous of what I could not see.

Of course the experiment failed. I was jealous. The girls are all so young. I know I am only twenty-three but most of those girls are sixteen and none of them is over twenty.

And the way you looked at the most endearing ones, when they would lean against the fountain and appear preoccupied. You were so enticed by them; you were living out a dream that had finally come true for you.

So I tried to end my jealousy and instead I feel confirmed in it. And I cannot forsake the memory I have of you—brushing up against these doe-eyed Italian girls who are only sixteen and promise you everything you've always wanted.

I know that most artists today make love to their models, that it's understood to the point of being commonplace, and many artists consider it a necessary inspiration. But the way you cannot stop looking at a woman, the way you must possess her at that very moment with your eyes, makes me think this is not just your artistic privilege that you are exercising. Sometimes it seems the sole motivating force of your work.

1887

Rodin,

I have now seen your illustrations for Baudelaire's *Les Fleurs du Mal*. Even though you complain you did not have enough time to execute them and many of the illustrations are adaptations of your old drawings of Dante's circles of hell, or sketches after your figures for the colossal door, I feel as if I am looking at something brand new and altogether different.

Your work always astounds me. I can look at a figure of yours over and over again, and each time find something so new and so alarming, I must ask myself if I really know you after all, or if I am just a lovesick young woman who cannot extract herself from love's unfortunate spell.

What do you think that love or sex or torment is? That is the question I ask myself after viewing these illustrations. There is no simple answer. There are only layers of answers. It is not just the way the drawing itself informs the page, it is the way the sketch adorns the poem, the way it hugs the margin or the way the devil's toe curls down upon a phrase. For after all, these are not simply drawings but illustrations, and you have placed them so they have a dialogue not only with the poem they decorate, but instead with the entire page. You have employed your genius so well at this; I say that anyone who complains you have no architectonic sense is a fool.

But here again, this placing of the figure with its back up against the phrases gives me yet another answer to my questions. I suppose it is a clever hoax to allow people to believe that because you are timid you are simple. You are anything but simple; you are the most convoluted soul I have ever witnessed. Perhaps that is why you intrigue me so much and I never tire of the excitement and new ideas your work brings me.

1888

Rodin,

I admit I was wrong when long ago I suggested you might benefit from sitting for a bust the way a composer benefits from learning to play an instrument. Clearly you cannot. It is irritating to try to concentrate on your bust when you cannot sit still, but mainly I feel sorry for you. I will finish this bust and it will be an acute and perspicacious interpretation of your head. But it seems you will never allow yourself the experience of being a model. By your impatience and irritability you prevent yourself from feeling what it is like to be scrutinized, to be devoured by someone's gaze, to be sucked whole into someone else's vision. This kind of surrender and abandon is so delicious, so complete, almost a religious experience. I am sorry you will never feel it.

1888

Rodin,

You see how my *Cacountala* is received in the Salon. I wish you wouldn't insist on always calling it *The Sur-*

render. That is not what it depicts. Your favorite moment in love might be the moment of a woman's surrender. That would suit your need always to dominate. My *Cacountala* depicts a moment of tenderness after love-making when the young woman is spent, and the young man is compelled by an irrepressible urge to express his tenderness for her. So you see, it is not what you think.

You rent La Folie Neubourg, the apartments of George Sand and Alfred de Musset, as if to say that two artists can love each other as equals. But then, you will not admit of knowing their union, or of them having rented the place, and you still will not leave Rose. I have agreed to live with you here because I am hoping that things will change between us, not because I agree to your conditions.

It's a pity, because the garden is so beautiful. Its wildness reminds me of the moor near Villeneuve, the Geyn, where as a child I used to take my brother Paul walking. On the moor I used to sit quietly and stare at the gigantic rocks, while they changed shape before my eyes. Usually they would change from one strange monster to another, but sometimes they would take the shape of jaguars or gazelle, or mimic the shapes of the clouds. Paul was always frightened of them.

It is much the same here, at the Folie. If I sit very quietly (I do this of course, after you have gone home to a wife you do not love), the wild, untamable bushes begin to change shape, they twist and entwine, much like your figures for the doors, and as they writhe, their relationships to each other change — much the way you and I are always changing.

Sometimes I envision you in the garden. Much time has passed. You are old. Your hair is completely white and your beard reaches down over your knees. You are kneeling, so the tip of your beard grazes the mossy garden floor. You are weeping. You finally realize that you should have chosen me and it is too late now. Your love was wasted on others. I ruined that well enough for you. Now you cannot take me out of your heart or your thoughts. So you've returned to the Folie, where other lovers lived a full life, to confess your own mistake, to try to leave the image of my face here. You want this garden to take back my soul, but even admitting your own folly will not be enough to achieve that. I will never leave you now, not ever. I will be with you always.

1889

Rodin,

What a decadent old house. I am almost afraid of walking around in it sometimes for fear of disturbing its previous occupants. I am glad we are giving ourselves another chance to be together, and that we are giving this house another chance. What an overgrown untamed place it is! Like our love affair, it would need a good weeding and some new paint to even begin to look presentable, but of course we will let it go.

I do not know what to make of these new drawings you are doing here. Is this the way you drew the circles of hell after Dante? You draw so quickly, paying no heed to what you are doing, and you move on to the next sketch so fast, as if you are an insatiable madman. You act as if you realize you have lost me once, and you are trying to seize me now to prevent it happening again. I have never witnessed such urgency. I feel that something very important is happening.

Perhaps I might understand better if I imagined you feel making these sketches the way I do fashioning your bust. Sometimes, when I am working on it, I feel it has a greater power over me than I do over it. Perhaps that is why, when you work on your sketches, you sometimes seem overwhelmed, like a man possessed.

1889

Monsieur Rodin,

You needn't worry that I am still working for you. You worked for others until you were forty and I am still only twenty-five. What I think troubles you is that I can model your figures with so much ease, that everyone prefers I mix their plaster; I finish my marbles before anyone else; and your graphite corrections are all superfluous.

I loved Cannes not because I cherish your artist friends (for Renoir, like the rest of them, is your friend not mine), but because I love the sea so much.

Yes, the sea. I know it means nothing to you, you who pretend to love Nature so much. But you only love what you can conquer; I love the sea because its vastness comforts me. It clears my thoughts. It provides me with a limit, but at the same time something in which I can lose myself.

What the cathedral does for you, the sea does for me. We are not so different, you and I, except you allow only those things that you can dominate. You dominate the cathedral by studying it; you master it by solving its mysteries. I love the sea for precisely the opposite reason— it cannot be tamed. I respect the sea; I allow it to be itself.

But I do not understand why they all made such a commotion about those birds. Certainly they could see how unhappy the poor things were, shut up like that, with hardly any air or light. I had to let them go. And to say that I am quaint and ingenuous to do so, when it is they who live in the provinces. They live in Cannes. I live in Paris now, where one cannot afford to be ingenuous.

1889

Rodin,

You were right to make me promises and take me away to Tours just now. It is the only way you could win me back. I don't mean to sound proud or cruel. It's just that everything in Paris reminds me of all the pain I've suffered on your behalf and there is no way to get relief from it, not even at our hideaway La Folie Neubourg. Here, for a short time, there is nothing to distract us, one from the other, and I have the time to rediscover why I love you so much and why I want to be near you even though it makes so much trouble in the end.

Even you seem to be rejuvenated by working here. You sleep better. Your stomach doesn't hound you. You concentrate better. You take solace in the countryside. I wish we could stay here indefinitely, living and working side by side, and did not have to return to Paris.

JUNE 1889

Rodin,

Goncourt was astounded when he heard the news. Monet says he is devastated. And now you have lost another good friend because you insist on having your way and shoving his paintings into the background. Monet insists both his work and yours could have been properly displayed but you were ruthless and would only pick locations at his expense.

I suppose it should give me some comfort to see that your other victims respond with the same sense of indignation that I have. But it only makes me wonder anew why you do it. It is so unnecessary. Both your sculptures and Monet's paintings could have been shown to advantage if you had been willing to go along with the placements you originally agreed upon.

I wish I knew how to make you understand, profoundly and irrevocably, that no one is threatening you. You don't need to make others suffer to gain the advantage. Yet I am at a loss to know how to accomplish this. I am close enough to see what harms you, but not ingenious enough to know how to alleviate it.

So will you make it up with Monet, or will you hold a grudge the way you usually do, coming to believe it was you who were wronged by him? I wish you did not persist in exorcising great men from your circle of friends every few months.

1890

Monsieur Rodin,

So what if I sat entranced and still in the face of Debussy's piano playing? I don't deny it. It is also true that he may be in love with me. We are companions he and I, nothing more. He treats me with kindness and as an equal, the very things of which you are incapable.

That is why you should be jealous of him, not because I am captured by his music, or because I have acquainted him with the Japanese Art I love so much.

You should not be surprised that young men of genius are attracted to me and do not look upon me as your student. You cannot prevent my contemporaries from noticing me. And you should stop tormenting yourself by wondering if I inspired Debussy's wonderful new piece "The Elusive Mademoiselle." Of course I did.

It is true Debussy loves me, but I am not going to marry him. I wish I could, because he offers me the companionship of equals that I want so much from you.

But I cannot marry him because I do not love him. Some say that I should marry him anyway, save my good name and my reputation, live among artists who are my peers instead of your decrepit friends who are members of the Academy in their hearts, even when they refuse to join. But I know it would ruin me to marry a man I don't love.

Also, he has another woman whom he has lived with since he was very young. She is said to be beautiful and have green eyes. Even her name, Gabrielle Dupont, is beautiful. Frankly, I am tired of The Other Woman. I know he says he loves me, but you said you loved me (finally) and that did no good for us either.

The story has come back to me of how you've stolen Pierre Louÿs' model from him. I don't know what to think about this. She was his only mistress. He even came to your studio and pleaded for her return but still you wouldn't surrender her. You can have any model in the Pigalle marketplace yet you steal them away from other artists. In a few weeks you will abandon this girl for some other you cannot live without.

1891

Rodin,

I am glad we can undertake the adventure of the Balzac monument together. It seems more like destiny than coincidence that our summer place in Tours is so close to the Chteau de Saché where Balzac wrote his *Lily of the Valley*, and we can combine some repose with a pilgrimage to seek out Balzac types.

I think you are right to search for them through his shape and not the reverse. I am sure if we look diligently we will find other men of his ilk, who fit the image you have in your imagination. Remember, it is what you see in your heart that matters, that must take precedence.

1891

Monsieur Rodin,

You needn't go with the others to Debussy's studio if my figure of the *Waltz* on his mantelpiece haunts you. I don't know why you visit his studio at all when you're always complaining that you don't like Debussy's music. He does not like your figures either, he dismisses them as gamey romanticism.

I think you persist in this association just to goad me, to remind me that he would have married me when you never will, and then to twist it into your jealousy, to hide the fact that it is you who have rejected me by not marrying me.

The Notebooks of Eduard Steichen #4
(1910)

1910

Picasso took some of the people in the Hôtel Biron over to the Jardin des Plantes last night. He is a friend of the curator's son, who lets him in and shows him the exotic animals. Picasso says he would like to have some tropical birds of his own.

Rilke is railing about the fact that the American Duchesse took Rodin to hear Caruso at the Trocadéro. He feels it's demeaning and absurd to expose Rodin to fashionable society. She's also taken him to the ballet, the opera and the horse races at Longchamps. It is not just the fashionable society and the activities Rilke objects to, it's the way the Duchesse curls Rodin's hair (which he has grown out for her), dresses him in a velvet beret and gloves the color of butter. Rilke feels she takes Rodin so far out of his nature she makes him ridiculous. Rilke believes that an artist should not try to make one's self belong socially by changing his dress or his companions.

Max Weber bought several of Rousseau's paintings two years ago, before he left for New York. Now he plans to exhibit them at the 291. It will be Rousseau's first one-man show. He's so thrilled. I wish I had arranged it myself as Stieglitz did the Picasso, and Rodin shows at 291.

1910

Cocteau has taken to his bed with an attack of neurasthenia
and won't receive anyone. He is driving the concierge
crazy. In the meantime his new book of poems, *The
Frivolous Prince*, has just been released, and everyone is
trying to contact him. A copy is circulating through the
house here. Rilke handed it to me without a word. But
someone has earmarked the page where one of Cocteau's
"Sonnets to the Hôtel Biron" appears. Cocteau is currently
chasing after that reptile, Count Robert de Montesquiou,
and the sonnet is supposed to make reference to him.

I don't understand why great poets like Rilke, and
poets who could be great, like Cocteau, are always pros-
trating themselves before older men who are either great
artists or men of position. Why do they do it? Don't they
have any pride? Is it the exuberance of youth? Rodin never
did it. Matisse didn't do it. And it's not just the fact of it
that troubles me, it's the way they debase themselves
flattering these men, imitating them, worshipping on
their altars, and these lizards invariably reject them or
somehow brutalize them in the meantime. I don't understand it. Apparently Cocteau is madly in love with this
half-baked Count (his mother is a stock-broker's daughter—hardly the aristocracy), and the Count just sees this
young boy whom everyone praises as a threat, so of course
he rejects him and calls him a young upstart.

Of course he is a young upstart, but why does this
scenario keep repeating itself between young artists of
potential and older men of standing? Does it happen in
New York?

1910

Rodin returned from his rue de L'Université studio this afternoon with good news: the flood ruined his Steinway piano but did not damage the *maquette* of his Whistler monument. He said it was an odd sensation to find some of his drawings floating in water, but none of the work was damaged. Then he began to discourse on the benevolence of Nature.

An interesting development has arisen out of Matisse's show at the 291 this year. Mrs. George Blumenthal, the wife of the director of the Metropolitan Museum in New York, purchased three Matisse drawings for the museum. This is the first time Matisse's work has been acquired for a museum and Matisse is thrilled about it. I'm pleased the transaction was brought about through the 291.

1910

Cocteau, in his ever ingenious plan to draw closer to Nijinsky, has just published *Vaslav Nijinsky, Six Poems by Jean Cocteau, Six Drawings by Paul Iribe*, as an answer to Diaghilev, who tries to prevent Cocteau from helping Nijinsky with his showers and rubdowns. Diaghilev likes the publicity but continues his suspicious supervision of Cocteau.

MARCH 1910

Rousseau is moping again over Apollinaire's review of his painting in this year's Salon des Indépendants. Rousseau says Apollinaire has no end of praise for Matisse for "freeing himself from Impressionism," but will only concede that other painters will like Rousseau's painting — which is a total departure from Impressionism. When Picasso (who is a friend of Apollinaire) suggested it didn't matter what Apollinaire thought, that Rousseau was the precursor to many young painters and someday everyone would realize it, Rousseau said he was wrong, that everything that happened in the Paris art world the next ten years depended on what Apollinaire wrote about it, that painters' careers would be made or broken based upon what Apollinaire wrote about them. Picasso tried to refute this, but Rousseau would have none of it, he just went into his room to paste Apollinaire's article in his scrapbook and write his rebuttal to it in the margin, as he does with all the press clippings about his work. Picasso went off down the hallway, grumbling that Paris is full of painters who care too much about what critics think of them.

April 10, 1910

Rilke has finished *The Notebooks of Malte Laurids Brigge*. He is leaving for Rome.

June 1910

Rodin went to a testimonial banquet to celebrate his promotion to Grand Officer in the Legion of Honor. Many of his friends are peeved with him for accepting the award, including Rilke, but three hundred people attended the banquet.

I postponed my trip to Voulangis this summer so I could see Stieglitz when he stopped in Paris on his way to Austria. I introduced him to the Steins and Vollard.

We visited the exhibition of Cézanne watercolors at the Bernheim-Jeune Gallery and Stieglitz liked it so much we asked to show it at the 291. It's been arranged for next winter, but they only agreed because we've exhibited Matisse and Rodin.

Picasso has left for Cadaqués on the Catalonian coast, with Fernande and the painter Derain.

AUGUST 1910

Camille Claudel has not used her room in the Hôtel Biron at all this summer or last. There is a rumor circulating through the Hôtel Biron that she leaves Paris for the entire summer and spends it in Tours where she has two sons, ages fifteen and sixteen. The sons are assumed to be Rodin's, though he denies their existence. So does Miss Claudel. Another rumor has been circulating that, before Miss Claudel leaves for Tours at the beginning of the summer, she destroys all the sculpture she has made the previous year. Since she works at her studio on the Quai Bourbon and not here at the Hôtel Biron, there is no way to confirm this.

AUTUMN 1910

In his review of this year's Salon D'Automne in *Poésie*, Apollinaire boasts of having always championed Matisse. This is true, but there is something about his bringing our attention to that fact which embarrasses me. In his defense, I can say that he mentioned something about the decorative power of Matisse's work, and I think that is a crucial point. I believe it is the decorative aspect of his work that makes it both important and underrated.

Autumn 1910

Picasso arrived in Paris from Cadaqués two days ago, but
it took him that long to reach the house from the train
station. Apparently some of his friends met him at the
station and they stopped in so many cafés and studios he
has only arrived this afternoon.

September 1, 1910

We had to take Rousseau to the hospital today. He cut
his leg and didn't tell anyone about it and we're afraid
blood poisoning has set in.

September 4, 1910

Rousseau died of the blood poisoning in his leg. The
hospital listed his cause of death as alcoholism. The
bastards. Everyone knows it could have been prevented.

1910

The composer Erik Satie has rented Rousseau's room at
the Hôtel Biron. Apparently no one has seen much of
him in twelve years, and he hasn't published or performed
any new music. The word around the house is that he is
a friend of Debussy and had to get away from him and
his music for a while, so he moved to the suburbs of
Arcueil-Cachan (he calls it Arcachan) and didn't tell anyone where he went. He rented a room with no heat or
water above a café called The Four Chimneys.

Now he's back. There are all sorts of stories circulating around the house about his twelve years of seclusion.

They say he was drinking heavily. They say he used to wear grey velvet corduroy jackets. Now he wears dark suits. They say he carried a hammer in his pocket for protection when he walked in from Arceuil-Cachan to Montmartre to play piano (that's how he earned his living). Now he leaves a lit clay pipe in his pocket. They say he went back to music school five years ago. He's forty-five! Whatever he did, it worked. Ravel and Debussy are playing his music and everyone is going wild over it.

There's something so exciting to me about an artist making a comeback after he's been quiet for several years. I almost like it more than the thrill of an older artist finally getting recognition, like Rousseau or Rodin. I'm not sure why I feel this way, perhaps I sympathize with what the comeback artist has lost and regained, or the courage it must take to face that failure and re-emerge from it, as opposed to an unrecognized artist, who has nothing to lose, and can only hope for the future. But I'm afraid I have no sympathy for a young artist who is successful, the way so many are today. I know they work hard and they may deserve the recognition, but it seems shallow or unearned. Maybe I am just a Romantic.

I asked Satie if he would like to write something for our issue of *Camera Work*. He immediately showed that puckish twinkle in his eye, and asked me if the article could be loosely related to Art. I said it could, that both Rousseau's and Matisse's would be. He said he would work on it in his leisure time. What leisure time?

Erik Satie's The Consolations, Introduction by Eduard Steichen

It is well known that, when Satie died in 1925, no one had entered his Arceuil-Cachan studio for fourteen years. When his friends finally entered, expecting to find a sanctuary, they found piles of manuscripts, musical compositions, clothes, food, refuse, books, newspapers, and Satie's pipes.

While sorting through this swamp of paper, carefully preserving original Satie musical compositions that no one knew existed, they also found a package, wrapped in brown paper, tied with string and marked in bold letters with one word: STEICHEN.

The package was mailed to me that same year at Condé Nast in New York City, where I was working as a photographer for *Vanity Fair*. Several of my colleagues were standing around when the package arrived, and hoped I would open it in their presence, but I pushed them out of my office and shut the door.

I ripped the paper off slowly and carefully. The box had a lid, and I lifted it off. Inside, on the top of a stack of papers, was a collection of five pipes, individually wrapped in newsprint. The pipes looked to be some of the ones Satie would keep lit in his pockets when he walked into Paris from the suburbs to play piano at the Chat Noir in Montmartre. But I could not be sure.

The stack of papers turned out to be *The Consolations*. On the cover page it said it was originally written for Alfred Stieglitz's magazine *Camera Work*, and later revised for Eduard Steichen's book project. It also said that it was *"based on The Consolations of Philosophy by Boethius, who wrote it while imprisoned by the Gothic emperor Theodoric, while awaiting his execution."*

The cover page was also decorated with musical notes that can be played on a piano, but have never been connected with any of Satie's known musical compositions, or anyone else's. It remains a mystery whether or not they are part of a larger composition by Satie. But when played they immediately remind me of the Hôtel Biron — its magic and tumult.

I framed the cover page of Satie's manuscript, and to this day it sits on my fireplace mantle, first in New York City, and now in West Redding, Connecticut.

The Consolations of Erik Satie

CHOOSING THE PROPER CURE

Doctors are quacks so it is important to choose the right one. Sometimes you can do this by selecting the proper cure for your ailment. The following cures are currently available, and these come with my opinions and commentary:

- *Travel, Change of Climate*: this is said to cure moral disease, profound sorrows, hallucinations and monomania. It does not help nervousness. It cures obesity in lymphatics but not others. It cures disordered imaginations, unbridled passions, jealous characters, worried dispositions and headaches, but only in thin women.
- *Taking the Waters*: This does not cure anything, but is satisfying if you wish to gamble or find your daughter a husband. Mont-Dore, Cauterets and Eaux Bonnes are said to specialize in sore throats. Saint-Sauver is said to specialize in neuralgia, hysteria and hypochondria. Plombières specializes in other female disorders. Luchon and Aix-Les-Bains will not cure you of gambling. You can only find the earth cure at Arcachon and Aix. It is supposed to be good for gout.
- *Chloroform, Ether and Alcoholism*: these kill pain, are

useful in reducing fever, and work well as a tranquil-izer. I do not recommend them in excess, except for the alcoholism.

- *Incarceration in an insane asylum*: cures old age, black-mail, unorthodoxy, and is very useful in getting rid of one's enemies. This is a very effective cure.

- *Invoking Saint Blaise, Patron Saint of Motorcyclists with colds*: I hear this is quite successful in curing a variety of ailments.

- *Throwing yourself at the mercy of your neighborhood sor-cerer*: I recommend blacksmiths for problems with the devil, cobblers for problems with women. For other problems, you may consult midwives, under-takers, or children who want to be priests.

- *Retiring to the country*: this cures people who are suffering from excessive ambition. When you retire to the country, take long walks, hunt, eat light food, undergo massages and warm baths, and engage in varied reading. Humiliate your pride and raise ob-stacles against your desires. Acquire modest friends without aspirations.

- *Severe Diets*: I approve of anything severe. Find a doctor who will put you on a series of severe diets, a different one each week. This is the perfect cure.

- *Fresh Air, Exercise, Water Drinking, Vegetarianism*: Hogwash. It makes you oversensitive and you're bound to contract every ailment that's tangoing through Paris.

- *Camphor*: It probably works, but think what it will do to your social calendar.

- *Deep Breathing and Spitting*: To me it sounds vigorous and calisthenics. Try it once.

- *Vaccination*: A tricky business at best.

- *Artificial Insemination*: I don't know what it will cure, but it sounds like an interesting idea.

- *Living on a boat in the Seine and playing music during meals*: it makes the fish terribly ill.
- *Electro-physiochemical treatments*: I hear they make you lose your appetite for cognac, and for this reason, I cannot recommend them.

HOPELESS CASES

If you're suffering from circular folly, dual folly, delirium of persecutions, hysteria, shoplifting, hallucinations, freewill, or insanity, there may be no help for you. On the other hand, now that the source of the emotions has been transferred from the stomach to the brain, the nervous intestinal system of insects is being studied, Bifurcation is being disputed, and Education has been recognized as a form of both suicide and homicide, maybe doctors can offer more hope.

ABOUT DOCTORS

If it's too perplexing to choose a cure, a simpler method might be to choose a doctor, and let him choose the cure. But if you're going to choose a doctor, there are some things you should know, and some recommendations I would like to make.

Dr. Broussais believes that all diseases are caused by inflammation of the intestines. I would recommend that painters see Dr. Broussais, since the only thing they do besides paint is complain of stomach aches.

If you want Dr. Ricord as your doctor, you must know which room to wait in. If you're an ordinary person, meaning possessing no memorable birthmarks and no money, you have to wait in a crowded room and you will be assigned a number. If you're a woman, you have to enter by a separate staircase, and you are advised to speak to no one. If you bring a letter of recommendation, you will be seated in a separate room with others like you. If you are a friend of the doctor, or a doctor, or a doctor of the doctor, or a doctor's doctor, you will be assigned to yet another room.

Another reason to visit Dr. Ricord is his collections. He has two Rubens and a van Dyke in the reception salon. He has a collection of busts of physicians in the library. In the same library he has a collection of surgical instruments. When members of the aristocracy fight duels, they have been known to select some of Dr. Ricord's surgical instruments as weapons.

A reason not to visit Dr. Ricord is that he believes syphilis is not contagious.

Dr. Piorry invented a method called plessimetrism, which means tapping on your abdomen to find out what's wrong with your organs. It's a very musical idea, and I recommend a recreational visit.

You may want to throw up your hands and choose your doctor according to his hobby. All doctors have one. Dr. Herard plays piano. Dr. Robin runs a metallurgical factory and reviews for the *New York Herald*. He was also a consultant to the Tsar of Russia. Dr. Brocq collects Impressionist paintings. Dr. Halle paints.

When visiting a doctor make sure to haggle over the fee and don't let him charge you more than ten francs. For dentistry, choose a dentist who began as a locksmith. They are the most sympathetic. Don't see any doctor who wears the *palmes academiques*. That's just a ruse to drive up prices. Doctors who require you make an advance reservation are respectable, but you may get nervous if you know about your appointment too far ahead.

SELF-DIAGNOSIS

If you prefer self-diagnosis and self-cure, I recommend the following reading: *The Natural History of Health and Illness*, F.V. Raspail 1848; *Treatise on Venereal Diseases*, Philippe Ricord, 1838; *The Moral Treatment of Madness*, Dr. Leuret, 1840; *Common Sense Medicine*, Dr. Piory 1868; *Manual of Health and Advice on the art of Healing Oneself*, Dr. Jean Giraudeau de Saint Gervais. These books can be found in any grocery store.

PERSONAL REMEDIES

My personal cures are as follows:
- *The white food diet:* It cures everything, but it is especially thorough in curing depression, lethargy, insomnia, neuralgia, indigestion, toothache, lack of discipline, failure of will, confusion, bewilderment, awe, bemusement, and obesity.
- *Five applications of the Ogives and Gymnopédies:* cures nose polyps. Prolonged applications cure liver disorders and rheumatic pain.
- *Throwing an acrobat out the window and founding a new religious sect of whom you are the High Priest:* This cures heart sickness and broken hearts.

A NOTE ON THE PASSIONS

The passions are currently divided up into three categories: The passion for wealth, the passion for glory, and the passion for debauchery. Artists possess the passion for glory. The passions are generally imprudent, and unhealthy. Passion leads to excessive ambition, and those who suffer from excessive ambition become pale, gaunt, bald, breathless insomniacs with heart murmurs, melancholy monomania and stomach inflammation, who eventually die of cancer, or apoplexy.

Those susceptible to ambition are bilious, or bilious-sanguine and melancholic types, who seek jobs above their talents, and exceed the boundaries of emulation.

However, since glory is a noble ambition, sometimes concessions must be made to those who thirst for it.

Recommended reading: *The Passions and Their Dangers and Inconveniences for Individuals, the Family and Society*, Dr. Bergeret, 1878, *The Medicine of the Passions*, Dr. Descuret, 1842.

How to Cope with Rising Rents

Rents have tripled since the turn of the century. The solution to this problem is simple. Acquire a fake aristocratic title. Hyphenate your name. Buy a pair of cufflinks, and have engraved on them the motto: "To Live is To Act." When you enter and leave your apartment building be seen carrying Paul Leroy-Beaulieu's bestseller *The Art of Investing and Managing One's Fortune*, and Louis Reybaud's potboiler *Jerome Paturot in Search of a Social Position*. Sit in prominent cafés and read these books.

Advice About Interior Decorating

Each room should be decorated in a different style, for example: the dining room Renaissance, the drawing room Eighteenth Century, and the library Empire. Painters simply use different colors in each room. Whistler had a blue dining room with darker blue dado and doors, a pale yellow and white drawing room, and a grey and black studio. My way is to have only one room. Only a bed fits, so I use it as a table.

The other problem with having rooms is that you must have furniture. Caned chairs are popular, but I prefer the washable beech kind one finds in hotels. Chests and four poster-beds are quaint extravagances. I recommend that plywood be used instead of furniture. If you must have your Victorian armchair, your pompadour, your English or Polish armchair, your Louis XIII, your bentwood, or your old oak François I, do not buy the real thing. Buy a cheap imitation at the Bon Marché or Galeries Nanciennes. For example, a real Renaissance sideboard costs 600 francs. At the Bon Marché an imitation costs 300 francs. I personally recommend the Henri II sideboard, which only costs 180 francs.

If you want bric-a-brac—enameled miniatures and porcelain—don't buy it at antique shops. They make it new, throw a little dirt on it, call it old, and sell it at ten times the cost.

Wallpaper is a delicate business. I am enamored of the enormous mural scenes like *The Lyon Saint Étienne Railway*, or *Hunting in the Forest*. But these are becoming increasingly difficult to find. Avoid those wallpapers that try to look like silk.

THE BEAU BRUMMEL THEORY OF FASHION

Velvet is out. The only truly tasteful suit to wear is the black or otherwise as dark as possible suit, without decoration. The true man is distinguished by the cut of the cloth. The differences are subtle. The cut should follow the natural line of the body. If you want to express yourself further, employ the neck cloth.

The embroidered jacket the Breton peasants popular-
ized is embarrassingly joyful. Do not be caught wearing
it. The habit of wearing three or four waistcoats is also
frowned upon. A passerby might think you're a smuggler.
Turkish boots are silly. Cossack waistcoats and short
English coats are ludicrous. Gold buttons catch the light.

Women squander their money and looks wearing
kimono coats and dyeing their hair the color of cows'
tails and egg yolks. They pile leaves, flowers, fruit, ribbons
and feathers on their heads and call them hats.
Women — don't do it. Wear culottes and Coco Chanel's
soft, loose clothes made from jersey. Cut your hair short
and wear trousers.

MYOPIA IN PAINTERS

Only fifteen percent of the general population is short
sighted. But fifty percent of painters are short sighted.
This explains modern art.

LE JOURNAL

My favorite newspaper is *Le Journal*. Their stories are full
of pornography, perversion, adultery, sadism, xenophobia,
nationalism, anti-Semitism and scandals. They are a
literary journal. Their main concern is that women flirt
too much.

THE COURTSHIP OF VICTOR HUGO'S NIECE

When Camille Flammarion was fifteen, he fell in love
with Victor Hugo's niece. He courted her until she left
her husband. They spent their honeymoon in a balloon.

When he was old enough, he took a young girl as a lover and the three of them lived together.

RENANISM

Renan wrote *The Life of Jesus* in a Lebanese hut. Clemenceau says he made us what we are. Renanism is a mixture of seriousness, mockery, unctuousness and blasphemy resulting in a dilettantism that is taken to the point of nihilism. Renan has been accused of transforming God into an interior decorator.

HAVING A CAR OR HAVING A CHILD

Much is said these days about whether to own a car or a child. Here are some things to consider:
- Owning a car increases your likelihood of divorce, and increases the tendency toward installment buying.
- Once you own a car, you will want another.
- If you own a child, you may not want another.
- Cars make loud growling and grating noises.
- Children make loud keening and gurgling noises.
- A car is less likely to criticize or judge you when it gets older.
- A car does not require a dowry or an education.
- A car will expand your movement.
- A child will limit it.

THE CONFLICT OF REASON AND PASSION

The Greeks invented it. Before them people did not distinguish between dream and reality, symbol and what it symbolized, body and soul, body and clothes, foot and footprints.

THE BRETON QUESTION

What is it?

ANGLOPHILISM

If you want to be an Anglophile, at every opportunity refer to your clothes as spencers, jerseys, waterproofs, macintoshes, and mcfarlanes. Tie your tie the way the English do. Carry your cane and mount your horse the way they do. Go to a tavern instead of a café. Be cold to strangers instead of polite. Attend the Jockey Club and gamble on horses. Dress your children in Queen Anne's clothes. Be seen reading Miss M.S. Cummings and Mrs. Elizabeth Wetherell's bestselling novels. Be funny, not witty. Drink beer not cognac. At every opportunity, use the words *beefsteak, fashionable, lunch, dandy, corned beef, pyjama, high life, baby, cocktail, breakfast, flirt, five o'clock tea, smoking, grill room,* and *shorts*. Send your sons to the Paris School of Political Sciences. Teach them to have pride and tenacity, a practical business sense, the ability to concentrate on their ambitions and achieve their goals.

HOW TO BECOME A BOURGEOIS

It is not how much money you make that makes you bourgeois; it's how you earn the money and how you spend it.

First, lay the tablecloth symmetrically. Serve dinner in its own room, not in the kitchen. Create a salon. Furnish

it with a piano, paintings, candelabras, clocks and bibe-
lots. Receive visitors here.

Pay for your children to go to secondary school, and
make sure they take up bourgeois professions. Your sons
should achieve the baccalaureate. Provide your daughters
with a dowry. Acquire a cultural education.

Know Latin and speak classical French. Do not allow
your wife to work. Your quarrel with the church is about
politics, not ethics. You believe that morality in women
means chastity, fidelity and duty.

Choose a profession that allows you to wear a dark
suit. In other words: no manual labor or physically dirty
work. In your manner, be polite. Give a good impression.
Cultivate distinction. Be conservative and understated.
Don't try to outdo other bourgeois. Simply keep up with
them.

How to Choose Your Cognac from a Variegated Flask

When you ask for a cognac in your neighborhood café,
the waiter will try to serve you the top portion. You want
the bottom portion because it contains more cognac. So
insist on being served the bottom portion. Be discreet.
If the waiter objects, pour out the top portions, serve
yourself the bottom portion, and pour the remaining top
portions back into the flask.

Love at First Sight

If your parents fell in love the moment they met, and
insisted on marrying against all odds, you will be con-
demned to a life of heartbreak, cuckoldry, bachelorhood,

and emotional violence that you should avoid at all costs. Do not marry. Do not take a lover.

THE DIFFICULTIES OF LEARNING RUSSIAN

If you are a shipbroker from Honfleur, it is essential that you learn languages. German, Portuguese, Spanish, Italian, Dutch, Danish, Latin and Greek are easy to learn, but Russian is impossible. Try as you may, you will not learn Russian. You can work as a translator, in Paris at the Foreign Ministry, at an insurance company, you can publish poems and articles on music in which you take Rossini's side against Wagner, but you will not learn Russian.

SPANISH PAINTERS

I befriend Spanish painters because we both must endure the same paradox in our lives — we like spicy food but we lack color in our palette.

THE COLOR WHITE

Isis's color is white. Sugar, grated bones, salt, mildew, cotton and fish without skin are white. Yesterday, a tainted oyster killed Péladan. The oyster was white. In my music I always long for white.

FAUCET SALESMAN'S MUSIC

Faucet Salesman's Music should endeavor always to keep the tap running. The water that comes out of this tap should be clear and sweet and simple. The Faucet itself should be free of rust and should make no sounds. Only the water should make sounds. Then the faucets will be easily sold. Only the faucet salesman knows the secret of his own music.

THE DUTIES AND RESPONSIBILITIES OF A CONTRAPUNTIST

Duties: To create music in which tedium is concealed behind malevolent harmonies. To greet poverty, who arrives like a sad little girl with large green eyes; to abandon charming and deeply inept music for boring and uninterestingly competent music; to sit by graciously while you are discovered through music you wrote twenty years ago, while the music you write as a contrapuntist goes unheard; to make poverty an aesthetic principle; to search for beauty through a minimum of means. To be tried, fined and sentenced on libel charges for defending your music.

Further duties: to become a progenitor of sublimities, to resign the high priesthood of the Cult of the Wound in the Left Shoulder of Our Lord Jesus Christ. To suffer being called a lunatic and being rejected three times from the Academy; to guard against the inflation of the spirit; to eat only white food; to end all ongoing quarrels with your brother and Willy; to face destitution honorably and move to the suburbs; to watch out for scorpions. To die of boredom and fail at everything you do; to squeeze the tips of your own fingers to make yourself cry; to resign your post in the Arceuil Soviet; to acquire and quarrel with protégés; to discover war-like love; to utilize telepathy whenever possible. To walk around your work several times until you can get it to go with you; to arrive yourself; to devise an elaborate system of shellfish; to exercise ironical conformism to advertise the virtues of the phonometer to lecture on musicality among animals to reveal the lack of truth in art to take your fingers out of your mouth; to succeed beyond your wildest dreams.

Letters Not Sent:
The Letters of Camille Claudel 4
(1892-1910)

1892

Monsieur Rodin,

   You pretend you don't know I am carrying your child. Then you let me come to the darling Islette early, before you have arrived, and stay after you've gone, as if you know I need time to plan and arrange things, enter into a conspiracy with Madame Courcelles concerning your child. You assent mutely to these proceedings, as if you understand what must be done, and consent to this grave undertaking.

   Sir, you are mistaken. I did not come here to put your child to rest as you so blithely assume, as if the events of the world were fashioned after your preferences.

   No. I plan to give birth to this baby. Why, you ask. I will tell you why. I will have this baby simply because it is yours. I know I am too proud and do nothing but complain, but the truth is I do love you. I'm afraid that I will never love anyone again this way. You see, I already speak of it in the past tense. If I cannot have you then, I can have your child. In this way I will never really lose you in body, the way I have lost the sight of you, lost the sight of your eyes, your squared-off brow. This way I will be able to enter your child's soul, the way I have never been able to enter your soul. I tried to win it, to lure it, to steal it. I tried to be frank and straightforward, but you will not let me inside.

I know the child will be a torment to me. I will have to hide him from Paris and my family. But I will love him frankly and truly, the way I love you, the way my father loves me. A child cannot hope for more.

1892

Rodin,

I am not surprised to be cradling your son in my arms. I knew I was carrying a son and not a daughter — but I would not have expected to be holding *two* sons. I should have known; I had grown much too large to be carrying only one of your children. I have named them both after you. The son who was born a minute older is named François and the one who was born a minute younger is named René. So now with your son Auguste, by Rose (whom you do not love as you love me, and should not have chosen over me), you now have three sons, each bearing one of your three names.

I have given them the Christian name of Athanaise. It was my mother's middle name and my maternal grandfather's first name. It's a beautiful name, isn't it? François Athanaise. René Athanaise. I chose the name because I did not want your sons tormented by having to carry your name or mine, and my mother's maiden name, Cerveaux, is too easily linked to me. Your sons will be safe and prosper under this name. My grandfather, who bore this name, was a doctor.

I am sorry you will never know that your two sons exist or get to see them face-to-face. (I'm sure, when they are old enough, they will want to sneak out to Paris to take a look at you). I am sorry I must be complicit in this lie you perpetrated that I came to Azay-le-Rideau to lose my children, not to bear them, and I have stayed so long because I cannot recover from losing them (when really it has taken this long to bring them to light).

Though I will not give up my art or my good name in order to raise your sons, they will be in good hands here with Madame Courcelles. I will see them as much as I can. They will know from the first that I am their mother and, as soon as they are old enough, that you are their father.

I will never slander you to them. The criticisms I level at you are between us. They will know your good qualities; I will answer their questions about your limitations as diplomatically as I can.

I have known all along that both my life and work were leading toward some great secret; now it is suddenly revealed to me in its many facets. I keep the secret from you that you have two sons by me. I keep the same secret from my family, Paris, the world. I keep the secret from you that I am breaking off our relation because of your sons. I keep the secret from myself that somehow, amidst all of this, my heart has died, and it cannot be reawakened.

1892

Rodin,

I am sorry you think my bust of you is wrong, the brow too noble, the eyes too sad, the nose too virile, the mouth too sensual, the beard too forceful and the overall effect too beautiful. I think it is perfect. I did not expect you to like it, or even approve, just as I did not like your *Thought* modeled after my face.

Just as, in your *Thought*, my face evokes the emotions you feel for me, so my bust of you does the same. The sadness around the eyes and cheeks, the longing in the forehead, that is what I feel when I look at you now. As far as beauty is concerned, you are beautiful. The tenderness in the face is of course not your tenderness, but the tenderness I feel for you.

I should not need to explain these things to you, you who pretend to understand everything about art.

MARCH 1893

Rodin,

It is probably best that you move to Bellevue with Rose. She will be happier in the suburbs and you will enjoy the boat ride to Paris. You will have the city and its diversions separate from Rose and perhaps the distance will spare her some of the humiliation and jealousy she must feel. She must be as unhappy as I am, and there is no reason to malign her.

I hope you will think of me when you go on long walks in the forest there, and become so troubled that your dog will wonder at it and press his wet nose into the palm of your hand.

Thank you for your kind letter about my two figures at the Salon. But to praise me for figures such as *Clotho* is to praise me for working in your style, following in your footsteps, remaining forever your student. I would prefer that you did not write to me.

Now that I am rid of you, and I am you know, I will pursue my own vision and everyone will see that it owes nothing to you, except you and your colleagues, who will remain forever blind and ignorant of my genius.

As I told you before in these letters, the real work I
have been hiding from you consists of tiny figures, miniatures of sculpture. My favorite is the *Gossipers*, several
women listening to another, garnering her secrets. A
screen encloses the figures. I envision this piece in onyx,
but of course I have no money for such extravagances.
There will be another group, very similar, of three young
girls holding hands under an enormous wave that has
risen up and is about to envelop them.

I am sure you will steal this idea from me after it is
exhibited, since you like so much the idea of possession,
especially Nature possessing young girls. But the air of
mystery in these tiny sculptures will escape you when
you try to copy them, even if you try to make the wave
into the image of God's hand.

Many other miniatures like these will follow: a girl
kneeling against a hearth, a girl gazing into the fireplace.
There will be a scene at the dinner table, farmers in a
wagon, children listening in astonishment to a violin
player, and many others I already have planned, if I can
survive forever on no money. Already my creditors hound
me, my mother and sister despise me, and my brother
barely helps me. Of course, you won't help. You watch
in secret glee while I sink deeper and deeper into indebt-
edness and shame, hoping I won't realize my genius.

1893

Rodin,

It seems only natural now that your sons are born,
that I should return to Paris and, instead of continuing
to live with my family, I should move into my studio on
the Avenue d'Italie. Since you have already abandoned

our Folie Neubourg and moved with Rose to Bellevue, I needn't worry about seeing you nearby at the Folie, or fearing I have misunderstood your decision.

Likewise, this should not surprise you. It was you who fled the Folie Neubourg while I was in Tours, so full with your sons. It was you who moved with Rose to Bellevue instead of installing her there alone while you stayed in Paris.

It is beginning to enrage me less that you remain with Rose when you really love me, and could only be happy with me, because I am beginning to understand your complacency, your fear of equality and true feeling. But I am becoming more and more infuriated by your inability to take responsibility for your own choices. Why do you blame me for not submitting to your whims? It is you who choose Rose over me again and again, who choose to live with her and legitimize her. It is you who refuse to marry me. Failing to act is a choice. Abdication is a choice. You might as well admit it. But then if you did, you would be admitting a shortcoming, a failure in your life, and you are not capable of that are you? Just as you are not capable of treating any woman well.

Tonight I am sitting in my studio staring at *The Waltz*, waiting for it to be packed up and taken to the Société Nationale des Beaux-Arts to be exhibited for the first time.

I wonder why you don't like this sculpture. Is it because it does not resemble yours? Is it because the young woman is embracing a young man her own age, and not someone older? Is it because the young man lets her be herself and does not try to dominate her? Is it because the young man is physically beautiful, well built, graceful and tender? Is it because the young man is so attentive in the way he's leaning toward the young woman, as if he is listening to her very being? Or is it simply because the couple slants precariously to one side, and creates an aura of tension you could not discover and display in your own work?

You are a stubborn intractable man.

1894

Rodin,

I wish we were still seeing each other so that I might console you about your *Balzac*. You have made a thorough pilgrimage into Balzac's life. You have walked the countryside where he lived, searching for types; you have read his biographies, looked through photos, even had a suit made by his tailor. You have made sketch after sketch and become disenchanted with each one in turn.

Now you believe you are lost, that all this searching has led you further and further from the man, and that in becoming so steeped in his surround you have lost his essence.

That is of course the danger, but that is not what has happened. As always you are simply impatient. You have perhaps become lost in details for the moment, and for the moment lost sight of the true man, but that is only part of the journey you are taking to find him. And you will find him. Be patient. Have faith in your abilities to find what you are looking for, to know when you have found it, and to persist until you do find it. It is no small accomplishment to create a monument to a man who is greater than yourself, and also make it a true work of genius. This is the task you set yourself. Of course it is going to take several years and a dozen sketches before you find what you are looking for. Why do we think it should be easy? Why do we think we should know the answer the minute we have gathered the information? Why do we think we shouldn't have to suffer, that this work should be full of success and glory and ease of execution?

In this muddle of information you have gathered you will rediscover the man you are looking for. Trust yourself to do it, and do not settle for less. Your heart will tell you when you have found him.

1894

Rodin,

I am having quite a pleasant time here in Guernsey with Monsieur Hugo's grandson, Georges. My only ill feeling is that if I am away from Paris. I should be with your sons. But Madame Courcelles convinced me that I was under too much strain having broken with you just before your sons were born, and I needed a complete diversion. She said everyone does at least once in their life and I should not be ashamed of it.

I do not understand why you would be so upset at my coming here that you would tell Roger Marx you no longer have any authority over me. Perhaps you think the Hugos your sole province just because of the bust you made of him ten years ago. But my acquaintance with Georges comes through my brother Paul, not through you, so you shouldn't believe you have the right of control over it.

1894

Monsieur Rodin,

There. I have done it. I have suffered your sons to sit for a bust, so you can at least see their likeness, though you still will not know they are yours. I have made the bust into a girl by giving it a braid of hair, to further prevent you from knowledge. The bust is called *La Petite Châtelaine* and is quite good. Both François and René were delighted with it, since they look the same. It is René's sense of wonderment I have captured in the expression. Being the younger, he seems to have the greater capacity for awe. They are only two now, and though I don't see them nearly enough, I see them as often as I am able, and Madame Courcelles is very kind.

It occurs to me, now that your sons are two, that I never explained in my letter why you will never know of them. It is so simple; perhaps it did not occur to me to mention it.

It is simply this: You do not want to marry me. After ten years that had become abundantly clear. Now, what if I told you about your sons, and you had offered to marry me? The indignity of it would have been too much to bear. I have my pride. So now you understand the reason.

You also might be wondering why I always refer to them as your sons instead of ours. There are two reasons. We share nothing now, since you have stolen my heart, my soul, my works of art, my particular figures, my lines, my poses, even my face. Since nothing is ours—it must be mine or yours.

Why are they not mine then? I don't know. I love them. I carried them. I see them as often as I can. But there is a way in which they are lost to me; I felt it the moment they were conceived, and continue to feel to this day. I don't understand it exactly, or I would explain it to you. Maybe some day I will understand better.

1895

Rodin,

I am worried about your health. If I were still seeing you, I would try to coax you away from all these banquets. I am sure you are eating too much. It is no wonder you are suffering from insomnia when in one sitting you can eat crayfish bisque, salmon, trout, leg of venison, fattened pullet with truffles, pheasant and partridge, lobster, artichoke hearts and asparagus tips, and you can drink a glass of Madeira, one of Pommard, another of Fronsac and another of iced champagne. No, of course you are depressed. The confusion to the palate alone must be overwhelming.

I have already written you what I thought of your *Balzac*, as you requested through the intermediary Monsieur Le Bossieu, so I don't think it fair that you complain I haven't given you all my thoughts on the matter. And of course this complaint reaches me as you intended it to. Why can't you accept the respectful praise I have already given you? Why is it never enough? Why, in addition to having loved and wanted you, do you insist that I admire you?

I don't think it is kind or polite to request that a woman reveal all her thoughts on a subject. Since when has that ever been required?

But if you must know the rest (and of course with your cunning you sensed it), I will tell you it here, since you will never read these pages.

I knew, when I saw your *Balzac*, that this was the true expression of your genius, your evil genius perhaps. The colossal doors and your tormented figures for them may be the perfect expression of your oeuvre, but this *Balzac*, which pretends to represent the prolific writer, is really an expression of your soul. It is the divine mirror reflecting back your face.

It told me two great secrets, one that I already knew and another I didn't. It told me that you do see yourself for the sacred monster that you are, and perhaps suffer for it. It also told me that we are finished, you and I. It made me certain of it.

1895

Rodin,

I warned you that my *Gossipers* would be a work of genius that even you could not fail to recognize. Now that you have seen it at the Salon du Champs de Mars, don't you agree that it is exquisite? I know you don't understand or appreciate the precious, you who are concerned only with that which is prolific or gargantuan. But here is the precious raised to the level of art, and I am pleased you have finally seen it at the Salon, even if you will find some way to claim authorship of it. Now I'm sure you can understand why I refused to let you in my studio to see the new work. You would have wanted desperately to steal it, and with all your money, supplies and apprentices (of which you offer me none), you could have easily reproduced it and exhibited it before I had the chance. At least now I have proven once and for all this new work is mine, and you must become ever more cunning and devious to invent a way to rob me. I'm sure you will succeed in the end, but in the meantime I take great pleasure in watching you realize, gazing at my new work, that I can, quite easily, create art that has nothing to do with you, or the love we had for each other, just as you created your Balzac. I had to prove it to you. At this moment I have never felt more triumphant.

1895

Rodin,

My brother Paul has returned from his consular position in America. He had the courtesy to invite me to dinner with his friend Jules Renard, but I'm afraid he no longer even pretends to tolerate me. Before I even speak, his entire expression changes and through the entire meal he looks as if he is trying to hold back a torrent of abuse.

I have received your request via Mirbeau that you be invited to his house the same day I am. Mirbeau of course can do whatever he chooses, it is his house. But I told him if you were invited that day, I would come another time.

I don't mean to be harsh, or reject you repeatedly. I know you are suffering as much as I am because of our separation, and my heart goes out to you. But please understand that I absolutely cannot see you again. I have explained all the reasons so many times before; I will not repeat them here. Please do not try, through whichever intermediaries, to arrange a meeting between us.

I will admit to you here, in this moment of sympathy between us, that life is indeed sad for me. I am able to continue to work, and I enjoy the work and my solitude. I spend whole afternoons copying in the Louvre or taking walks around unfamiliar parts of the city. The people I see there give me ideas for new groupings, and thus inspired I go back to my studio and work. But I must confess that I have little heart for seeing my old friends. The Daudets are kind enough to invite me, and the Schwobs and Pottechers often ask me to dinner, but even when I try to go, I end up standing outside in the hedges staring in the windows instead of going inside.

It is not simply that I have nothing to wear. Sometimes this is a real hindrance or an embarrassment and if I do not earn some money soon it will become a real problem. But that is simply what I seize on when I am angry, because it is simple and clear. Something much deeper is wrong. It is as if my heart has died. I can't believe this is true since I am still able to work. But I can no longer be around people. My whole body rejects it. I become sullen and withdrawn, if I am able to go at all. The only people I can stand to be around now are your sons. They are so delightful. They are the only things besides work that bring me joy. I'm afraid I am overcome with sadness at no longer being near you. That must be it. Being near others must remind me I am not with you, and aggravate the wound. At least here alone in my studio, working, I can find some peace.

END OF DECEMBER 1895

Rodin,

I am worried about your reaction to Bing's opening exhibition at his Galerie de L'Art Nouveau. Perhaps you were overcome by an impulse to support your friend de Goncourt. But to say that an international style is barbaric! To defend the maintenance of a French style at all costs!

I know you are a conservative when it comes to politics and life (except in your dealings with women, in which you make an exception for selfish reasons). But I never thought you would become conservative in your thinking about art. Your whole life you have dedicated yourself to making innovations in art; you have shocked the public and critics with your innovations. Do you now disallow others to make these same innovations? Or do you make progress in art in spite of yourself?

You have not stopped searching for a new truth in art. Your struggle with the Calais and Balzac monuments is proof of that, as well as your quick sketches of the female form. So I do not understand why you can no longer afford that search to others. Don't you see that your criticism of an international artistic style is just as narrow minded as the critics' reaction to your own work?

I know that eventually you will become part of the older generation of artists, and young artists will feel the need to reject your style as I have, and find their own. But I was not aware that your vision would be narrowed and you would no longer be able to appreciate progress and innovation in art.

After all, internationalism is where art in Paris is headed. Everyone comes here from other countries now. In the next ten or twenty years the new art that is formed will have to be, by its very nature, international. That is the future. I can't believe you don't understand and welcome this as the next innovation. Should innovation stop with your own work? Is your truth the only truth?

I suppose what I am really afraid of is that this new conservatism of yours signals an end to innovation in your own work. I hope this is not true.

JANUARY **1896**

Rodin,

I hear you have actually bought the Villa des Brillants in Meudon. Frankly I was surprised by the news, I did not realize you had so much money. It sounds like it must be a very spacious house, if you have room in the out-buildings to make coops for Rose's canaries. The view of Sevres, St-Cloud and the Seine as far as the Trocadéro sounds exquisite. And you already have a studio with skylights. What could be more convenient? And with such an expansive house you will have all the room you need to display the art you've been collecting, your friends' paintings on the second floor, your Oriental bronzes and Egyptian statuettes in the bedroom, your own pieces in the studio.

Rose will continue to be completely away from Paris and your escapades, and you too will continue to be able to get away from Paris when the strain becomes too great, but now to your very own house.

Since I know your fear of fires, I worry about how you will be able to heat and light such a big house. Does it have gas or electricity? Those vegetable oil lamps are so inconvenient.

I also hear that, now that you have moved into the house, you do not seem so tired and you are beginning to work again. I am glad of it. I envy you finding a place of your own where you can be comfortable and at peace. Only then can we find the concentration we need to sustain our work. I envy what you have made for yourself. I wish I could share it with you, especially the peace.

1896

Monsieur Rodin,

I have moved from l'avenue d'Italie because I needed a change of air. I am not trying to "hide" from you as you claim, though I have asked you not to send me messages and invitations, and I do wish you would stop.

I left l'avenue d'Italie because it was rendering me melancholy. It was too near the Folie Neubourg, and our good times together, when you began, for a moment, to treat me kindly, and I still hoped you might realize I was your salvation, and that you should stay with me.

Now you are lost, and I am alone and a bit sad. So I moved to brighter quarters, where perhaps I can forget about what might have been possible, put out of my mind the euphoria that would have been our life together, working side by side.

It is best now to rid myself of all possibilities that remind me of you. That is why I began my new work, my true work of secrets in miniature; they give me so much pleasure. Perhaps I can find peace here with my new work, and will no longer have any reason to run away.

Since you will not listen to my polite requests, I have directed Monsieur Morhardt to tell you quite plainly not to visit me anymore. I have been trying to explain to you since your sons were born and your *Balzac* was conceived — it is over between us. It is cruel to force me to employ intermediaries.

And even if it did not pain me to see you and prevent me from making progress with my new work which I love so much, I am by now so broke trying to pay off creditors, I have no decent clothes in which to receive you, or go out with you.

December 1897

Rodin,

You needn't be chagrined by these new rejections of your work. I know they come from all sides. You should be accustomed to it by now, but I know you expected that at least other artists would understand your work.

Ignore the Swedes. They are embroiled in politics of their own and their rejection of the *Interior Voice* has no bearing on its merits. The Symbolists are blind and ignorant when they say your work isn't really human. They should be able to appreciate your art, but they are bold and their need to reject older forms renders them unable to see what is novel in your work.

The reactions to your Victor Hugo monument at the Salon must be accepted in the same light as all your previous scandals there. Just as they did not understand the modeling of your *Age of Bronze* twenty years ago, they are outraged by the unfinished qualities of the monument. Instead of realizing that is the direction your art is headed, and hailing it as a stroke of genius, they criticize it as a craftsman's flaw, as if you don't know what you are doing.

I know how dispiriting this barrage of criticism must be, but I am afraid the truth is that your work will always outrage everyone, and you will remain trapped inside the world of your own art, looking out at all the scandalized and famous people, young and old, artists, critics and public.

JUNE 1898

Rodin,

I think it was right to keep the Balzac monument once the committee had rejected it, rather than sell it to the group of artists who had raised money by subscription to buy it. But it was wrong to do it for the reason you chose: that the group of artists who wished to buy it was pro Dreyfusard. You should have chosen to keep it for artistic reasons, not in order to avoid being embroiled in a political squabble.

I understand you are not political by nature (neither am I), and so you don't wish to involve yourself in political issues. But decisions about your art should be made for artistic reasons only, not for any reasons peripheral to art. I am anti-Dreyfusard as you are, and may lose my friendship with Monsieur Morhardt because of it, so I sympathize with your position at the same time as I voice my opinion.

It is time we addressed this question of you stealing my works. I should not have to remind you, sir, that you worked as a decorative artist for Carrier-Belleuse and an artisan with Van Rasbourg. You were more than a bit upset when these men claimed your vases, your caryatids, your colossal figures as their own.

So you should not be surprised to learn that I am outraged to hear you plan to exhibit my works as yours. It is easy for you, the great Parisian master, as they call you, to go to the Universal Exposition, and accept the praise and acclaim for my sculptures. Who would believe me, a struggling sculptress, over you, the great master? I will not be surprised if I go down in history as your student, and as a natural result my *Cacountala* is believed to have been modeled from your *Eternal Springtime*, my *Young Woman with a Sheaf* is believed to be copied from your *Galatea*, my *Old Helen* is believed to be a study of *She Was Once the Helmet Maker's Beautiful Wife*, that my *Torso of a Crouching Woman* was borrowed from yours, that my *Man Leaning* is a variation of your *Thinker*, that my *Waltz* is done as a homage to your *Kiss*.

We both know, don't we, that you have stolen all these works from me, that mine was the initial conception, the original pose, the innovative line, and it was you who

copied, in the name of your colossal doors, and believed
it just, because you, as you claimed, were the master and
I the student.

But do not be misled. I am putting my lawyers to the
great chore of unmasking you and they will work long
and hard at the task. I am not naïve. I know that the truth
may not be revealed in your lifetime or mine, but someday
the truth will be uncovered. Some day the world will
know that not only did you steal my heart, my will, my
position in society, my reputation, my potential as a great
artist; you stole my very work, one by one, you expropri-
ated my figures. And they will be made to realize that
you did not do this unknowingly or unwittingly or even
nobly for the sake of art, you did it ruthlessly and delib-
erately to subjugate me.

Someday they will see who you are. For now, I am
forced to suffer the torment of reading the praise heaped
on you for my sculptures. I am asked to watch silently
while you receive all the adulation and glory for my work.
And then you reproach me for being bitter.

And the plot does not end with theft. You must thwart
my commissions as well. First you blocked the commission
your colleague Puvis de Chavannes tried to secure for
me, to install my *Clotho* in the Luxembourg Museum in
his honor. I knew very well why that project died. Now
you are attempting to thwart Monsieur Morhardt's efforts
to secure for me the commission for the Alphonse Daudet
monument.

Why do you do it? You know I cannot pay for clay and
marble and armatures with the meager sums I receive
to fashion lamps and ashtrays. You know I will never be
able to support myself making busts if I am not legitimized
in the public eye by a commission.

But you neglect to speak to Léon Daudet and Monsieur Mirbeau as Morhardt asked you to, because you know your neglect will quickly ruin the project and they will ask someone else. Then you pretend to have forgotten. And since you have pretended so long to be my mentor, Morhardt believes you. He doesn't see through your plan to destroy me. But I do. And I warn you. You will not manage it. I will survive, on pure bitterness if that's all that is left to me, and I will have my day. It is you who will be ruined, ultimately. It is you the great master who will be shown as a liar and a thief, thwarting an innocent young girl's career and then pirating her creations. Raphael was avenged the thefts of Perugino, Van Dyck was avenged the thefts of Rubens. I too will be avenged.

Although you insist on persecuting me, and sometimes succeed in blocking commissions that would otherwise be awarded to me (witness the Chavannes tribute and Daudet monument), I still prevail.

With the kind patronage of Maurice Fenaille, who is not easily tricked and does not believe your lies, I have been able to complete the *Wave*. And what a beauty it is. I have even been able to have a copy made in onyx as I dreamed of.

Of course you will steal it the minute you see it exhibited, and turn the great *Wave* into your hand or some such vain, silly nonsense, but I will know the beauty of it is mine, and Monsieur Fenaille will know. Even though I have exhibited in three salons for fifteen years, I show at two galleries, the critics praise my work and proclaim me the greatest French sculptor and publish homage to my work, I still cannot secure the commission that would give me the financial safety to proceed with my work, legitimize me in the eyes of my family and the public, and provide me with a wardrobe that would allow me to leave my studio without being ridiculed by urchins and whispered about by neighbors.

You needn't grieve so much about losing me. I know how unhappy you are. Of course the news gets back to me; for example, the display you put on at Monsieur Morand's lunch the other day, in which you frightened his children.

I wish you would admit that it was your decision, instead of making everyone believe that I abandoned you. You were the one who would not live with me, who would not leave Rose, who would not marry me. It was your choice, not mine.

Yes I have moved to the Quai Bourbon and what of it? I needed to be farther away from you, closer to the Seine, surrounded by water. And furthermore my landlord evicted me for not paying the rent.

1899

Rodin,

I don't know how to make you understand that all your little attempts to help me make me more and more unhappy and I must be completely alone and completely free of you if I am ever to recover from losing you. Still you send me these Scottish sculptresses asking for lessons and saying you have recommended me.

I don't want to see you. I don't want to receive messages from you from intermediaries. I do not want you to try to obtain commissions for me. I do not want to exhibit with you. I do not want you to arrange for articles to be written about me. And I do not want you to send me students.

I suppose you cannot put yourself in my place. Imagine you are me. You are trying to get over a man who for fifteen years has dominated you and your work and treated you badly. You find that your only solace is to be alone and work at your art. Any memory of that man reminds you not only of your present hurt, but the fifteen years of humiliation and unhappiness at his hands.

Yet this man will not leave you alone. Every day he does something to make you think of him. You ask him in every way imaginable to stop but he does not. Now he sends you young sculptresses, the age you were when you fell in love with him, so you will be reminded of that. What must I do to make you stop?

So your painter friend Fritz Thaulow has told Henrik Ibsen "everything" about us, who in turn has written a play on the subject, which has just been published. When the play is staged in Paris, will you attend the opening?

I am almost tempted to go with you, if you do go, more as an act of defiance than a gesture of approval. Of course I do not approve. My sculptures should be exhibited, but my personal life should not be interpreted (by an infamous misogynist no less), and displayed to the world.

We do busts and monuments of dead artists without their consent, and the results are often revealing and outrageous to the public. Your *Balzac* (your only true work of genius, which could not have been conceived if I had not inspired you to undergo the preparatory exercise of your colossal doors) is the prime example. It is too revealing for many, no wonder they are outraged. And the busts we do of live artists, even commissioned, are never really approved of or sanctioned—again, because they are too revealing.

But our busts and monuments are not interpretations, they are not an attempt to convey information—they are works of art, and stand alone without reference, regardless of how they were inspired.

So why doesn't Ibsen's play invoke the same immunity? Perhaps I suspect him of bad intentions, of setting about to spread gossip and innuendo, instead of to create art. Perhaps I am wrong and simply resent the sacrifice of my personal life in the service of art. I suppose I should have to read the play and decide for myself if it transcends the merely anecdotal. But since I am sensitive to being the play's subject, I am not sure I could objectively judge.

1900

Rodin,

I do not know what to think of your new liaisons with young women of position. I wonder what it is like for you now to conquer a young woman. You have such a reputation. Do they expect it, and feel snubbed if you do not approach them, and so you feel obliged? Has it become a form of introduction, like exchanging names? Do you still feel the same thrill of possession you once did in the lean years when you were alone with Rose and had not yet exercised fully your artist's prerogative? Or is it less urgent, less frantic, more of a subtle pleasure that a pipe smoker or a connoisseur of rare cognac might feel?

I wish I knew if anyone, at this moment, truly touches your heart. Is it the aristocrat Sophie von Hindenburg, or her daughter Helen? Is it the American dancer Isadora Duncan? The painter Jelka Rosen who reads you Nietzsche? The Scottish sculptress Kathleen Bruce?

1902

Rodin,

I wish you would stop celebrating your success at the Universal Exposition and get back to work. I am worried that you will never work again, now that you are content and so busy socializing. That would be a great loss for art.

You are never in your studio anymore. It seems all you do now is travel. I don't know how you tolerate it. First you are off to Grez to visit Jelka Rosen, the painter who reads you Nietzsche in translation. Then you visit the Thaulows in Quimperlé. Next you're off to Italy to visit the von Hindenburgs at the Villa Margherita in Ardenza, and allow them to take you sightseeing in Serravesa, Lucca, and Pisa. Then you're off to London to be honored by the Victoria and Albert Museum, and the students at the Royal College of Art, next to Prague, to preside over your exhibition there. Then to Vienna to make an appearance at the Secession exhibit.

And when you are in Paris, you spend your time attending banquets in your honor, humoring young artists who are enthralled with you, lunching with the aristocrats and socialites who buy copies of your figures from the colossal doors and commission their own busts. In the meantime you are being passed over for national commissions to do monuments because all your previous monuments remain unfinished or have been rejected by their sponsoring committees, and you have not produced one figure of importance since your Balzac five years ago.

Whereas many of the artists today are known when they are in their twenties, you were not known until your forties, and now you are past sixty. But a late success is no reason to stop working in order to relish it. Nothing is more important than continuing to create art. I thought you had more conviction. I did not know you could give up your work so easily.

1902

Monsieur Rodin,

It is absurd to persist in this thinking that I am ruining my chances for success by refusing to exhibit with you. If I continue to show my works next to yours, in Prague or whatever city invites it, I perpetuate this notion, in the minds of art critics and the public, that I am your student. I refuse to go down in history as your student, sir, and if this means waiting until I can show my work alone and be recognized for the artist I am, I will wait.

I also object to this myth you insist on perpetuating, that you want to exhibit my sculptures with yours to make me famous, that you are giving me opportunities. I suppose it would be too much to ask that you be frank about your aims — that would spoil your plans to ruin me. I will ask my lawyers to find a way to make you stop, even though I am penniless and can only pay them with copies of my work.

1905

Rodin,

As more time goes by and my brother rises in the ranks of the ministry, he becomes more and more incensed with art, especially modern art. He seems to have made you the target of his abuse and vilification, and wants to make an example of me.

I have no way of preventing him from publishing these articles about us in *L'Occident*. He also attacks the Fauves in his latest article. I told you twenty-four years ago that he had an aversion to art. Since he was only a child when we moved to Paris for my sculpture and I fell in love with you and became your student, he connects my current situation as a neglected artist to you, even though we haven't seen each other in thirteen years.

You must try to forgive him. He has never felt any passion or known any love; he does not understand the need to make sacrifices for art. All that is left to him is to try to fit us into his narrow scheme of things. That is his only hope of understanding us.

It hurts me that he reviles you, and tries to make an example of me, but he is my brother and I love him. In any case, put your mind to rest — he has taken a post in China and is leaving soon. Perhaps he will change his notions there, or simply forget about us.

I have just finished carving my *Cacountala* into marble. You will be pleased you have already exhibited *Eternal Springtime* and *Fugit Amor*, so people will believe my piece is inspired by yours, not the reverse.

Mine is the better sculpture. It is modulated perfectly; it is not marred by sentimentality like *Eternal Springtime*, or excessive zeal like *Fugit Amor*. This perfection is not created by the surfaces or the modeling but by the lines. The lines in your *Eternal Springtime* are too rigid, and those in *Fugit Amor* too arabesque. Mine are somewhere in between, in that area you cannot find because it is too subtle, too precise. You haven't the patience to find it nor the tenderness to recognize it if you did.

The rumors you hear about me are only partially true. In the summer I lock up my apartment and leave for several months without telling anyone where I am going. I am going to the Islette to spend some time with your sons, so obviously I cannot tell anyone. And who would really want to know? My father, bless his poor heart, might want to know where I have gone, but my mother and sisters hound him so for loving me I could not bear to tell him.

As far as smashing my sculptures to pieces — that is also true. They are not the originals. I let the gossip-mongers believe that to keep them off the track. I keep the original plaster cast in one safe location, and a bronze copy of each figure in another. It is true that this deception of mine is extremely costly, not only in time and money but in the damage it does to my good name, but I feel forced into this to preserve my art in the face of my mother and sister's vengeance and my brother's and your thirst for revenge.

I am not the desperate lunatic you had hoped I had become, just a destitute artist, struggling not only against poverty and the public's indifference, but the vicious intentions of my family and yourself to destroy me.

Your sons are big strapping fellows at the great age of thirteen. They have, by some gift of Providence, escaped your childhood faults of weakness, shyness, and frailty and show no signs of assuming your adult faults of vanity, egotism, or an oppressive attitude toward women. They also seem to have escaped my sin of hubris. You should consider yourself lucky to have two sons who are both free of your faults, and their mother's.

Today I wrote my dealer Eugene Blot and turned down his invitation to accompany him to the Salon d'Automne because I am so poor I have nothing to wear.

My family and colleagues complain about how much I stay locked up in my studio, but I beg for money so that I might pay the rent, buy some clothes and look respectable, but no one helps me. Yesterday I was forced to borrow money from an acquaintance to pay the fines levied against me for not paying my creditors and this acquaintance accused me of keeping a lover.

And of course you do nothing to help me, you who have grown rich and fat from the Universal Exposition. You could easily help me now if you really wanted to save me from disgrace and embarrassment, but of course you don't want to see me succeed as an artist, because then you would be revealed as a fraud and a thief.

1906

Rodin,

I never thought I would be ashamed to have known you but the rumors I've been hearing lately make me feel just that. All of Paris is talking about your intimacies. Each one is discussed in great detail, savored on the palate like a fine wine. Many people say that you are clinically insane, that you suffer from erotomania. At the same time a whole other group of stories are circulating, about your belligerent acts against the young men you employ to work as your secretaries and apprentices, and the way you end long friendships with other great men over trifles.

Finally, and this perhaps is the most damaging, the news is circulating that you no longer sculpt or create any works of art, instead you draw one sketch after another, of young women engaged in the solitary act of giving themselves pleasure.

I was afraid when you stopped working six years ago. I thought then that I simply grieved the loss for art. Now I see what I really feared was that, if you stopped working, your lust for women would overtake you.

I know how much I and the other women who loved you have suffered from this disease of yours. I did not realize you suffered from it too.

1909

Rodin,

Gwen John is an excellent painter. But she suffers over you like I did. She wants a relationship of equals, as I did, and as always, you will not give it to her. I know how unhappy and single-minded she is. I hope it will not destroy her.

I worry less about the American Duchess. She is a shrewd businesswoman and I know she is making you money by raising the prices of your sculptures. It gives me a particular pleasure to hear the other members of your circle detest her and spread rumors that she is poisoning you slowly with arsenic, now that she has taken over your diet. I am also thrilled to hear that she talks so much it drives everyone crazy, that she dominates the household by playing Gregorian chants much too loud on a gramophone, that she orders you around, dresses you, and arranges your hair, as if you were a small child. She is the first woman who has ever been domineering and oblivious enough to degrade you.

Don't think you've captured me for good now that I've acquiesced, at your urging, to take the rooms next to yours in the Hôtel Biron. I still keep my old studio, and house my religious icons in it, though that's a secret.

1910

Rodin,

It was you who prevented Judith Cladel's article praising my work from being published in *La Fronde*.

How clever of you to show an *Aurore* in Italy that is not mine (and furthermore is not a good piece of work), attribute it to me, and then arrange for it to win the gold medal. If you were not trying to ruin me, enrage me and drive me mad, I would applaud this little escapade as the supreme practical joke.

The Notebooks of Eduard Steichen #5
(1910-1913)

NOVEMBER 1910

Rilke is back from Rome and is making us all suffer now
that, after *Malte Laurids Brigge*, he seems unable to write
anything. He wanders around the house spouting apho-
risms out of context; he visits perfume shops and comes
back reeking of geranium oil. He is even further depressed
by the death of Tolstoy. He is leaving again, this time to
Algiers and Tunisia, in hopes that a change of scenery will
help him write again.

DECEMBER 20, 1910

Picasso is calling Braque "Wilbur." This puzzled me so I
started asking around the Hôtel Biron about it. No one
understood the joke except Matisse, who says Picasso is
alluding to Wilbur Wright. Apparently he feels Mr.
Wright's flying machine is the perfect example of a Cubist
object.

An exhibit of Picasso's early work opened at the Vollard Gallery today. There was something very rustic and
ingenuous about the entire affair. No invitations to the
opening reception were sent out, no catalogue was issued

for the show, and the pictures were unframed. I suppose
this corresponds to Picasso's distaste for exhibitions.
When he greets a fellow painter he never asks them where
they are exhibiting, or who is representing them, or if
they have sold any work. He only asks: Are you working?
How is the work going? What are you working on?

END 1910

Agnes Meyer, a reporter from the *New York Sun*, wants
to start a contemporary magazine called 291 to complement the gallery. She, Stieglitz and de Zayas have established themselves as the editorial board. Mrs. Meyer is
also sponsoring a show of Brancusi marbles at the 291.

WINTER 1911

The Cézanne watercolor exhibit at the 291 has drawn an
incredible amount of outrage and criticism, the most
we've ever had, I think. Of course those familiar with
contemporary art think it's the best we've ever shown.
Some of the visitors to the gallery did notice the fake
Cézanne I painted for the exhibit. They felt it was much
more literal than his other work. People even asked to
buy it. I'm terrified, and I've asked Stieglitz to burn it
immediately. I won't rest until I hear that he has.

Cocteau has just met Anna de Noailles and I'm afraid
he's already begun to talk like her—i.e. without stopping.

Matisse has returned from Morocco. He let me see
his new paintings. They are truly remarkable. He has
succeeded in making color an end in itself. But he doesn't
seem to realize what he has achieved, or if he does, he is
not content with it. It seems color is just one of the many

problems he will address in his career as a painter. For the moment he seems to have put it aside and is struggling with the composition of his paintings.

FEBRUARY 24, 1911

Apollinaire gave my paintings at the Devambez Gallery a perfunctory review in *L'Intransigeant*. Now I know how Rousseau must have felt. Of course now that Rousseau has died and the painters Apollinaire believes in won't back down about him, Apollinaire writes the unqualified reviews of Rousseau that would have made the poor man happy.

1911

The Irish sculptress Nuala O'Donel, who was a student of Rodin's and a friend of Malvina Hoffman, purposely gassed herself yesterday in her studio. She's dead. Miss Hoffman is quite shaken by it. A rumor is circulating through the Hôtel Biron that Miss O'Donel was despondent because Rodin no longer came to see her work and didn't seem interested in it anymore.

I wish we could all stop caring what other people think of our work. Surely we have a million examples, right here in the Hôtel Biron, of how dangerous it is.

1911

Cocteau has managed to get himself hired by the Russian Ballet! He is painting publicity posters and writing advertisements for magazines. I knew he would insinuate himself into their company somehow.

I accompanied Rodin to the opening of the Société Nouvelle Salon at the Georges Petit Gallery. Rodin is its chairman, so he should not have been surprised by the work exhibited there. Nevertheless, he stood for a very long time in front of Jacques Blanche's portrait of the dancer Vaslav Nijinsky, as if he had never seen it before. I envy Rodin's capacity for awe.

Our show of Picasso watercolors at the 291 caused even more commotion than the Cézanne exhibition. But there have been some buyers, among them Arthur B. Davies, a painter who frequents the 291, and Stieglitz himself.

MAY 14, 1911

Rilke is back from North Africa and he still has not written anything since *Malte Laurids Brigge*. He is seriously considering giving up writing altogether.

Rodin, who never had a dry spell in his life until after he turned sixty, is trying to convince Rilke he has no right to quit, that it would be an arrogant rejection of his obligations in life to do so.

Rilke was respectful to Rodin but in private said Rodin is no example, that he has let his life become "grotesque and ridiculous." He wouldn't let Rodin's age or ill-health serve as an excuse, as Matisse thought it should. I think Rilke still admires Rodin too much, and as a result can only be disappointed by his humanity, his foibles, and the infirmities of his old age.

MAY 1911

The American Duchesse claims that some street toughs broke into Rodin's rooms here at the Hôtel Biron a few nights ago, held him at gunpoint and tried to steal some of his work, but she brandished her own pistol and frightened them off. No one believes her. But now several people in the house are worried about Rodin's collection of revolvers. The collection seems to be quite large, which no one realized before. The Duchesse has acquired a guard dog for Rodin, hired a detective, and sits up in an armchair while the master sleeps. She's driving everyone crazy.

SUMMER 1911

Picasso is summering in Céret in the Pyrenées. He is staying in an abandoned monastery surrounded by a wild garden, where he has taken all the rooms on the first floor. Sounds like Rodin here at the Hôtel Biron!

Braque, Max Jacob and some other friends are visiting him; Matisse even plans to go down there. Picasso writes us that he likes the Catalan people and Max Jacob is earning extra pocket money by reading their horoscopes in the local café. The town's butcher gave Picasso a red curtain he had admired, and Picasso has hung it in his studio.

JULY 1911

Yesterday Rodin presided over a meeting of the women's society called the Internationales, to honor Valentine de St-Point. Homage to Rodin was read at the meeting. Miss de St-Point was blasted in the press this morning for her novels. *Le Cri de Paris* said the first one is about a woman achieving sexual satisfaction; the second incest, the third self-gratification, and they ridiculed Rodin for admiring her, implying he was duped by her novels' eroticism.

SEPTEMBER 21, 1911

The tenants of the Hôtel Biron are talking about a suggestion made by Apollinaire in *L'Intransigeant* that a Warranty Office be created for artwork, which would regulate and supervise payment of a percentage to artists when their work is resold at a higher value.

Rilke thinks it is an idea before its time, but hopes the system will eventually be employed. Picasso thinks it is a high-minded idea but impossible to execute, and that dealers would find some way to circumvent it. Matisse said that painters should think about creating art for its own sake and not try to become rich off of it — that profit is the artist's downfall.

1911

Max Jacob's novel *Saint Matorel* with four etchings by Picasso has been published. Kahnweiler, the gallery owner who sometimes shows Picasso's work, had it published.

Rodin has been complaining lately that he's thirsty all the time, so his doctor told him to drink milk instead of wine. The American Duchesse is administering it to him. The tenants of the Hôtel Biron are grumbling that this doctor is a quack. The doctor doesn't pretend to know what's wrong with Rodin, only how to cure his thirstiness. We'll see. Picasso is also ill and has been advised by a different doctor to remove all spices from his diet.

Matisse has cancelled his painting classes. He says he is not a teacher, only a painter. He says he failed to dissuade his students from imitating his style, and instead helps them learn the fundamentals in order to find their own direction. He seems discouraged and disheartened by the whole experience. The students are very disappointed he has decided to quit, and are trying to change his mind, but he won't be budged.

Rodin gave a lecture on cathedrals today to another ladies' group. He shocked them by going into raptures comparing the Gothic cathedral to a woman's body. He used some rather suggestive language. I always thought one could speak rather romantically in French and get away with it—in English any emotion always sounds more vulgar—but apparently I am wrong, because the ladies were shocked. Rodin was oblivious to having offended them.

DECEMBER 1911

Rodin is working on three different busts of Clemenceau but the ex-prime minister won't sit for him as much as Rodin would like him to. Clemenceau doesn't like the busts; he says the first one looks Japanese.

JANUARY 1912

Rodin and the Duchesse have gone to Rome, to preside over the unveiling of *The Walking Man* in the courtyard of the Farnese Palace. The Duchesse has also arranged for Rodin to meet with John Marshall, a representative of the Metropolitan Museum of Art in New York.

1912

Cocteau's third book of poems, *The Dance of Sophocles*, has been released. I'm afraid Andre Gide has given it a bad review, implying that Cocteau thinks too much of himself. The talk around the Hôtel Biron is that Gide is a Jansenist and Cocteau is not, and this difference prejudiced Gide's review.

Everyone seems to be taking the Cubism that Picasso and Braque started and running off with it in all directions. The Dutch and Russians have developed something called Orphism now that attempts to arrive at pure abstraction in color and form. Picasso hates this; it doesn't include enough of the messy reality that is his raw material. Gris and Leger are working on a cylindrical form of Cubism (no irony intended). The Futurists in Italy and the Vorticists in Russia claim to have been inspired by Cubism. Picasso says Cézanne started everything, and Picasso, for his part, just tries to take art a step further whenever he can. He and Braque are working on high analytical Cubism now. I'm sure Picasso and Braque will take the work to its furthest point and then move on to something else the way Matisse does, while their followers spend the rest of their lives mulling over the ramifications of Cubism.

Satie's career is definitely re-launched. A few months ago Ravel played a few of Satie's works at the Société Indépendante Musicale, and Debussy played something called *Gymnopédies* at the Cercle Musical. Roland Manuel just performed the *Prelude de La Porte Héroïque du Ciel* at SIM. Now the critics can't stop praising him.

Satie was pleased at first, but now he's annoyed because people only want to hear the work he wrote before he went into seclusion. He says those pieces are all twenty years old. He wants his new work to be performed.

FEBRUARY 1912

Rodin and the Duchesse have returned from Rome. I'm afraid the Duchesse made a nuisance of herself again. She insisted *The Walking Man* be placed in the very center of the Farnese Palace courtyard, where it blocks traffic, and nowhere else. Camille Barrière, the French ambassador, did not want the figure in the courtyard at all and certainly not in the very center where it would be an obstruction. But apparently he gave in.

The Duchesse's digestive problem was also aggravated by the trip. (She cannot keep any food down.) She had to leave the table repeatedly during meals when she was dining with the Marshalls. I imagine this made it very disturbing and unpleasant for them. The tenants of the Hôtel Biron have nicknamed the Duchesse "The Infection" and want her out.

Rodin hadn't been to Rome in thirty years. He said he enjoyed sightseeing alone and being honored with banquets. He said that everything is so big there, the men so expressive, the women so natural; he wished they wouldn't dress in Paris styles.

1912

Since the ballet *Scheherazade* was such a hit, Diaghilev plans to stage another Oriental ballet and has asked Cocteau to write the libretto.

Picasso and Fernande have ended their association. Fernande said their life changed so much after Picasso became successful and financially comfortable that she no longer knew how to be his companion. Picasso has taken up with a girl he calls Eva.

May 13, 1912

The premiere of Cocteau's ballet was a failure. Cocteau is wandering around the garden sulking, and various tenants of the Hôtel Biron are watching him from their windows, wondering what they could say, if anything, to console him. I imagine that if anyone understands what the public failure of a work of art feels like, it would be Rodin.

May 28, 1912

Everyone is in an uproar over Nijinsky's *Afternoon of a Faun*. Debussy did the music and the libretto was drawn from Mallarmé's poem. Nijinsky was wearing a skin-tight leotard with faun spots on it, a little tail protruding from the back and a cluster of grapes in front to serve as a fig leaf. He portrayed a faun who is haunted by some nymphs who leave him a scarf to remember them by. Apparently, in an unrehearsed gesture, he lay down on the scarf and aped the sex act at the end. Rodin thought it was quite beautiful.

May 30, 1912

Rodin was so thrilled with Nijinsky's performance of *The Afternoon of a Faun* two nights ago that he went backstage afterward to congratulate the dancer. The next day Rodin was willing to sign his name to a defense of that performance, written by Roger Marx, that was then published in *Le Matin* as an answer to Calmette's article in *Le Figaro*, which attacked Nijinsky's performance as filthy, bestial and lecherous.

Calmette's answer to Rodin's article appeared in this morning's *Figaro*. He's a shrewd editor; I'm not surprised he has so much power. Instead of dwelling on Nijinsky's performance, he attacked Rodin, saying that he displays his lewd drawings of women in the chapel here at the

Hôtel Biron and the French state has purchased the Hôtel so the taxpayer can subsidize Rodin while he lives here, at a cut rate, desecrating the place.

Rodin is going to retract his *Le Matin* article but that will only anger his friends and remind them of his refusal to sell his *Balzac* to a group of pro-Dreyfusards fifteen years ago. His enemies will add desecrator of churches to his other sins.

Summer 1912

Picasso took Eva to Céret for the summer but Fernande was staying there with the Pichots, so Picasso and Eva left for Avignon and ended up in Sorgues, a town just to the north. Braque and his wife have joined them.

Nijinsky has been coming over to pose for Rodin. Today Diaghilev caught them napping in Rodin's studio and flew into a jealous rage. Cocteau was delighted. He says Rodin is the only one who, by virtue of his position and power, could make Diaghilev feel truly threatened, and he assured Rodin that Mr. D. would never let Nijinsky return to pose. Rodin acted wounded, claimed nothing unusual had occurred and complained he is not far along enough in his sculpture to do without Nijinsky.

The tenants of the Hôtel Biron say Cocteau is looking at Rodin in a new way now and has begun to wear lipstick for him.

August 1912

Picasso painted a picture on the wall of his rented villa in Sorgues that he wants to preserve, so Kahnweiler is having the wall removed and shipped to Paris. Picasso has also asked Kahnweiler to move his belongings from his studio to another in Montparnasse so he and Eva won't return to the studio where he stayed with Fernande. He plans, however, to keep his room here at the Hôtel Biron.

September 30, 1912

Stieglitz sent me the *New York Times* article on Rodin's break with the Duchesse which was published two weeks ago. They portrayed her as domineering and unreasonable and Rodin as duped by her aristocratic title.

Rilke is complaining that Rodin is depressed because he doesn't sculpt anymore and doesn't know how to regain his dignity now that the Duchesse has made a fool of him.

After many letters and desperate pleading, Cocteau has finally met Gide. Cocteau was hoping for a mentor and a good review of *The Dance of Sophocles* but I'm afraid Gide was as petulant as ever and simply told Cocteau to change his handwriting. (Cocteau uses purple ink and employs a florid style copied from Anna de Noailles). Cocteau is hurt, as could be expected.

October 14, 1912

In a couple of articles that appeared this week, one in *Le Temps* and the other in *L'Intermédiare*, Apollinaire has attempted to explain Cubism to the public. I'm afraid he spends too much time defending it, defending his defense of it, and insisting that it is a French form of art. (Parisians won't like any form of art if they suspect it to be un-French, and Apollinaire, who is Polish, shares both this reasoning and this weakness). But he does say something about the history of Cubism and what it attempts to do. This may help the public appreciate it more.

MARCH 1913

To celebrate the closing of the Armory Show, the students at the Art Institute of Chicago have burned in effigy Matisse's *Blue Nude*.

After the vicious attacks on him by critics in the *New York Times*, Matisse takes this new development very hard. I believe he was hoping that at least the young art students in America would appreciate his work, but even they are outraged by it. It made me wonder if he misses his own students now, who appreciated his innovations and wanted to copy him. When I asked him, he conceded he misses their sympathy but felt he had made the right decision closing the school, because he had expended so much energy trying to understand what each student was trying to do in his painting. He said he couldn't be a teacher and painter at the same time.

Rodin is putting his finishing touches on the Clemenceau bust. Clemenceau is complaining he looks like a Mongol general. His wife doesn't like the bust and has advised Clemenceau not to accept it. Clemenceau tells everyone he doesn't like Rodin because he's vain, stupid and cares too much about money. Rodin complains that Clemenceau is surly and condescending.

Rilke is back from trips to Austria, Spain and Venice, and is celebrating the demise of the American Duchesse. Rilke quibbles with the reasons Rodin banished her from the Hôtel Biron (he is perpetually disappointed with Rodin's reasoning in the area of human relations) but is feeling too victorious about her dismissal to let that bother him.

Everyone in the Hôtel Biron is debating the rumor that before she left, the American Duchesse systematically poisoned Rodin's milk with arsenic. No one denies Rodin is ill, but there is considerable speculation about the cause.

MARCH 1913

I arrived back at the Hôtel Biron today after a long morning of photographing Paris, to find Camille Claudel gone. Rilke informed me that Miss Camille Claudel has been locked up in a lunatic asylum! Her own brother, the writer Paul Claudel, and her mother arranged it. In France any family member can obtain a doctor's certificate authorizing internment and that's enough to put you away for life. Only your family can get you out again. It's terrifying! According to Rilke they arrived, waving their certificate, and pointing her out to the hospital bullies who came to help incarcerate her.

I knew Paul Claudel was a prig and disapproved of his sister's profession as a sculptress, her failure to marry, her affair with Rodin twenty-five long years ago, but I had no idea he would do anything like this. People in the house say Miss Claudel's sister and mother also disapprove of her, and it was only her father who kept them from doing this. A week after her father died, they locked her up!

Miss Claudel does act a bit oddly at times but certainly no more so than a hundred other artists in Paris (men) who are considered only eccentric. She has harmed no one. She was working and is well respected among other artists.

Afterward Rilke, Cocteau, and Matisse all stood around stunned, staring at each other. That is when I arrived back. Now people in the house are waiting to see what Rodin is planning to do about this. Only some kind of public outcry could possibly get Miss Claudel released.

END OF MARCH 1913

Rodin has cleared all Camille's belongings out of the room he was letting her use, and he has offered it to Nijinsky!

MAY 1913

Cocteau has just witnessed the "scandal" at the opening of the Russian Ballet's *Rite of Spring*, and he's now suffering from the misconception that all great art is sprung from the desire to rebel. Several tenants of the Hôtel Biron would like to tell him otherwise, but Diaghilev has asked Cocteau to astound him, and right now Cocteau's primary motivation is to do just that.

1913

In a further effort to astound Diaghilev, Cocteau is trying to induce dreams. To do this he eats several boxes of sugar then stops his ears with wax and lies down. He does this twice a day. The rest of the household is awaiting the results with great trepidation.

JUNE 1913

Picasso has returned to Céret for the summer. He has written to Apollinaire that his father died, Eva is ill, and that he has taken Max Jacob across the border to Spain to see the bullfights.

Rodin has returned from a trip to Knole to visit his friend Lady Sackville. She took him to a Louis XIV costume ball. He wants to do Lady S.'s bust, and complains she treats him like her father. (She is fifty-one, he is seventy-two). He also profited from the visit by choosing a site in the Victoria flower gardens for a copy of the Burghers to be installed.

Fall 1913

Cocteau has just returned from Normandy with the results of his sleep experiments. The book is called *The Potomak*. It's about a winged gelatinous monster who lives in an aquarium under the Place de la Madeleine and eats gloves and spelling errors. In the book, Cocteau and his friends visit the monster. Cocteau claims the book started out as drawings and its subject is really the molting of intelligence as revealed by occult characters experiencing an entire range of deep confusions. Cocteau keeps insisting that this book is his first major breakthrough, because where before all his books were the product of consciousness, this one is the result of sleep. He says he owes it all to *The Rite of Spring* and has dedicated his new book to Stravinsky. His poetry publisher, *The Mercure de France*, has agreed to print it.

Nijinsky got married to one of the dancers in the Russian Ballet on their tour to South America. Diaghilev didn't go because he's afraid of traveling by boat. Cocteau says Mr. D. will be more upset by being replaced by a girl of twenty-three than by losing Nijinsky, and will find some way to dismiss him from the company. Today Nijinsky brought his new wife over to the Hôtel Biron to meet Rodin. Cocteau won't speak to Nijinsky anymore and stayed in the sacristy. I think Cocteau loves the intrigue of the Russian Ballet; it makes our house full of artists seem so tame by comparison.

NOVEMBER 1913

Apollinaire published reproductions of Picasso's Cubist constructions in his new magazine *Les Soirées de Paris*. Now all his subscribers are cancelling.

Matisse's *Portrait of a Woman* in this year's Salon D'Automne has received rave reviews from Apollinaire in *Les Soirees de Paris*. Apollinaire has knighted Matisse as the first Voluptuary since Renoir.

Rodin is working on a bust of Lady Sackville. He is fascinated with her long hair (down to her thighs) and has asked her to go to the Riviera with him this winter. Rodin invited the Count of Montesquiou over to watch the sittings, but complains he talks too much about himself. Rodin has hired a man to serve them tea and cakes while wearing white gloves. I think he's the produce man!

DECEMBER 1913

There have finally been some articles in the Paris newspapers about Camille Claudel's incarceration in a lunatic asylum. But since October Paul Claudel has been in Hamburg on a diplomatic assignment and won't respond to any of the accusations. People in the house have asked Rodin to do something but he won't. I think he remembers the Nijinsky imbroglio last year and the Dreyfus affair many years ago, and refuses to take any public stand on any issue that might draw personal attacks on him.

Rilke is outraged and thinks it is the most selfish and immoral thing Rodin has ever done. Other people in the Hôtel Biron think Rodin might prefer to have Camille out of Paris because he seems to feel victimized by the women who love him, and wish they would go away, but does not seem to have the will to send them away himself, as with Rose or the Duchesse.

I wish there were some way to get Miss Claudel out of that asylum. It frightens me to think this can happen. Cocteau says Gwen John was acting awfully peculiar when Rodin stopped seeing her, but no one locked her up. Rilke explained that away by saying she is English and the English have a way of letting all their emotions out at once and acting totally wild for a few weeks. Then they return to normal as if nothing at all had happened. Rilke always attributes behavior to nationality, or "race" as he calls it. Picasso says the difference between Camille Claudel and Gwen John is that Gwen John's brother chose to comfort her instead of lock her up, and Picasso would never do such a thing to a sister no matter how strange or embarrassing her behavior. Cocteau said Camille and Rodin ended their affair twenty years ago and it is romanticism to attribute her demise to that, but others in the house, including Rilke, said that her brother Paul still blames Rodin for ruining her reputation and steering her toward a career in sculpture (even though she had already established it as her profession before she met Rodin), so it is her brother who makes the connection, not us.

Letters Not Sent:
The Letters of Camille Claudel 5
(1913-1917)

1913

Monsieur Rodin,

It had occurred to me that after my father died my sister and mother would immediately execute whatever plan they had already devised to get rid of me, and my brother Paul would acquiesce, pretending to be distressed by it, so his colleagues in the world of letters would not blame him. But since I did not know that my father had died, I was not prepared for this sudden incarceration.

I think it apt that you chose an insane asylum. I am sure my sister and mother were planning some way to end the disgrace they felt in having a sister and daughter who had given herself up to a beast and let him destroy her; I am sure it was you who planted the specific idea in their mind of an asylum in the provinces.

An asylum will be more likely to prevent me from creating art, because the cries of these tormented souls will distract me. An asylum in the provinces will prevent my colleagues from coming to my aid. And an asylum is better than a prison or a convent or the family's country home, because it discredits me in the most convincing way, it throws doubt upon my ability to create art. You were quite ingenious in your choice, sir.

I blame myself: for falling in love with you, for believing that since you were a great artist you could also be a great man, for hoping that the fact you finally loved someone deeply and irrevocably would make you kinder, for deluding myself that since you enjoyed women so much you would treat them as equals. I blame myself for not ceasing to care, when I realized you were a ruthless man who brutalized women.

After you I was smart enough never to love completely again, the way you had promised yourself after your sister, never to give yourself completely again. But where you were able to shut out your mistake, I let it poison me and make me bitter. I blame myself for that.

Finally, I blame myself for letting you get this far in your attempt to destroy me. You, who complain so much about your apprenticeship, only had to fight indifference. You did not have a family and a teacher who were in league together to destroy you.

I blame myself for my lack of cunning and deceit. I should have pretended to you that I had no grand aspirations, and to my family that I was chaste. It is my great failure in life that I could not fool you or them. I was not capable of deceit.

1913

Rodin,

My doctors have just told me why I have been incarcerated and I must congratulate you on the evil genius of it.

What cunning! To set up sophisticated plots to undermine me and my work, not because you intended to carry out my demise by these obvious machinations, but in order to have me suspect it, so later you might have me incarcerated for paranoid delusions that you yourself orchestrated.

This is truly brilliant, really too marvelous for words, heady in its genius. It makes me euphoric just to think of it. If it weren't so completely vile and base, I would be quite delighted by the intricacy of it. And I accused you of not appreciating the precious! Surely this ploy is the most precious imaginable.

I suppose you are so smug you didn't count on this outcry in the Paris press against my incarceration. I hope you are afraid that this plan is about to backfire and the world is already discovering what you've done to me. I hope you're living in terror of the fact that instead of silencing me you have given me a voice.

All I wanted was to be an artist. I never wanted to hurt you or reveal what a monster you are. I loved you. I would never have harmed you. So you have brought all this shame down on yourself for trying to harm me.

By reading all the wonderful true things that are being written about me in the Paris press, I have acquainted myself with the law of 1838, which allows a family member to lock up another family member for life, with only a doctor's certificate, after which only a family member can secure the poor soul's release. I applaud you on making use of this ingenious law and thereby diverting blame from yourself to my family.

I was overestimating my sister Louise by believing her only motivation was protecting her good name by removing me from the eyes of Parisian Society. But now that I consider it, it seems only fitting that my sister Louise would want my inheritance. How clever of you to point out to her how much more dangerous I might have become to her, had I received my inheritance, and no longer destitute, I had been able to attend the exhibitions of my artwork. I know others in the press and art world think only my mother and brother Paul are to blame, but you and I know they are all three working together. So we have another secret.

1913

Rodin,

Your sons are horrified by your monstrous deed of incarcerating me, and it will alter their opinion of you forever. They are threatening to denounce you publically, declare themselves my sons, and have me removed from this asylum immediately, so they might take care of me, but I made them promise not to. Even if they could prove they are my sons, they most probably could not get me released over the protests of my sister, brother and mother.

I have devised an elaborate system for working here. Your sons must first smuggle the clay in to me. This is not too difficult, since I am still working in miniature, and therefore I do not require much. I must work at night so the Sisters will not notice. Many of the madwomen in the asylum are insomniacs, so they have seen me working and tried to warn the Sisters, but the Sisters believe they are just raving. I don't mind working at night; it is easier to concentrate, but that means I am tired all day. Luckily, the doctors are not suspicious of this. They take it as a good sign—the body's way of healing the mind. Your sons are also assigned the task of smuggling the figures out of the asylum. This is not too difficult, since the figures are so tiny.

Your sons want to take the figures to my dealer Eugene Blot, to have them exhibited. But as much as I trust Monsieur Blot, it would be extremely dangerous to show the figures now. I fear the reprisals of yourself and my family. I prefer to wait until we are all dead, until only my sons remain, and then allow them to exhibit the busts. They are not happy with this plan because they want me released, and they are convinced an exhibition of my work would prove my sanity. But I am not so much worried about my release now as I am in securing a place for my art in history, and I am convinced this is the unfortunate choice I am forced to make.

Your sons have plasters made of my *maquettes* and, when they have money, René has them copied in bronze and Sandro carves them in marble or onyx, which is the material to which they are most suited. You would be proud of your sons; they have become quite dexterous craftsmen — René at enlarging and foundry work, Sandro at stonecutting. And at the same time they manage to continue their studies in law, architecture and art, while they visit me faithfully and handle my affairs skillfully. I cannot imagine how they do it.

I thought my imprisonment in this asylum would not be much different than the imprisonment of poverty, but I was wrong. My poverty was a choice I made for my art; this asylum is not a choice. At the Quai Bourbon I could not go out because I had nothing suitable to wear; here I cannot go out because the doors are locked. There I lived in the company of many independent but affectionate cats, and a few curious but harmless neighbors; here I live surrounded by keening women.

There, at the Quai Bourbon, I was free to work night and day, my only distraction being my creditors. Here at the asylum I am forced to work at night, in secret, smuggling my supplies in and my completed figures out, constantly interrupted by the litanies of these poor women.

At the Quai Bourbon the public was indifferent to me, and my family thought of me as nothing more than a common prostitute because my relations with you did not end in marriage. Nevertheless, my colleagues, some critics and dealers looked upon me as a great artist, the most promising young sculptor in Paris. Now that I am confined to this asylum I am thought of at best as a victim of my family's retribution. At worst my very being is questioned; my ability to create art and to live in the world is thrown into doubt.

There are different types of incarceration. Though I did not realize it at the time, of those possible incarcerations poverty was the most benign. And certainly, this asylum must be the most degrading. I am sure that was your purpose. For it was not enough to get me out of sight—you needed to break my spirit, and my family wished to punish me. A convent, a debtor's prison, or sequestration at the family country home in Villeneuve— these were not enough to ruin me, and you knew it.

1915

Rodin,

I wonder how you feel about this war. I hear that, after becoming disenchanted with life in London, you've moved to Rome where you have made an ice cream parlor into a studio, and no one speaks French. Are you bored? Do you sulk because attention has been diverted away from you, because no one comes to visit you or hold banquets in our honor? Or are you concerned about your cathedrals being destroyed? I wonder if you will survive this war.

I have had the privilege of changing residences many times, but I have never had the unique experience of changing asylums. I am being transferred from Ville Evrard to Montdevergues. They say it is because of the war, but I know it is because you want me to be further from Paris, and you've used the war as an excuse to execute your wishes. I was causing too much trouble for you at Ville Evrard; it was too easy for me to smuggle letters in and out, to speak with friends who went to the press.

I know you're hoping to discourage me and make it even more difficult for me to obtain my release, but I assure you this will only make me try harder and put you in even greater danger of exposure.

I am concerned primarily with desperate fundamentals. Will the asylum food make me so sick I will be forced to subsist on potatoes and eggs I cook myself? Will the Sisters be abusive or simply silent? Will the other inmates be more wretched than those at Ville Evrard? Will I be punished when I am caught smuggling mail in and out of the asylum, when descriptions of my plight are read in the Paris press, when friends are caught visiting? These are now my pathetic concerns.

But I will not give up. Even though they have sent me further away, I am trying to have myself moved to an asylum in Paris. I know you will do everything to prevent this, because, if I were in Paris, my friends, colleagues and the press would be reminded of my plight. I know your influence is strong and I probably won't succeed in having myself moved to Paris.

In the meantime, both the doctors at Ville-Evrard and here at Montdevergues have repeatedly written to my mother and brother to inform them that for a long time

I have been well and healthy, and that I should be removed from their care. Of course they refuse to release me and they are the only ones who legally can. I am telling you this to prove to you that even the doctors understand that I am quite sane and I am being kept here for no other reason but vengeance. My sons have obtained copies of these letters and have sent them to newspapers and my friends in order to exonerate me from the charge of madness. How France loves to dismiss women as mad.

I have also heard about your meager fund for my internment that contributes 500 francs per year to keep me here, about one sixth the price of a single bronze copy of *Fugit Amor*. I take this as your way of saying you wish to keep up a slight pretense of feeling sorry for me, for those who are stupid enough to believe it, but that you really intend to gall me by this insipid gesture.

1917

Rodin,

My sons have told me that you are going to die, and that amidst the chaos that reigns at the Hôtel Biron, Judith Cladel is pushing forward a plan to evict the other artists and transform the house into a museum to exhibit your works. Your sons have also told me that you have requested, should the museum be established, my room at the Hôtel Biron be used exclusively to show my works. They tell me Mathias Morhardt supports this plan. So even on your deathbed you cling to this notion that my artwork should live only in your shadow.

I will write Mlle Cladel and Monsieur Morhardt and emphasize to them once again that I do not wish to exhibit under your auspices, and doing so would be against my

expressed wishes. I will further suggest that they use that
room to exhibit all the works you stole from me (though
the room is much too small for that), and to document
the criminal way in which I was incarcerated and am
being held against my will.

The Notebooks of Eduard Steichen #6
(1913-1914)

DECEMBER 3, 1913

As expected, Diaghilev has dismissed Nijinsky from the Russian Ballet. Everyone is furious. Nijinsky is taking it very hard. He is having trouble sleeping, seems lethargic, unhappy, lost. Miassine has become Mr. D.'s new companion.

JANUARY 1914

Apollinaire has nicknamed Picasso "The Bird of Benin" after some bronze bird with a butterfly in its beak that originates from there. He used the Autumn Salon in Berlin last fall, and an article in *Les Soirées de Paris* this month to glorify Rousseau. I like the publicity it gives Rousseau's work, but I am suspicious of Apollinaire's motives. He is so excessive in his praise, it's as if he's embarrassed by the fact that he was lukewarm about Rousseau at first, and he's either trying to make us forget his error, or he's trying to make amends for it. Either way, it makes me uncomfortable.

I'm also disturbed by the way Apollinaire insists on perpetuating myths about Rousseau. He says his work was discovered when it was not. He says his work was encouraged when it was not. He loves to retell only those anecdotes that make Rousseau seem quaint and naive, like his arrest and belief in ghosts. Why do critics insist on making myths out of artists? Why can't artists just be regular people who happen to paint or sculpt or compose music, and also happen to possess a cross-section of the oddities of human nature, just like other regular people?

Vincent van Gogh's letters have just been published in Paris and people in the Hôtel Biron are reading them. Rilke was quick to point out that, when van Gogh lost his mind for brief periods, it was his choice to seek help in an asylum and he knew he could get out whenever he felt ready.

Camille Claudel's doctors have said already that she is well and still she cannot be released without her family's consent, which they will not give. Matisse pointed out that van Gogh had committed violence to himself and others and still had a choice whereas Camille has not hurt anyone and was locked up against her will. Picasso reiterated his brother theme: van Gogh had a brother who tried to help him where Camille's brother seems out to destroy her.

Cocteau was struck by the fact that, when van Gogh was doing what is believed to be his best work, he considered himself a failure. This sparked a discussion about the possibilities of judging your own work, and the necessity to keep on working when you don't know if it's good or not.

We eventually got back to talking about Miss Claudel. No one knows what to do. If the doctors in the asylum can't get her released and the uproar in the press doesn't produce results, we are all at a loss to know what to do. Her family says she has a persecution complex. My goodness, wouldn't anyone who was locked up against their will and against the advice of their doctors?

I do hear that someone managed to smuggle her papers and artwork out of her Quai Bourbon studio before her family destroyed everything. Her sons visit her daily in the asylum and are sneaking in supplies so she can work at night in secret. (She is forbidden to do her artwork in the asylum!) Her dealer Eugene Blot is planning an exhibit in hopes this might force her release.

FEBRUARY 1914

Nijinsky has a contract with the Palace Theatre in London for the spring season. He and his sister are rehearsing here in Paris, but no one thinks he will be able to make it without Diaghilev. Mr. D. is making as much trouble for Nijinsky as he can. He's taken court action to prevent Nijinsky's sister from dancing with him on the grounds that the Russian Ballet has not accepted her resignation. Nijinsky is a nervous wreck and some people are afraid he might snap.

MARCH 1914

When Cocteau can't satisfy his need for intrigue by observing the clashes within the Russian Ballet, he inevitably ends up creating his own. Cocteau ran off to Switzerland a few weeks ago to convince Stravinsky to write the music for his new ballet *David*. Of course Diaghilev found out, and he's furious because he thinks Cocteau is trying to take Stravinsky away from his work on *The Nightingale*, which Diaghilev already commissioned. Stravinsky patched it up with Diaghilev by promising to finish *The*

Nightingale before he begins work on *David*. In the meantime, Cocteau wants to go back to Switzerland to work with Stravinsky, but he keeps making dates and cancelling because he is afraid of the epidemic of scarlet fever there. When he does finally insist on going, it's usually because Stravinsky has wired him not to come—either because he hasn't finished *The Nightingale*, or because his wife is too sick, or because he's off to Berlin on business. I'm sure Cocteau is driving him crazy.

Max Jacob has just published a book of poems called *The Siege of Jerusalem*, with illustrations by Picasso (three etchings and dry-points), and published by Kahnweiler.

MARCH 1914

Nijinsky came down with influenza and was unable to fulfill his contract at the Palace Theatre in London. He is trying to persuade Diaghilev to pay him his back salary from the Russian Ballet, but apparently nothing was ever written down. Mr. D. paid Nijinsky's food and hotel bills and reinvested the remainder of Nijinsky's salary back into the ballet company. Nijinsky also earned enormous sums that he never received to dance at private parties.

APRIL 1914

Rodin has returned from three months in the Riviera. His book *The Cathedrals of France* has just been published, but as usual Rodin cannot enjoy an untarnished success. The Paris Municipal Council passed a resolution that prohibits municipal libraries from purchasing the book. Rumors and criticisms are circulating that the text was not written by Rodin, that the drawings are rudimentary and beneath a schoolchild. Several prominent Paris writers believe the book is a hoax. Reviews are appearing which cite numerous errors of fact and claim Rodin doesn't know anything about cathedrals. Some people think his critics are just angry that he has not used the book to take a stand about the church-state battle, but they should not be surprised since Rodin has always avoided political issues.

Cocteau finally went to Switzerland when he was least welcome and has just come back. The word around the Hôtel Biron is that the meeting was a disaster, even though Cocteau pretends it wasn't. Apparently Stravinsky is not really that interested in *David* and is still trying to finish *The Nightingale*, and Cocteau behaved badly. I think Stravinsky is embarrassed by Cocteau's slavish adoration and by his persistence.

MAY 1914

Charles Morice, the Symbolist poet and editor of Rodin's *Cathedrals of France*, gave a reading from the new book today at the Hôtel Biron. Rodin seemed to like it best and acted as if he had never heard it before.

Nijinsky is well again and has vowed to keep dancing but hire someone else to administer his company. He went to the premiere of the Russian Ballet's season at the Opera, but everyone was cold to him, including Cocteau. People say the Russian Ballet has no magic now that Nijinsky has been thrown out.

JUNE 23, 1914

Picasso is hopping mad. His friend Apollinaire just published an article in *The Paris Journal* that says all the

Montmartre painters have moved to Montparnasse, where they get high on cocaine, wear American clothes and frequent cafés. He even lists which painters frequent which cafés!

Nijinsky and his wife had a baby girl and named her Kyra. Diaghilev invited Nijinsky back into the Russian Ballet, but only to save the company, which no one likes anymore without Nijinsky. Nijinsky tried to go back but everyone was so cold to him at rehearsals it broke his heart and he has quit again.

1914

Cocteau is sulking over his break (as he calls it) with Stravinsky and insists that, despite the failure of *David* and Stravinsky's indifference to him, he will cherish their time together in Switzerland the way Nietzsche cherished his time with Wagner at Tribschen. In private Stravinsky says this is all rubbish and that he was never close to Cocteau in the first place, so there can be no break.

Maurice Rostand has "broken" with Cocteau because Rostand has discovered Proust has been a friend of Cocteau all along. Apparently Cocteau didn't tell Maurice or introduce him, even though Proust had seen Maurice at the Opera and had requested Cocteau introduce them.

People in the Hôtel Biron have been speculating on why Cocteau hasn't tried to exploit his friendship with Proust the way he has with Diaghilev and Stravinsky. The consensus of opinion seems to be that it's because Proust is a stay-at-home. He's not in the public eye, so there's no opportunity for exploitation. An idea has also been ventured that Proust is too much like Cocteau, frail and vicious.

When Cocteau gets older, I wonder if he will draw young men of talent into his circle and treat them as he wished to be treated by Diaghilev and Stravinsky. Or if he will punish them by rejecting them, in order to exact retribution for the humiliation he suffered by fawning over great men who neglected him. Maybe both. Or perhaps he'll play the young boys off each other for sport. I'm afraid he has a malicious streak.

MID-JULY 1914

Cocteau has met some of the other Cubists and suddenly people in his circle feel threatened, because he can't mix socially with his aristocratic friends and the Cubists at the same time.

Rodin had dinner at the American Embassy with Theodore Roosevelt, Henri Bergson, Edith Wharton and Cornelius Vanderbilt.

AUGUST 2, 1914

French soldiers have confiscated Rodin's car, horse, workmen and advised him not to ship any sculptures to London. They've given him forty-eight hours to move all his artwork into the cellar. Rodin is very unhappy about this. The Great War has started. What will it mean for us? For art? For the community here at the Hôtel Biron? Already we are affected.

SEPTEMBER 1914

Cocteau has organized a convoy of ambulances and left for the front line. Rodin and Rose went to London with

Judith Cladel, but people in the house say they've heard reports that he is not happy there.

Picasso and Eva have returned to Paris after their summer in Avignon. Picasso is very irritated by the war. He said when he saw Braque and Derain off at the railway station in Avignon last month he was afraid he'd never see them again. Kahnweiler has fled, we assume to a neutral country. Apollinaire applied for French nationality and, when he received it, joined the artillery. Picasso is calling the war a gross display of human stupidity.

NOVEMBER 1914

Rodin and Rose have moved to Rome, where Rodin is drawing from the model in an ice cream parlor (!!!) during its off hours. Apparently it is a large rotunda with columns and marble tables, which he likes very much, but otherwise he is bored from lack of social opportunities. People say he's sulking because no one pays attention to him anymore now that the war has begun.

Diaghilev has asked Nijinsky to dance with the Russian Ballet in New York but Nijinsky's citizenship forbids him to leave Europe during the war.

NOVEMBER 1914

Stieglitz wrote me that *Camera Work* is going to fold and he won't be able to use our articles right now. He did say though that he plans to start another magazine some time in the near future and hopes we won't give the articles to another publisher. The tenants of the Hôtel Biron insist they have no intention of giving away their manuscripts. Picasso, Matisse, Satie and Nijinsky aren't finished with theirs and plan to continue working on them. So do I. Rilke suggested I write to Miss Claudel with the news and ask her to hold on to her manuscript for possible future publication by Stieglitz. If Stieglitz cannot publish them, I will find a way to do it myself. I am adamant about this.

Matisse's Brief Lives,
Introduction by Eduard Steichen

After leaving Picasso in Vallauris in the spring of 1954, I headed south to Golfe Juan and then west to Nice. Matisse lived in a suburb called Cimiez and had not long to live. It had been forty-six years since, as a young man, I had arranged for the showing of his work at Stieglitz's 291 Gallery.

I'll tell you a secret: Matisse has always been my favorite 20th century painter. For all Picasso's exuberance and abundance and ground breaking, Matisse seems more honest, more emotionally complex, his landscapes and portraits delve deeper into the human psyche. I know this will be dismissed as my penchant for the decorative — so be it.

Lydia Delektorskaya was expecting me, and let me in. Matisse had been confined to a wheelchair since his surgery for colon cancer, but was still directing assistants and clipping his now famous *Jazz* cutouts from his chair.

The Master smiled when he saw me. He was sitting in his wheelchair, covered in a blanket. His color cutouts surrounded him. As I expected, he would work until the end.

So, you have become a big man now, he said and gave out a little laugh. I supposed he was referring to my job at MOMA, directing the photography department. Or perhaps he was referring to my portrait work for *Vanity Fair*, back in the 20s.

Matisse motioned to Delektorskaya, who brought me a tattered manuscript.

My friend, Matisse said, looking at me over his eyeglasses, *it is the best I can do.*

I told him I was sure it was more than enough.

Is it? he said. Matisse looked around his studio. *Is it ever enough?*

I nodded. I told him it was.

Because I am plagued with this idea, the Master continued, *that it has not been enough.* He motioned with his hand to the work in progress that was going on around him.

Delektorskaya came up to Matisse and adjusted the blanket over his legs. She gave me a sharp look. She was an angular woman, with dark eyes, her hair in a bun, wearing a simple gray shift dress.

Rest assured, I said. *You've given us more than anyone.*

Matisse winked at me.

Delektorskaya pinched my elbow with her hand as she escorted me out.

Forgive me, she said at the door. *If he talks too long, inevitably he comes to his daughter Marguerite.*

Marguerite? I said. She had worked in the French Resistance during the War, had been held at the Ravensbrück concentration camp, and tortured.

He mustn't think of it, Delektorskaya said, as she opened the door for me. *It will make him ill.*

The Brief Lives of The Tenants of The Hôtel Biron by Henri Matisse

INTRODUCTION

I name the biographies set forth here *Brief Lives*. The reasons are many. Some of the artists portrayed in the following pages are still mere boys, and the lives they have lived so far have been brief. Some have achieved brilliance for a short moment, only to falter forever afterward. Others may enjoy fleeting moments of brilliance surrounded by intervals of mediocrity. Some have already died and some may die young. Still others may succumb to a surfeit of grief or bitterness and live out their lives in darkness. Some may enjoy a brief moment of fame or glory, despite the fact that most of their work is pure genius. And still others may have so much to do, so much to discover, so much to invent, that one lifetime is not enough, and even if they live into old age their lives will be cut short long before their innovations are complete.

HENRI ROUSSEAU

Those people who ridiculed Rousseau belittled only themselves. People made fun of Rousseau because he was not educated in art and was therefore an outsider. Rousseau was not an innocent, but his soul was innocent.

Rousseau never traveled to the jungle in Mexico or anywhere else. Picasso has stolen Rousseau's ideas and many more artists will steal them after the war. But they will not give Rousseau credit for his innovations the way they give Cézanne credit, because they are embarrassed by Rousseau's childlike nature.

Even now that Rousseau is dead, other artists are still embarrassed by his ingenuousness, guilelessness and naïveté because they are afraid they might be like him. But they are too self-conscious to be like Rousseau. We would all be lucky if we were more like Rousseau. Our art would improve. We would be happy and flourish.

Rousseau understood color much better than Picasso does. Picasso did not discover Rousseau in 1908. He was first esteemed at the 1905 Autumn Salon where Vauxcelles labeled me a Fauve. At his first exhibition in 1885 Rousseau's paintings were slashed.

Rousseau did not begin to paint until after he retired. He took his portraits seriously. Rousseau invented the portrait-landscape. Rousseau painted Marie Laurencin fat because he thought she didn't like him.

Rousseau always believed in ghosts and spirits. All his wives and children died young.

Other artists must deny Rousseau's whimsy in order to deny his genius, so they go on pretending Rousseau was serious. He wasn't. Lawyers produced Rousseau's *Merry Jesters* in court to prove his imbecility, while mothers of artists commissioned him to paint snake charmers. His cows are much too big; his football players cast no shadows. His moon has a face and his monkeys toss a milk bottle. In particular the cubists have stolen his mandolin. He was not afraid to take the couch out of his studio and use it in his painting of Jadwiga's dream.

Rousseau told everyone that all great art was Egyptian and all foreigners were American, but this was just a code he used to simplify his speech.

Rousseau always wanted to paint like an academic painter, but he could only paint like himself.

At the end of his life Rousseau was not afraid to love a woman who did not love him. Max Weber loved him. I loved him and do still.

When Rousseau painted babies, their heads were always much larger than their bodies. This is true of babies.

Rousseau was a man who dreamed awake. All Rousseau's paintings are these waking dreams. No wonder he believed in spirits. If the Hôtel Biron acquires a ghost, it will be Rousseau's.

AUGUSTE RODIN

The Rodin predicament reminds me very much of The Emperor's New Clothes. In public everyone says what a great master Rodin was. What an artist. But alone in their rooms they are embarrassed. They remember him as a doddering old man who was entirely too interested in certain amorous attributes of the female form. Still, in public they go on pretending he was a great man. The problem is that Rodin just died, and one either dwells on his ignominious old age, or finds him impossible to summarize.

Rodin never had enough studios or residences at one time to satisfy him. Even the Hôtel Biron was not enough.

Rodin made his own myth. He pretended to be victimized and guileless and believed his own story. That is how he became bitter and resentful. It makes no difference that Rodin's sister died, or that he grew up in

Paris, or that he was rejected by the École des Beaux-Arts, or was exiled to Belgium during the Prussian War. He would have prevailed no matter what happened or failed to happen to him. For many artists life is a series of lucky or unlucky accidents. Rodin was neither lucky nor unlucky. He was singular in purpose.

Rodin is the bridge between two centuries. The old artists can only see the outrageous and incomprehensible future in his *Balzac* and *Gates*. The young artists can only see the insipid and academic past in his *Kiss* and *Eternal Idol*. It seems he can't win, but he has.

The *Gates of Hell* is the most modern of all Rodin's work. Since Rodin is the Hugo and Balzac of French sculpture, it is appropriate that he designed their monuments. Rodin knew about African Art before I did; he knew about Japanese Art before it became popular; and he discovered the secret of Puvis de Chavannes. When people talk about Rodin's work, they like to talk about nature and motion. I have nothing to say about either.

Rodin didn't create his own scandals, but he knew how to use them to his advantage. Though Rodin denied politics, the Balzac affair was really the Dreyfus affair. Likewise, his separate pavilion at the 1900 exhibition, Hugo's monument, Camille Claudel's incarceration, his reversal on Nijinsky's *Afternoon of a Faun*, the rejection of the Calais monument, Rodin's funeral, the possible establishment of a Rodin museum here at the Hôtel Biron, where Rodin allegedly committed sacrilege by exhibiting erotic watercolors in the sacristy—all these were and are political events.

People think that, because Rodin's work shows genius, it should also show worldliness and sophistication. They are shocked when it does not. Many of his works were never finished. This is not the point. Incompleteness is a quality of his work, not a fault.

People make too much of the American Duchesse. She was not important. She only humiliated Rodin in the short run. Each person assumes only he knows which woman Rodin really loved. A would-be biographer believes that Rodin went to the grave never having known love for a woman. A lady with a fake aristocratic title selects as Rodin's true love an obscure Italian model from his early years in Nice. A former amanuensis insists on some obvious choice like Camille Claudel. An art critic theorizes that Rodin could never love a woman who loved him, or obeyed him, or responded to his advances. A fellow chevalier in the Legion of Honor thinks that Rodin's true love was always Rose.

Rodin never loved anyone but Helene von Nostitz, daughter of Sophie von Hindenburg. I saw him pass her photograph, which rested atop a glass case of fake Egyptian artifacts in his sitting room here at the Hôtel Biron. If you saw the way he gestured toward this photo, so painfully, as if his whole life had been a failure, you would believe me. You would throw away all your other theories.

To Rodin everything was sex: art, women, nature, love — everything.

Rodin mistreated women but he did not disrespect them. They were the only thing that mattered. They knew this and that is why they were susceptible to him. He appealed to their vanity. He also appealed to their sense of mystery. Rodin was one of the few artists — like Michelangelo — who had mystery inside him and needn't go looking for it. Instead he was driven by it. Rodin was only comfortable with art and women. Rodin was capable of loving anyone. So it is no wonder that at the end of his life Rodin became openly obsessed with women's most sexual characteristics. From the beginning of his life he had carried a single idea in a single direction—from male warriors to Dante's hell, to Adam and Eve, to fraternities of religious men, to solitary men bigger and bigger than life, and this is where it finally and inevitably led him.

Rodin would have been a better artist if he had stayed with Camille Claudel. But either way, Rodin would have ruined Camille Claudel. Rodin never had any idea what his sons could have meant to him. Rodin should have loved Nijinsky. He should have had Camille Claudel released from the asylum.

Rodin was a redhead. The redhead has no business trifling with women. The redhead is unkind to all women. If a woman's first love is a redhead, she will never recover.

It makes all the difference in the world what Rodin's statue of Balzac is doing under his robe.

To Rodin anything was possible. That is why he was so shocking and so successful. In the future he will be accused of everything.

CAMILLE CLAUDEL

Camille Claudel gained a lot of weight after she had her two sons, but she did not go crazy and her voice did not change. Her sister Louise is jealous of her even now, and incarcerated her to take her money and property—a country house. People say she could have married Debussy. It's true he wanted to marry her, but she could not have married him.

Camille's *Cacountala* is much warmer than Rodin's *Eternal Idol* and shows a great understanding of what love is. The *Eternal Idol* does not understand love, only worship, which is a form of hatred.

Camille Claudel's tiny figures called *The Gossipers* and *The Wave* constitute a new kind of art — the art of telling secrets. No one will take up this art for a long time.

If Camille Claudel did not have a famous brother and a famous lover, her art might be respected and she might not be incarcerated.

We think that Camille Claudel must have made a mistake to have such an unfortunate life. But she has not made a mistake. We have made one. Because she is a woman, we don't believe her talent. We indulged her when she was younger, thinking she would go away. When she didn't, her family locked her up. She is Nijinsky's sister, not Paul's. She is more akin to Nijinsky in having the kind of genius people are intent to destroy. If we have learned anything from Camille Claudel and Nijinsky, it is this: if people are intent to destroy your genius, get away from them. Get away from everyone. Do not love anybody. Who can obey this warning?

The reason George Sand could write and take Chopin as a lover and Gwen John can be a painter is because people let them. Camille Claudel does not understand that. Camille Claudel thinks it is through some fault of her own she is being thwarted and punished. She blames herself and so pretends to blame Rodin.

I would prefer to say Camille Claudel is a great French sculptress than to have to say Camille Claudel is Paul Claudel's sister, was Rodin's student and lover, and has been locked up by her brother, sister and mother in an asylum where she does not belong. Do I have to say that? Who is forcing me to say that?

I wish there was some way to get Camille Claudel away, both literally and figuratively, from Rodin and her family, and keep her away. So she could fulfill her art: the art of telling secrets.

I do not know enough about Camille Claudel. I know absolutely nothing about Camille Claudel. She is beyond me. She is beyond us all. If only we could get there.

When women can no longer stand the way they are treated, they will remember Camille Claudel and use her as an example.

EDUARD STEICHEN

Eduard Steichen is the only artist in Paris who constantly does things for other people. For Alfred Stieglitz's 291 Gallery in America, he arranges for shows of French paintings. For Stieglitz's magazine *Camera Work*, he arranges for monographs to be written on Rodin, and articles to be written by painters on why they hate photography. For Rodin, he photographs his *Balzac* so that one day other people might understand it. For me, he explains how my paintings utilize the Purkinje effect. For Cocteau, he arranges an introduction to Rilke, so the younger poet might have an older poet to adore. For the Hôtel Biron, he arbitrates discussions among the tenants so everyone remains on speaking terms. For Picasso, he convinces the other tenants that monkeys and turtles should be allowed to roam the hallways. For Nijinsky he tries to appease Diaghilev that his prodigy is loyal. For the war he stays up for three nights in a brewery and develops reconnaissance photos.

I predict that Steichen will continue to do things for other people for many years. When he goes back to America, he will probably return to portrait and fashion photography. But one day, when he is middle aged, and begins to see his brief life slipping away from him, he will decide he is fed up with doing for others. He will drop everything and everyone and become utterly selfish. He will even get divorced. Then he will do his best work; something completely his own. And people will stand in awe of it and say: That—that is art. In this way he will prove that photography is art. This has not yet been proved. But we will call it art here for the sake of discussion.

Steichen is the ultimate representative of his art form. He is a persuasive spokesman for art photography. He defends the rights of its practitioners to employ silhouettes, blurriness, accidents, and technical modifications in order to further their art. He avidly supports this notion that photographs should be exhibited as fine art, and that painters should not dominate the juries of photographic salons. He is a pioneer of color photography and color photography as art.

But Steichen is also smart enough to know when to remain silent. He has not said anything about the feud between Stieglitz and Day, or the expulsion of Gertrude Kasebier and Max Weber from the Photo-Secessionists.

Stieglitz made Steichen possible. Steichen knows this. Steichen's genius lies in his ability to get what he wants out of people and landscapes. To do this he must know what he wants and how to get it. Eventually Steichen will be forced to break with Stieglitz but by the time he does he will no longer need the older man and Stieglitz will be unable to hurt his career.

Steichen knows color. Despite his willfulness, Steichen has no ill intentions. Steichen has no outside impediments to his work within the art photographic community. He was welcomed and praised from his very first salon submission and made important by older men in his profession. In the art world this would be highly suspect, but in photography it is not.

Steichen's only impediments are the lure of commercial portrait photography, and the dismissal of photography as fine art—but even there he has supporters in Rodin, Shaw and Maeterlinck. Steichen is a good painter but painting no longer lures him.

Steichen organized all the shows of the Hôtel Biron artists at the 291 Gallery in America. In this way Steichen has brought the art of the tenants of the Hôtel Biron to the Americans.

Steichen himself is not really an American. He was born in Luxembourg. No one knows this.

Steichen admits he has no idea what the name Photo-Secessionist means, even though he is one.

PABLO PICASSO

Picasso is Spanish. He started Cubism. He's perfectly willing to admit that he has no idea what he's doing. It's everyone else who is afraid to admit it. I introduced him to African sculpture.

Our quarrel is overrated. I am his nemesis. He wishes he understood color as well as I do, but won't admit it. We have split art in two, and each is carrying it in his own direction. He resents me for this, but it is for the best. Neither will be more important than the other.

Picasso has not yet learned how to stop working. He will have to learn. He is prolific in everything—food, women, work. But this is not a yearning to annihilate himself as some say, but to make himself.

Since Picasso creates fashions instead of following them, he can risk being unfashionable. He can throw a party for Rousseau. He can design the sets for *Parade*. He is willing to move on, to realign, to take risks.

As a result there are periods in Picasso's art. Already people want to claim that some are more important than others, that the periods before the *Demoiselles* and since his new pastoral painting are less important than his Cubism. They are not. His periods aren't separable from each other. They are stops on a journey. The journey is important, not the stops.

What is his art to Picasso? Research. Just that. Only that.

Likewise, the woman in Picasso's life represents the period he's going through. With women, as with art, Picasso is looking for something he will never find. He knows this and he knows the point is to keep looking. Critics are wrong when they say Picasso's hatred of women is evident in his paintings of them. Picasso's paintings of women aren't about women. They are about art.

Picasso's eroticism is already evident in his Cubist paintings, but no one will notice it for a long time.

Picasso is affected by his surroundings. His paintings change whenever he changes his studio in Paris or his summer home in the country.

Picasso was not affected by his sudden wealth or fame, but like everyone he is profoundly affected by the War. Despite the War, he is very young to have had so many close friends and lovers die. Since childhood, Picasso lives in a constant state of grief and revelry, as if he were always at a wake.

The War has ruined everything for now, and it will ruin some artists permanently, but it will not ruin Picasso.

Picasso will not give titles to his paintings and yet he creates new names for the women he lives with. Picasso's Eva is dead but even so, what do Fernande, Eva and Olga have in common? Their future without Picasso.

As willful as Picasso seems toward other people, he lets his art rule him. It is the only thing he allows to rule him.

Almost all artists suffer at one time or another with indigestion and trouble with the law. Picasso has already experienced both of these.

Many artists lack confidence. Picasso does not. He doubts his work, but he never doubts himself.

Picasso is not afraid of otherness. All his friends are poets.

Erik Satie

Everyone agrees Satie is the most insulted, derided and ridiculed composer of his generation. But they also agree he's oversensitive.

Everyone says that Debussy was Satie's greatest friend. Debussy allowed Satie to dine with him but made him drink inferior wine. Satie wanted to adapt a Maeterlinck play and Debussy thought it was such a good idea he obtained permission for himself before Satie could even ask. Debussy could have introduced Satie's music to the public but chose not to. When Ravel finally did it, Debussy was angry and surprised anyone liked it.

Satie's irony does not mask his bitterness. It often vents his bitterness. And when he is whimsical and puckish, he is not hiding anything. He sees the world that way. Are people of Honfleur born of Scottish mothers never puckish? Why can't people be who they are? Why must they be protecting themselves?

Satie is a fetishist. He could not be without some form of affectation. Satie's personal eccentricities extend much farther than his dress. Instead of bathing he scrapes himself with a pumice stone. Weekly, assiduously, he sends all his collars and handkerchiefs out to be laundered, but he will not clean his room or hire anyone to do it. He likes to carry lit pipes and hammers in his pockets, since the umbrella is always on his arm. He hates the sun and stays up all night.

No one understands Satie. Satie is the only one who doesn't try.

Satie does nothing but write. He sits in cafés and composes music in sets of threes, using different colored ink, writing in a calligraphic hand, and including copious marginal directions to the musicians, which he believes are essential to the piece but forbids to be read aloud during a performance. He also invents ideas for music he never composes, and writes the ideas down in his notebook.

Anyone who goes back to school at forty is either courageous or humiliated. Satie was both. He wanted to improve his music, and become known for his new innovations. Instead he has improved his music and become known for his old innovations. He pretended to be bitter about this but was secretly flattered and wrote more during that time of flattery than before or since. This proves that the artist is too susceptible to discouragement and encouragement. It is obviously a dangerous thing and should be avoided at all costs.

The reason Satie's new music is not recognized is . because one is not permitted to change one's character in France, and therefore he was not really permitted to go back to school and write different music, even though he did it anyway.

Furniture music is the music of the future. But no one knows it. *Socrate* is Satie's best work so far. But no one realizes it. Satie is the only artist I know whose work flourishes during the War, but no one admits it.

Twenty years ago Satie moved to the suburbs and, except for his room here in the Hôtel Biron, he has lived there ever since. Satie prefers the gloom of the suburbs to Paris and I have no idea why he condescends to loiter with us painters. He confessed to me that he learns more about music from painters. But he may have been flattering me.

Satie is childlike but is not a primitive and should not be compared to Rousseau, though he often is. Satie is childlike and shrewd; Rousseau was never shrewd. Satie should not be compared to anyone.

No one likes Satie's music because they are afraid he is playing a joke on them and he will get the last laugh. Satie's music is no joke.

If Satie hadn't played the piano at the Chat Noir and L'Auberge du Clou, he would never have had a mistress. He is afraid that if he were ever comfortable his music would no longer be any good. That is why he refuses to live with a woman, or have his room cleaned, or accept large sums for his music to be published. This idea that he might be cuckolded or that women don't understand him is rubbish.

Socrate is Satie's only humorless work. I already said it might be his best. He could not have written it until Debussy died. Satie is a miniaturist in music. His triptychs are three-sided, sculptural music. He insists on spareness because he is tired of this Decadence and Romanticism and German music, even though he was against the ban on German music when the War started.

Satie is the only artist I know who has successfully avoided ordinary life. He lives in a world of his own construction.

Satie happened in France. He could not have happened in any other country.

RAINER MARIA RILKE

Rilke longs to write, but has extended periods when he produces nothing. He longs to be loved by a woman in a particular way, but cannot determine what that way is. He longs to be understood, but that is too much to ask.

To Rilke, no one is ever pure enough, right enough. He applies these standards to his own work. This overly critical sense prevents him from working. It forces him to suffer long intervals when he tries but cannot work. He repeatedly tortures himself about his inability to work. He sleeps and wakes up refreshed. In an access of gratitude, he falls into a swoon and writes, without stopping, an immortal work of literature.

Rilke believes that he is a Carinthian. He believes that everything originates in the blood. Most exiles who travel aimlessly and have no country feel compelled to invent their origins and create elaborate personalities based on them, as if this excused their odd behavior.

Rilke is especially fond of women, children and animals, because they rely on their intuition. He wants to make childhood into a cult and childlikeness a necessity for grownups.

Rilke travels to get away from himself, not to find himself. Rilke is a procrastinator. He will do his best work when he knows he is about to die.

Paris is the closest thing that Rilke has ever had to a relationship. Paris attracts and repels him. He tries to get away but comes back. He will always come back.

Rilke subsists on a monthly income from his German publisher Anton Kippenberg, and from an anonymous Austrian donor who is a woman. All Rilke's great friends are women. Women are drawn to him and he needs a fascinating woman nearby at all times. But when she gets too close, he withdraws. For Rilke withdrawal is a creative act.

Everybody praises Rilke's *The Notebooks of Malte Laurids Brigge* for its evocation of Paris. No one even notices that it is the most apt treatise since Shakespeare on the difference between loving and being loved.

Rilke has sought out great artists to admire, but his obsessions last only long enough to answer his immediate question. With Tolstoy the question was: *Must one be an artist?* With Rodin: *How do I live?* With Cézanne: *How do I reconcile the intuitive with the intellectual?* And with Gide: *How do I reconcile life and art?* Now that Rilke has found partial answers to all these questions, he may not have the need for a great man-artist in his life again, and may never acquire another love of this kind.

Rilke believes in the voluptuous soul and understands the painterly idea of the body as landscape. Of all the writers in Paris he is one of the few who understands the correspondences among the arts, respects the visual arts, and uses concepts drawn from the visual arts for his own work.

Art is more real to him than life. Rilke's greatest struggle is to reconcile life and work. So far he has failed.

Rilke is only attracted to people he hopes might understand him. The only thing that matters to Rilke is the life of the emotions. Rilke makes you see through his eyes.

JEAN COCTEAU

Cocteau adores other people with a headlong abandon that is typical of impetuous youth. But he is no longer a youth. He will retain this childlike quality into old age, and complain that he is still too young.

Cocteau prefers to love men who are reluctant parties. He used to love men much older than himself, but now that he is approaching thirty he has begun to love boys. Cocteau will provide all the love and guidance for these boys that he wanted when he was a boy. Of course they won't want it.

Cocteau has been accused of being a dilettante and a dandy instead of a serious artist. But he will be one day. His most impressive contribution to art so far is his organization of the event called *Parade*, in which he induced Picasso and Satie to collaborate. I imagine Cocteau's real genius will be revealed in his old age, in some masterpiece of staging, in some collaborative effort, perhaps in some ultra modern field of art that has not yet been invented.

No one enjoys suffering. But suffering has become a habit with him, and he craves it the way he craves love. I'm afraid Cocteau might be prey to other addictions besides love. An artist should not expect to be understood, but Cocteau is one. I am afraid that as a result he will become bitter and resentful. Bitterness and hatred spell ruin for the artist.

We are all searching for something; Cocteau is searching for himself. Cocteau claims his artistic collaborators at the Hôtel Biron are his friends. They claim he is not. They will probably continue to collaborate over the years, and continue to bicker over whether or not they are friends. Cocteau is one of the few Parisians at the Hôtel Biron. He marvels at how so many foreigners can reap so much artistic indulgence, inspiration, fame and glory from his native city. Secretly, he envies them. Like many artists, Cocteau feels lonely and insecure and will probably always feel that way. His morbid desire to please may be his way of showing how much he fears this.

Cocteau does his best work under the influence of romantic love. This will be both his glory and his downfall. Cocteau has no friends, only lovers. He wants sons and will try to make his lovers his sons.

HENRI MATISSE

I am not afraid to use my intuition. I use it all the time and for everything. I have been working very hard throughout the War and I am about to change directions entirely. My wish is about to be fulfilled.

I refuse to develop the bitterness I see destroy other artists. I am what I am. That is enough. In my art I seek oblivion in its various forms — oblivion, the thing without limits.

My use of color is never arbitrary. It is designed to make us see objects and their relations to each other in a new way. It is designed to bring out the heart — mine, yours, the one of the canvas.

Only Steichen understands my use of color. I am indebted to him even though I disapprove of photography.

Simplicity is not a choice. It is my direction. I have no choices, I have only to be diligent and follow my direction. No one else is going in my direction.

I travel to get away. Illness is a place I have traveled to, and will again. My family is a solace to me. I just want to understand myself.

Fauvism is the critics' way of explaining the incomprehensible but inevitable next step. I understand Cézanne better than anyone. I am a purist but I am never decorative. Deny the effect my painting has on you: color, purity, bliss. Everything that is happening to me is happening right now.

I do not paint my desire, but the quality of my desire.

Why am I telling you all this? Shall I go on?

VASLAV NIJINSKY

People like to say that Nijinsky is only emotional, only instinctual, only physical, only intuitive, that he is really an animal or a creature from another world. This is untrue. Nijinsky can only express himself through motion.

Everyone is so thrilled because, when Nijinsky leaps, he pauses for a moment in the air before coming down. In the future Nijinsky's secret method will be revealed and all the dancers and athletes will be required to learn it.

What should thrill people is his choreography, his ingenuity of movement, his ability to transform himself into the character. Of course it doesn't.

No one appreciates Nijinsky's choreography — it is too modern for the moderns, more advanced than any other art form. The most scandalous and innovative of his dance movements have been improvised. They have come directly from the character Nijinsky has allowed to overwhelm him. The only reason *Afternoon of a Faun* was so shocking was because no one could deny that for a moment Nijinsky became the Faun.

Like the painters here at the Hôtel Biron, Nijinsky hates prettiness. His choreography shows that. Nijinsky becomes the music when he dances and wants his audiences to understand his ballets as physically as his choreography of it. Nijinsky is looking for something beyond prettiness — what we are all looking for.

The public is fascinated by the strength of Nijinsky's legs, but his real power is in his abdomen. This is why Rodin loved him. There is no power in the extremities.

In this period of showy decadence, Nijinsky is the only performing artist who is truly erotic. This is another reason why he is profoundly disturbing, and yet another reason why Rodin loved him.

Nijinsky is aware of the tension between the Greek and Egyptian, and used it in *The Rite of Spring*. Nijinsky insisted on preserving his childlikeness and innocence, because he knew it was essential to his art. Nijinsky's work is perfect because he achieved a perfect synthesis of his own nature and his training.

Geniuses who are able to abandon themselves can be controlled. They never know when to accept protection and when to fight it. When Nijinsky was well, he protected his mother and sister vehemently but did not know how to protect himself. After Diaghilev threw him out, Nijinsky tried to start his own company and manage his business affairs but is only a genius at dance and choreography. We like to think it is bad luck that the first person he finds—Diaghilev—will not let him flourish and then destroys him. We would like to think it is bad luck that he cannot manage his business affairs himself, and cannot find someone else after D. to do it.

Diaghilev and his dancers did not destroy Nijinsky because he left D. and married a woman. They destroyed him because he is the best dancer—not of their time, or up until this day. Nijinsky is the best dancer ever. They realized this and so they destroyed him.

It is easy to destroy genius. There is no glory in it.

Nijinsky did not go mad because Diaghilev rejected him. Nijinsky went mad because after D. he could not find another opportunity to dance and choreograph. And so his heart died. You cannot live through a war like this one when your heart has died.

You may blame Diaghilev if you like. He was the instrument of Nijinsky's destiny. Nijinsky was incapable of making his way alone. Someone else might have enabled him to dance a full twelve years instead of only six, and to choreograph and teach another fifty. Or, someone might have come along who could not help Nijinsky at all, and only the Russians would have known about him. We cannot know who the others might have been. What we know is that Nijinsky danced for six years and choreographed for only two. He is the only real tragedy at the Hôtel Biron.

Nijinsky is at home in the water. He loves weightlessness. He seeks oblivion. Don't we all.

The Notebooks of Eduard Steichen #7
(1914-1918)

DECEMBER 1914

Cocteau is back from ambulance duty on the front lines. He is trying to get Maurice Barres to publish an article in *L'Echo de Paris* about the bombing of Rheims. He feels too much has been said about the cathedral and not enough about the human suffering.

Max Jacob has converted to Christianity and was baptized. He asked Picasso to be his godfather, and Picasso agreed to it.

APRIL 1915

Rodin has returned to Rome to do a bust of the Pope. I hear he is unhappy though because the Pope only granted him three sittings when he had requested twelve, and the Pope would not let him look down at the top of his head, or at the back or sides of his head.

Nijinsky was given permission to go to America to dance for Diaghilev but they are already fighting. Nijinsky wants Mr. D. to pay him his back salary before he agrees to dance.

Fall 1915

Rodin has returned from Rome but complains of the cold. Coal is in short supply.

Cocteau continues to publish his magazine *Le Mot*. He wants to stage *A Midsummer Night's Dream* at the Cirque Medrano and use music from Satie's *Gymnopédies*.

Matisse has been back from his summer home in Nice for several months now. In America only the rich summer in the country and winter in the city, but here all the painters do it, and they are not rich. I suppose it also seems odd during wartime, when all established rituals of behavior have been suspended, but the painters in Paris, including the tenants of the Hôtel Biron, travel even more than they did before the war started.

I had the opportunity to go down to Matisse's studio and take a look at his new work. I don't know what to make of it. All the pictures are done in different styles; composed in different manners, use color and brushstrokes differently. I am not sure what Matisse is after, and I am not sure if this variety is a search for something in particular or a symptom of the disruption of the war. In either case Matisse is furiously at work; he knows he is after something, but he does not know what it is. The most curious feature of his new work, and the only thing I can see in common among this wildly variant work, is his use of erasure. Matisse scratches out certain forms on a canvas, but leaves their traces visible. Someday this technique will be the rage in New York. I must tell Alfred Stieglitz about it. There is something fussy and irritable about it that would appeal to a New York painter.

DECEMBER 1915

Picasso's companion Eva has died. He is taking it very hard.

Cocteau is in raptures. He has fallen in love with Picasso. He says the experience was one of the majo revelations of his life, on par with seeing Stravinsky's *Rite of Spring*. He has focused all of his admiration on Picasso now. A few days ago he visited the painter weaing a harlequin costume concealed under a trench coat. Bu Picasso seemed to like the idea and even kept the cotume. Picasso may be the first great man who is generous enough to let Cocteau adore him.

Cocteau would like to collaborate on a ballet with Picasso. This has made him realize that Diaghilev doesn't know anything about Modern art, and the painters from Montmartre never go to the Russian Ballet. From this he's beginning to understand that there really is an artistic right and an artistic left in Paris, and no one has been successful aligning themselves with both, and that's what his aristocratic companions were arguing about so vehemently when he made friends with the other Cubists.

JANUARY 1916

Some charcoal drawings by a woman named Georgia O'Keeffe arrived by mail at the 291 a few weeks ago, and the photographs Stieglitz made to show them to me just reached me here in Paris. His note says the photos do not do justice to the drawings, but I think they would be the most amazing things I have ever seen, if I could actually see them. The drawings are abstract, and convey with astonishing power and forthrightness what it must feel like to be a woman. Stieglitz wants to give this Georgia O'Keeffe a show.

Matisse brought me down to his studio to see the culmination of his experiments of the past year. The painting is called *The Piano Lesson*. It takes elements from Cubism, Orphism, and abstraction, and integrates them. The result is beyond categorization, except to say that it is a Matisse. His remarkable use of color is also in evidence. There's a feeling of foreboding in this painting that I have never seen before in a Matisse, and may never see again, based on his newer work. He is now doing paintings of models lounging in his studio, and he seems quite content with them. But we both know this satisfaction is only momentary. Matisse is like an advancing army. He is regrouping, gathering his forces. The next campaign will be launched soon.

Picasso is sketching portraits of Max Jacob and Apollinaire with his head bandaged in his hospital room.

APRIL 1916

Cocteau is trying to convince Satie to collaborate with him on a ballet called *Parade*. He's taken voluminous notes and left them with Satie. He's also been posing for Picasso. I believe he still entertains the idea of Picasso also collaborating on the ballet. Picasso is trying to get Cocteau to go to the Italian hospital here, to visit Apollinaire who is suffering from a head wound he got in the trenches. Cocteau likes Picasso's instinct of trying to bring people together, but Cocteau says he's heard that Apollinaire doesn't like him and he doesn't think it would be appropriate to go visit him. But Picasso has been introducing Cocteau to other painters, among them Modigliani and Max Jacob. Cocteau seems to like that but says everyone, except Picasso, is suspicious of him because of his Russian Ballet associations.

Picasso gave up his studio in Montparnasse to take a house in the suburb of Montrouge. Since Satie still has an apartment nearby in Arceuil-Cachan, they often walk home together in the middle of the night. Transportation is impossible with this war on.

MAY 1916

Nijinsky was a big success in America but Diaghilev and the Russian Ballet have left for Spain without him. He and Mr. D. fought the entire time and Diaghilev does not want him to dance for the company anymore, even if it ruins them. Nijinsky's wife says Diaghilev is trying to ruin Nijinsky. Nijinsky's nerves are so frail I'm afraid this is quite possible.

AUGUST 1916

Rodin had another stroke and fell down the stairs at the Villa Des Brillants in Meudon.

Picasso has agreed to do *Parade* with Cocteau and Satie. Cocteau is thrilled. He feels that Picasso painting for the Russian Ballet will be the scandal he's longing to create, the collaboration of the artistic left and right that everyone claimed was impossible.

SEPTEMBER 1916

Cocteau is sulking about *Parade*. Apparently Picasso and Satie enjoy working together so much Cocteau feels left out. The talk around the Hôtel Biron seems to confirm this. Satie seems to like Picasso's ideas about the libretto better than Cocteau's. Third parties are trying to get Picasso to assuage Cocteau's hurt feelings.

September 1916

Picasso talked to Cocteau and convinced him that all three of them see eye-to-eye, and Satie is simply confused by the different approaches of Cocteau and Picasso. Cocteau has agreed to allow Picasso to clear things up with Satie. The situation has reached that point where it's impossible to tell who is lying to whom, but Cocteau appreciates Picasso's gesture to placate him, and I'm sure he appreciates the intrigue, even though in this case he would not admit it.

October 1916

Diaghilev agreed to send some of his dancers back to New York to dance with Nijinsky but he did not do it in time for adequate rehearsals. Nijinsky's nerves are a wreck from trying to manage, choreograph and direct the company — something he vowed never to attempt again. The dancers are giving him trouble; they even organized a two-day strike. Some people believe Diaghilev asked them to cause Nijinsky grief and sabotage his work. Considering Diaghilev's malicious streak, this is altogether possible.

December 1916

The senate passed a law making the Hôtel Biron into a Rodin museum and accepting all of Rodin's works as gifts to the French state. There was still a lot of objection to it. Some senators called him demented and his work dangerous and offensive. The erotic drawings in the chapel were discussed again. But the law finally passed and Rodin has not heard about the charges against him. I hope they will not evict us until the war is over. We are all too busy to stop and reflect on what this loss will mean to us. Or perhaps we try not to think of it.

DECEMBER 1916

A banquet was held in honor of Apollinaire. Cocteau and Picasso attended. A fight broke out between the Cubists and Dadaists. When the banquet ended, Cocteau went to Diaghilev's New Year's Eve party, where he argued with a Cubist.

JANUARY 1917

Parade is scheduled to debut in May. Diaghilev is buying Cubist paintings. Mr. D. wants to rehearse *Parade* in Rome but Satie doesn't want to go.

Rodin married Rose so if he dies first she will have some financial protection. I don't think he even knows what is going on—Judith Cladel arranged it.

Cocteau and Picasso have left for Rome to work on *Parade*. Satie stayed behind.

FEBRUARY 14 1917

Rose died in her sleep early this morning.

MAY 18, 1917

Parade premiered this afternoon at the Théâtre du Châtelet. The crowd was probably more mixed than it has ever been for a Paris premiere of the Russian Ballet. Diaghilev's society people were there, a notable group of counts and princesses. But the Montmartre and Montparnasse painters showed up for the first time (Diaghilev sent them free tickets), and there was a large contingent of Russian soldiers on leave.

The audience liked Picasso's drop curtain—a very sweet depiction of a winged horse, a harlequin, and some circus people sitting around backstage. But, when the curtain rose and Satie's music started, everyone went crazy. It sounded like a circus. A few of the dancers were dressed up in these cubist towers. The dancers jumped up and down and tripped over themselves.

Of course the counts and princesses booed; the painters shouted *Vive Picasso! Vive Satie!* from the upper balconies; and the soldiers joined in the bedlam. People said the ballet was "un-French" and inappropriately gleeful during wartime. Fist fights erupted and people shouted death threats against Diaghilev, Picasso and Satie. Women brandished their hatpins. Throughout the spectacle, Satie sat in the first row of the balcony applauding madly.

JUNE 1917

Young composers have been flocking to Satie since the scandal of *Parade* has made him esteemed in the art world. Today Satie's protégés gave a concert at the Hôtel Biron. Blaise Cendrars organized it. Satie calls his troupe The New Young Ones and plans to organize a public concert for them at the Vieux-Columbier Theatre.

But Satie is no longer following the line of thinking he set up for his protégés when he composed *Parade*. He has gone in a completely opposite direction. He's working on very sober music that he deems appropriate to Plato's *Dialogues*.

Nijinsky is in Spain working with Diaghilev. They seem to be getting along but Nijinsky has become a Tolstoy fanatic (i.e. peasant farming, vegetarianism, asceticism) and his wife is afraid Diaghilev is using the Tolstoyans to break up their marriage. As a result, she doesn't want Nijinsky to go to South America with Diaghilev.

JULY 1917

Nijinsky refused to go to South America with Diaghilev, so Mr. D. had him arrested in Spain for breach of contract and forced him to go to South America against his will. Nijinsky's wife still maintains that Diaghilev and the Tolstoyans are trying to ruin their marriage. Picasso, who is still close to the ballet because of his new companion Olga, says that Diaghilev is not in league with the Tolstoyans and Nijinsky could have gone to South America willingly without fear of further entanglement with them. Picasso did admit though that Diaghilev probably does have plans to break up Nijinsky's marriage, more out of spite than love.

Picasso is worried that Nijinsky has become a little too fanatic about this Tolstoyan philosophy and, without the possibility of working harmoniously with Diaghilev, he is afraid the strain might be too much for Nijinsky and he might lose his reason. What a choice — a family and insanity or losing your family and working with that viper Diaghilev!

AUGUST 1917

Nijinsky is dancing in Rio and Buenos Aires with the Russian Ballet but once again everyone in the company is doing their best to sabotage his work. He keeps having "accidents" and hurting himself. It's really frightening. He's stepped on a rusty nail on stage, had to avoid a falling iron beam, and in *Petrouchka* fell from the puppet's booth which was not properly secured. Nijinsky's wife suspects foul play and has hired a detective.

Picasso has returned to Paris with Olga, who has left the Russian Ballet.

NOVEMBER 12, 1917

Today is Rodin's 77th birthday. He has pneumonia and no one thinks he will pull through. It's a pity he has to die because there is not enough coal, but a lot of people are dying in much more horrifying ways because of this war.

NOVEMBER 17, 1917

Rodin died this morning. His last words were in praise of Puvis de Chavannes. He also mentioned his "wife in Paris who needs money." Most people assume he was referring to Camille, but he could have been speaking philosophically about the Duchesse.

I am not going to deliver an elegy here; nothing I could write would be adequate.

More backlash from the *Parade* scandal: Jean Poueigh is suing Satie for a lewd postcard Satie sent him as an answer to Poueigh's vicious attack on Satie in his review of *Parade* in *Le Temps*. Satie lost his appeal today and Cocteau, who appeared as a defense witness, was fined for threatening Poueigh's lawyer. Satie has been fined a thousand francs and must serve a week in prison.

The Russian Ballet has returned to Spain without Nijinsky, who is no longer under obligation to them. Picasso is afraid Nijinsky will never dance again, and fears for his health, which seems to be failing from trying so hard to live both with and without Diaghilev.

1917

The tenants of the Hôtel Biron have been listening to Satie work on his new music and of course everyone is talking about it. No one can even agree on what it is. Picasso says it's humorous, but Matisse insists it is only humorous on paper by virtue of the titles, directions and marginal notes. Cocteau brought out his copy of *Sports et Divertissements* to prove his point. Cocteau insists that *Sports et Divertissements* is the supreme collaborative effort of calligraphy, painting, poetry and music, and wishes he could do something comparable in his lifetime. Matisse tried to explain to the rest of us Satie's economy and individuality in his keyboard style, his use of dissonance and spare two-part counterpart, his appoggiaturas and sonorities built up on fourths, but none of us know enough about music to understand him. Picasso insisted on the humor again, saying that the textual comments only mirror the irony and whimsy in the music itself. Nijinsky said he thought if Rodin were still alive he would like Satie's new music, but Rilke balked at the idea, and said if Rodin couldn't understand Wagner or Debussy, he certainly wouldn't have understood Satie. When Cocteau suggested you can like art without understanding it, Rilke conceded that this was true in principle, but that Rodin could not have.

I have joined the US Signal Corps Photographic Section under Major Barnes. Barnes is returning to New York to run the School of Aerial Photography so I will be in charge of operations here in Paris.

JANUARY **1918**

Satie is once again despondent over his friend and nemesis Debussy. He was very hurt last year when Debussy never sent him any word congratulating him on *Parade*. He finally sent Debussy what appears to have been a very nasty, retaliatory letter. Now of course Satie regrets it.

The other tenants of the Hôtel Biron say that Satie is not angry simply about *Parade*, but about his entire friendship with Debussy. Satie has always been the broke one, the unrecognized one, and now that his work is acknowledged it still remains on the fringes, unaccepted. Though he would not choose to compose any other music than what he has created, he still resents his position, and Debussy of course is his hair shirt, the constant reminder of the position he wanted to be in.

But Debussy is very sick, and may even be dying, so Satie of course feels terrible that he caused Debussy any unpleasantness. What a tortured friendship that must be.

Picasso continues to be afraid that Nijinsky is losing his mind. Nijinsky flies into rages at his wife, walks head-long into traffic on the streets and repeatedly draws pictures of red and black eyes. Sometimes he walks through the streets carrying a cross. Nijinsky and his wife are leaving for Budapest to get help.

Picasso says he has never seen so many examples of human destruction as the result of lost or thwarted love as have passed through the Hôtel Biron: Camille Claudel, Rose, the Duchesse, Gwen John, Nuala O'Donel and now Nijinsky. He says that some things, like work, may be more important than love, but nothing is more painful, not death, not illness, not even the failure of work. Of course he blames it on women. Rilke agreed with him up to that point. Rilke, our resident supporter of women's rights, blames it on men. They got in an enormous argument over it, neither one of them would back down, and gross generalizations about the differences between the sexes were flying all over the house.

January 1918

Picasso has taken a studio on the Right Bank on a street full of art dealers. His new dealer Paul Rosenberg (Léonce's brother) has opened a gallery nearby. Paul Guillaume, who held a joint Picasso-Matisse exhibit, has his gallery in the rue du Faubourg-Saint-Honoré. Picasso's continued success seems assured.

April 1918

I've returned exhausted from the Meuse-Argonne offensive where we worked day and night out of a brewery building to produce French intelligence photos by the time they were needed.

Summer 1918

Apollinaire has married. Everyone hopes his health will improve.

Picasso is summering in Biarritz, drawing portraits of the Rosenbergs and painting murals with Apollinaire's verse on them.

Picasso married Olga in a civil ceremony with Apollinaire, Max Jacob and Cocteau as witnesses. He has promised her an Orthodox Russian ceremony.

Late Fall **1918**

Apollinaire has died. Picasso is so overcome with grief he has asked Cocteau to send out the notices to newspapers.

Late Fall **1918**

We received our eviction notice. We have a month to vacate. Everyone is making plans. Matisse has decided to move to the South of France permanently, most likely to Nice. Picasso and Olga plan to winter in Paris in their new apartment on the Right Bank, and summer at the Riviera. Rilke is leaving for Munich right away; he doesn't even plan to ship his possessions. He says we can have what we want and the French government can dispose of the rest. In honor of the Armistice I have burned all my canvases in a big bonfire and have resolved to give up painting entirely. I plan to concentrate on photography, which I feel I'm better at. I am going to Voulangis for a time and, when I've recovered from the war, I plan to return to Paris, and eventually, to New York.

Stieglitz has written me that he would like to re-commission our articles. He is starting a new magazine called *MSS* and would like to publish the articles in it. But I'm afraid we cannot find the manuscripts. Rodin was reading them shortly before his last illness, and Rilke suspects they were locked in the basement with his other possessions, which are now the property of the French State. We've discussed asking the government for them but Picasso is afraid they would claim them as their property and suppress them. Matisse suggested we wait until we might be able to retrieve them safely. Everyone has agreed to do that. No one was happy that Rodin was reading the manuscripts. They said I had no right to show them to him. They all blame me.

I have written to Miss Claudel, who has her manuscript in her possession, to tell her of the situation. Since Satie, Nijinsky and I were not finished with our manuscripts when we gave them to Rodin to read, and continued to work on them, we too have at least a portion of our manuscripts in our possessions.

Letters Not Sent:
The Letters of Camille Claudel 6

(1917-1943)

1917

Monsieur Rodin,

So you have died then. I did not think you would out-live the war. Your youngest son René brought me the news. He comes to visit me almost every day. He has told my keepers that he is an art student who worships me and desires to be my apprentice. When Sandro comes to visit, he claims to be René. I do not want my keepers to know that there are two of them. Your sons invented this ruse. They are clever boys, all of twenty-five. They escaped the war because of their short sightedness and dyspepsia, which they know they inherited from you.

René has told me that on your deathbed you asked for me. I still do not believe him, but Sandro, who was also at the bedside (he was hired on as a marble cutter in your studio to replace the men who had left for the war), claimed you asked for your wife. When one of your sycophants explained that Rose had died several months before, you became irritable and said it was your wife in Paris you wanted.

I told René that Sandro was mistaken, that there had been so many after me, you were undoubtedly asking for the American Duchess or that English painter. But

René insisted to me that Sandro heard the sycophants around the bedside murmur my name; they all agreed that I had been your greatest love.

I know why you were calling for me. You wanted me to forgive you for all the sins you committed against me: theft, adultery, prevarication, subjugation and now this incarceration. Don't think that even on your deathbed I would forgive you. I will never forgive you. And it is not because I have no heart. Your crimes are too great.

Are you a different person now that you are dead? Are you a kinder and better person? Do you see the errors of your ways, and all the harm you have inflicted on people?

1918

Rodin,

I hear the copy of *The Waltz* I gave Monsieur Debussy has been stolen. Did one of your sycophants perpetrate this crime? Does this mean that even though you are both dead you still can't tolerate a former lover possessing a figure of mine? If I had married Debussy, I would be a respectable widow now.

My brother Paul has blamed our mother for ruining me by favoring our sister Louise. I wonder how many lives are dominated by this problem. For example, would you have treated Rose and me so poorly if your sister hadn't died of love for Barnouvin, if you hadn't blamed yourself and promised never to love so completely again? Would I have let you get the upper hand with me, if I hadn't been hoping to earn that love away from Rose, the way I failed to earn my mother's love away from Louise? Would Debussy have loved me if he weren't trying to win me away from you? Would Rose have loved you if she weren't trying to constantly to win you back from models?

1926

Rodin,

My brother Paul has been made an ambassador. He has purchased the Château de Brangues near Grenoble. When my brother speaks of me, it is as if I am already dead. He continues to use me as an example of why a young person should not choose art as a profession. He made me an example. If he had not locked me up, I would simply be an artist, working in solitude in the face of public indifference.

1929

Rodin,

My mother has died and she will soon be joining you in that hell of malice, revenge, jealousy and hatred against me, which was certainly your own making.

1932

Rodin,

I received the kindest letter today from my dealer Eugene Blot. He says you and I, and three or four others of our generation, showed greatness and authenticity. So at last we are admired as equals. I told you the day would come.

M. Blot goes on to describe me as a woman of great beauty, mystery, sensuality and genius. He goes on to tell me you cried over my portrait and I was the only one you truly loved.

I wonder if it is true. It might be. When you met Rose, you were too young to love. She was beautiful at first, and shared your life, but she was really your housekeeper, your model, your studio apprentice. It is hard to love someone who works for you.

Then I came along—I was young and beautiful, you were forty and about to become successful in your career. Do you ever wonder if it was your love of me that inspired you to make those figures for the colossal door? That was the step you needed. You would never have created your *Balzac* without the doors, and you would never have executed the doors without me. Already people are attributing your success to me. After me, you were famous, and so the women you met then were the rewards of fame and once again inferior.

If you loved me because at that moment in your life between obscurity and fame you were in the best position to love, then you loved me most. I showed you how to love without surrendering. Isn't that what you wanted after your sister died? Monsieur Blot assures me that I have suffered too much on your account, and that nothing would justify your conduct, but that time will put things right.

1935

Rodin,

You are now almost twenty years in the grave. I am writing to tell you that my work is being exhibited with great prestige and distinction at the Exposition des Femmes Artistes Modernes. I am hoping that perhaps now, when the artists and critics are beginning to soundly reject and even forget your work, mine will finally be able to be noticed. It is not enough for you to die, so my art can flourish, it seems your reputation must also die. As much as I despise you and what you've done to me, I find this unfortunate. But perhaps after my work is recognized and flourishing, your reputation can enjoy a rebirth, and our work can coexist as equals in the world of art, as we should have done as lovers and artists when you were alive, and I was not incarcerated.

I am not going to die yet but I have finally succeeded in erasing myself. I have tried to grow smaller and smaller in this ludicrous world of the asylum, so that one day I might cease to exist, and at that moment I would finally have some peace.

After many years of effort and discipline, I have finally achieved this. No one looks at me, speaks to me, or even utters my name. I have become invisible. I could probably even work on my sculptures in the daytime now without trouble. But it has become a habit to work at night and there is no point in changing that now.

This success has brought me peace. I don't know what exactly I have achieved—a different way of seeing, another plane of existence perhaps. It feels almost mystical, the way the nuns would feel if they were allowed to practice their calling without restraint. It reminds me of those Japanese watercolors I saw at the exhibit of 1883. This feeling must have been commonplace for them, part of their daily life. There is something Eastern in this peace. Does this mean I am about to die?

When I was first incarcerated, I was terrified by the idea that the grief might be too much to bear. Now I realize that the true horror was that I could bear the grief, and I did bear it. It would have been much easier if I had died of it.

1943

Rodin,

I am going to die now. I will not be joining you in hell, because, as you know, my sins of hubris, martyrdom, bitterness, exaggeration, and the excessive way I cherished my own victimization, hurt no one but myself.

I have arranged for my sons to steal my body from the asylum after I die, and bury it under the window of my room at the Hôtel Biron. I am not abdicating to you. I do not see the Hôtel Biron as a museum for your works, even though since 1919 that is what it has become. I see the Hôtel Biron as a house in Paris where, for just a few years, several great artists lived under the same roof and pursued their art. They didn't always agree with each other, sometimes they didn't even like each other, but they respected each other as equals. I want to be a part of that now, even though it is too late.

I have entrusted all my artwork to my sons. I have asked them to reintroduce my work to the public, only when they believe the time is right, i.e., conducive to the world recognizing me as a great artist, on a par with the other artists of the Hôtel Biron. If, during their lifetimes, this moment in history does not arise, I have asked them to pass this duty down to their own children. For, I am in no hurry now to be recognized as a great artist. I know I am one, and that someday the world will know. I have plenty of time now. I am sure you understand this. Wasn't it you who said that patience is a form of action?

I have told my sons that I want to be remembered as a student of Alfred Boucher, along with Chagall, Modigliani and Lipschitz. If I am remembered in connection to you at all, I wish to be remembered as the only woman you really loved, the one whom you betrayed and lost.

Nijinsky's Spiritual Exercises, Introduction by Eduard Steichen

In the snowy winter of 1950 in London, I went to the psychiatric clinic where Nijinsky spent his last months. He had been incarcerated in several hospitals in Switzerland and elsewhere since the 1920s and had been treated for schizophrenia without much success.

I had made an appointment, so I was expected. A nurse led me to his room. I did not think Nijinsky would recognize me, but when he turned from his window and saw me, he gave me his great smile from the old days and opened his arms to me.

My brother, he said. *How long it has been.*

He gave me his chair at the window, and sat down at the foot of the bed near me. In the intervening thirty years he had not lost any of his dark beauty or Slavic charm, only his youth, hopes and of course the worst, his dancing. But ironically, his reputation was stronger than ever.

Nijinsky went to a large mahogany wardrobe that stood at the far side of the room, knelt down, and searched under a pile of blankets. He pulled out a manuscript, bound with a rubber band. He hugged it to his chest as he walked back to me, and with both hands, set it gingerly in my lap.

I think you will like this, he said. *It is something of a revelation.*

He smiled again and cocked his head to one side, as if he had asked me a question.

Despite his success and the enduring strength of his reputation and contribution to dance, Nijinsky's life always seemed to be the most tragic of all the tenants of the Hôtel Biron.

I leafed through the manuscript without really looking at it or reading the words. Nijinsky watched me intently.

I discovered something, Nijinsky said, motioning toward the manuscript.

Yes? I said.

Nijinsky nodded. *Only you will know*, he said.

I didn't remind him that I planned to publish the manuscripts. I didn't want to insult his dignity.

I stood up. *It is so nice to see you again*, I said in parting.

Yes, my brother, Nijinsky said, and showed me to the door. *One last time.*

The Spiritual Exercises
of Vaslav Nijinsky

PURPOSE

The purpose of these exercises is to help the exercitant
understand what feeling is.

PARTICULAR EXAMINATION OF CONSCIENCE

As soon as he wakes up in the morning, the exercitant
should resolve to understand feeling. After the noon meal
he should ask himself what he has felt since waking. He
should review each instance. In his review he should ask
himself which feelings he failed to understand and how
he might allow himself to understand feelings in the
future. He should renew his resolve to try again.

After the evening meal the exercitant should repeat
his examination for the period from the first examination
to the second.

The exercitant should compare each examination
period to the previous one, each day to the previous one
and each week to the previous one, noting his improve-
ment.

GENERAL EXAMINATION OF CONSCIENCE

The exercitant should review the difference between the existence of feeling and the lack of feeling. Under the category of feeling he should distinguish among:

- love, affection, sentiment
- passion, fervor, ardor
- excitement, stimulation, exhilaration, titillation
- agitation, perturbation, turbulence
- trepidation, disquiet, restlessness, unrest
- tension, strain, nervousness
- arousal, provocation, pique, anger
- irritation, exasperation, aggravation, discomposure
- frenzy, rage, fury, delirium, hysteria, vehemence
- patience, indulgence, lenience, forbearance
- sufferance, endurance, stoicism
- fortitude, self control
- resignation, meekness, submissiveness, passiveness
- impatience, anxiety, eagerness, fretfulness, intolerance
- susceptibility, responsiveness
- sympathy, tenderness
- awe, amazement
- hate, loathing, repulsion
- gratitude, pity, fear
- remorse, guilt, penitence shock, horror
- pride, vanity
- sadness, bereavement, grief, loss, friendship, companionship
- bemusement, intrigue, romance, excitement, lust, anguish, loneliness
- listlessness, lethargy
- numbness, paralysis, stupefaction

- composure, calm, serenity, placidity, tranquility
- equanimity, poise, aplomb, equilibrium
- self possession, self restraint, confidence, assurance
- sedateness, soberness, sobriety, staidness
- suppression, repression, nonchalance

The exercitant should remind himself of the difference between feeling and false feeling, feeling and forced feeling, feeling and faked feeling, feeling and mocked feeling.

Under the category of lack of feeling he should distinguish among:

- apathy, catatonia, unresponsiveness, impassiveness
- indifference, neglect, insensibility, unconcern
- frigidity, coldness, callousness, obliviousness
- heartlessness, spiritlessness, dispassion

The exercitant should remind himself of the difference between lack of feeling and defensiveness, lack of feeling and the appearance of no feeling, lack of feeling and shock, numbness, restraint, etc.

THE EXERCISE PROGRAM

The First Exercise should be performed upon waking, the second after lunch, the third after dinner, the fourth before going to bed. If this regimen is too strenuous, the exercitant should perform one exercise each day upon waking.

Other exercises like these four can be devised by using the other emotions discussed in the General Examination of Conscience. The exercitant should simply ask himself the inevitable questions.

The exercitant should continue an exercise until he is no longer learning from the exercise, at which time he should substitute one of his own devising. The exercitant should continue the exercise program until he understands feeling, or is no longer learning from the exercises. If the exercitant becomes too exhausted to continue, he should rest for one day, or one week, or whatever period of time he feels is necessary and appropriate, and should begin the exercises again.

FIRST EXERCISE

Remember the first person you ever loved. Imagine her eyes and her hair. Imagine her looking at you. Recreate the moment you realized you loved her. Imagine the room, the weather, the way the light hit. Remember what you said and what she said.

Remind yourself of what you want and desire.

Review your life. Recall to mind each person you have loved, looking upon them year by year, period by period. To help yourself do this, recall to mind the place and house where you lived, the people you knew, the work you performed.

In each instance, imagine the beloved. Imagine his face and hair, his eyes and body. Conjure up his smile and his look of doubt. Imagine a room or a place. Imagine yourselves together in that room. Imagine what he would say to you and you to him.

Do this for each person you have loved. And in relation to each person, consider who you are. Were you older or younger than the beloved? What did the beloved teach you? How did the beloved make you suffer? What were your greatest moments of consolation and desolation?

How were you a better person for having loved him? A worse person? What did you learn?

Let yourself be struck with amazement when you consider how your love for this person affected and changed you.

SECOND EXERCISE

Remind yourself of what you want and desire.

Review everything you have seen, heard, smelled, tasted and touched in the previous exercise. Try to draw some knowledge from this.

Remember the first person with whom you were in love. Imagine her face, her eyes, her body. Imagine her laugh and her anger.

Imagine how you felt when you first realized you were in love with her. Imagine how you felt the first time you touched her. Imagine the way you felt the first time you made love to her. Imagine the way you felt when you knew you would not see her again.

Imagine how you felt when you made love for the last time. See the place where you made love. Imagine its length, depth, and breadth. See her undress and stand before you. Look at the look in her eyes. Look at her looking at you. Hear the cries you both made. Taste the tears, taste the taste of her skin. Sense the touch of you touching her. Sense the touch of her touching you.

Review your life. Recall to mind each person you have been in love with, looking upon them year by year, period by period. To help yourself do this, recall to mind the place and house where you lived, the people you knew, the work you performed.

In each instance, imagine the beloved. Imagine his hair and eyes and skin. Imagine his laugh. Imagine him looking at you. Imagine his body against yours. Imagine yourself touching him. Imagine him touching you.

Imagine yourselves in a room or a place. What does he say to you? What do you say to him?

For each person with whom you were in love, imagine how you felt about him when you first met. Imagine how you felt when you realized you were in love. Imagine how you felt when you first made love, when you quarreled, when he hurt you, when you knew you couldn't have what you wanted, when you parted.

Ask yourself: What did you gain from being in love with this person? What did you learn? How are you changed?

Let yourself be struck with amazement when you consider how your love for this person affected and changed you.

Imagine you are a man in love with another man. Imagine you are a woman in love with another woman. Review each of the people you've been in love with. For each, imagine that person is a man. Imagine he is a woman. Imagine falling in love with that person if you were a man, then if you were a woman, if he were a man, if he were a woman. Imagine you are a child in love with a grownup. Imagine you are a grownup in love with a child.

THIRD EXERCISE

Review everything you have seen, heard, smelled, tasted and touched in the first two exercises. Try to draw some knowledge from this.

Remember the first time someone you loved died. Imagine how you learned of the loss. Imagine how you felt in the days and weeks that followed. Imagine what the things around you looked like. Imagine what people said to you, and what you said.

Review your life. Recall to mind each person you have loved who has died, looking upon them year by year, period by period. To help yourself do this, recall to mind the place and house where you lived, the people you knew, the work you performed.

In each instance, imagine where you were when you found out. Imagine how you felt. Imagine the days and weeks that followed. Imagine what things looked like then. Imagine what people said to you and what you said. Imagine what you thought about the person you lost. Imagine yourself letting go of that person. Imagine how you felt then. Imagine yourself grieving. Imagine how you grieved.

For each beloved you have lost ask yourself how that loss affected or changed you. Ask yourself what you have learned.

Remind yourself of what you want and desire.

Let yourself be struck with amazement when you consider how your grief for these lost loved ones affected and changed you.

Imagine your own death. Imagine the place and the time. Imagine how you would die. Imagine what you would say and who would be there. Imagine if you are afraid or not afraid.

Imagine your death as you fear it.

Imagine your death as you would like it.

Remember each time you thought you were going to die. For each instance, imagine where you were. Imagine the circumstances that compelled you to believe you would die. Imagine what you thought about. Imagine how you felt when you realized you would not die.

Remember the times you wished you were dead. For each instance imagine the circumstances. Imagine how you felt. Remember how you imagined your own death. Imagine the moment you stopped wishing for your death. Imagine why and how you stopped wishing.

Remember the times you have wanted other people dead. For each instance imagine the circumstances. Imagine how you felt. Imagine what you did and said. Imagine how you wished the person dead. Imagine the moment when you no longer wished the person dead.

Fourth Exercise

Remind yourself what you want and desire.

Review everything you have seen, heard, smelled, tasted and touched in the previous exercises. Try to draw some knowledge from this.

Remember the first time you had power over another person. Imagine who that person was, what she looked like, how her hair felt, how she looked at you. Imagine what you did and said to dominate her. Imagine what it felt like to dominate her. Imagine if you were kind or cruel when you dominated her.

Review your life. Recall to mind each person you have dominated looking upon them year by year, period by period. To help yourself do this, recall to mind the place and house where you lived, the people you knew, the work you performed.

In each instance, imagine the person. Imagine how he looked, how his hair felt, how he looked at you. Imagine what you did and said to dominate him. Imagine what it felt like to dominate him. Imagine if you were kind or cruel when you dominated him.

Remember the first time someone had power over you. Imagine the person, what she looked like, how her hair felt, how you looked at her. Imagine what she did and said to dominate you. Imagine how you felt. Imagine if she was kind or cruel when she dominated you.

Review your life. Recall to mind each person who has dominated you, looking upon them year by year, period by period. To help yourself do this, recall to mind the place and house where you lived, the people you knew, the work you performed.

In each instance, imagine what he looked like, how his hair felt, how you looked at him. Imagine what he did and said to dominate you. Imagine how you felt. Imagine if he was kind or cruel when he dominated you.

Imagine the people you would like to dominate. For each person, imagine what he looks like, how his hair would feel, how he would look at you. Imagine what you would do and say when you dominated him. Imagine what you would feel. Imagine if you would be cruel or kind when you dominated him.

Imagine the people you would like to have power over you. For each person: imagine what he looks like, how his hair would feel, how he would look at you. Imagine what he would do and say to dominate you. Imagine how you would feel. Imagine if he would be cruel or kind when he dominated you.

For each instance above, imagine how the other person would feel when you dominated him or were dominated by him.

Remember what you want and desire.

Let yourself be struck with amazement when you consider how your power over other people and their power over you has affected and changed you.

Praise for *The Tenants of the Hôtel Biron*

Laura Marello writes, through the voice of Eduard Steichen, that "... all these powerful artists are so invulnerably weak." Rodin, his lover Camille Claudel, Picasso, Rousseau, Nijinski, Matisse, Rilke and others, all tenants of Hôtel Biron, and all brilliantly and excitedly human, presented by manuscripts fictionally collected. The result is an appropriately cubist look at each, because we see each from several subjective vantages. This is a brilliantly conceived work of reflective and self-reflective parts. With Marello we get to imagine, as war is coming on, the confusions and certainties of competing artists, conflicting and collaborating geniuses in a world of misunderstood avant-garde where gallery patrons sometimes slashed canvases. The tenants, as a "decadent" group in much of the public eye, were entropic, burning up on mutual energy but producing lasting art and reputation. And there is a love story at the core: Rodin and Claudel, medieval in its passion and constraint, physical and spiritual amidst wild theologies of art. As each character speaks to us from manuscript and letters, their mutual story moves on. Chaucer would have loved it.

—**Paul Nelson**

Laura Marello is a masterful and brilliant writer. Backed by strict scholarly research, her novel *The Tenants of the Hôtel Biron* brings us a perceptive and unique understanding of the people whose lives crossed in the Hotel Biron: Rodin, Claudel, Picasso, Satie, Matisse and other fascinating characters from that time. This is a compelling story on a real and imagined Paris—the ravishing bohemian Paris of the early 1900s.

—**Jennifer Clement**

Printed in April 2012
by Gauvin Press,
Gatineau, Québec